Knight Literary Journal

VOLUME II

Knight Literary Journal

VOLUME II

CHARLES CUTTER, EDITOR

Copyright © 2004 by Knight Media Strategies Inc.

Cover photo by Susan Stanton

ISBN: Softcover   1-4134-4842-9

All rights reserved. No part of this book may be reproduced or transmitted in any form or by any means, electronic or mechanical, including photocopying, recording, or by any information storage and retrieval system, without permission in writing from the copyright owner.

The short stories contained herein are works of fiction. Any resemblance to actual persons, living or dead, is entirely coincidental.

This book was printed in the United States of America.

To order additional copies of this book, contact:
Xlibris Corporation
1-888-795-4274
www.Xlibris.com
Orders@Xlibris.com
22854

Contents

The Dragon in the Photograph 7
by Mark Johnston

Back Roads 13
by Annamaria Formichella Elsden

The Greatest 18
by Ron Sheasby

The Atlantic Ocean and Other Things 31
by Chris Reed

A Red Bicycle 44
by Kathryn Hamilton

Bi-Coastal 59
by J. R. Carpenter

Hot Mango Chutney 68
by Theresa Martin

Uncle John 74
by Tom Henighan

Brunch 85
by Dawn Ladds

Horseshoes 96
by Jason Ockert

Snakes 106
by Mark Vogel

All the Colors of the Rainbow 121
by Mike Hood

The Painter 134
by Joseph M. Ditta

Power Play 142
by Evelyn Shakir

Playing with an Invisible Deck 153
by Jessica Somers

George Goes for A Walk 160
by Caitlin Hicks

The Trash Bag Kid 169
by Connie Noel

Fisherman's Daughter 179
by DeAnna Jarrell

Reunion Underground 181
by Jewel Seehaus-Fisher

The Ballad of Geezer Malone 190
by Evelyn M. Perry

Franny & Mary 209
by Heidi Wohlwend

The Day My Life Fell Apart 219
by Mimi Reddicliffe

Authors' Notes 225

The Dragon in the Photograph

by Mark Johnston

I am sitting at the kitchen table, working on my daughter's dragon costume for her school play. When I was in school, I was only in a play once. In the fifth grade. My class put on a very abbreviated version of *William Tell*. A paper of pins, two thimbles, a spool of green thread, and a pinking shears lie in front of me on the table. Bobby Gordon got to play the part of Tell's little son. He was the smallest boy in our class, and he often cried after recess. The other boys would push him around, or laugh at the thick glasses he wore (they called him "Mason Jar"), or make nasty remarks about his sister, who got caught making out with a tenth grader in the projection booth.

George left for work two hours ago, and Amanda left for school a half hour after that. When I drank my morning tea and watched the news, a bird flew past outside. He seemed to fly over the surface of the tea, but of course it was only a reflection. In *my* class play, I was the wind during the storm of the *William Tell Overture*. In one week, Amanda will be the front end of a dragon. She will come out on stage, followed by a little girl who will "play the part" of the tail. Amanda will roar threateningly at another little girl who plays a damsel in distress. A knight dressed in silver armor, Amanda has told me, will walk onto the stage, brandish his sword, scare the dragon away, and save the damsel. Bobby Gordon peed his pants on the stage when Aggie Mach pretended to shoot the apple off of his head.

There was a very disturbing item on the news. A couple who lives across town got into an argument, a "domestic dispute" they called it. The wife accused the husband of having an affair. The news reporter, dressed in an expensive topcoat, calmly reported how the husband stabbed her thirty-seven times, including on the arms and legs. They found her lying dead on her living room floor with the knife in her throat. They showed a picture of the wife dressed in a green party dress that was almost the color of Amanda's dragon costume. When I saw this picture, I thought of how George had pricked the yolks of his eggs, gently, with his fork, and how he had used his knife to spread jam on his toast.

Amanda's costume has to be big enough to fit over two girls. It is of green felt, with large yellow spots on each side. The kind of baize green that is used on the tops of pool tables. I have made the scales to go along the back. I cut the triangles with the pinking shears to give them an extra edginess. I have used pieces of coat hanger to make them rigid. There will be a huge red tongue as well. It is supposed to be like fire, but I don't know how I can make it do anything more than loll out of the dragon's mouth. I'm afraid it won't be as terrifying as it ought to be. The tail tapers down to a blunt point. It will have Fiber-Fil inside. Amanda's partner will use a stick to make the tail sway back and forth menacingly. The felt alone cost thirteen dollars.

Bobby Gordon stood against a wooden pole one of the fathers had donated. Mrs. Rappaport made him take off his glasses because, she said, there were no glasses in William Tell's day. I remember he tried to argue that there were no gym shoes, either. Bobby was frightened because he couldn't see what they were doing to him. They had to tie his hands loosely behind his back, around the pole. The pole could be turned by a stage-hand. On the side opposite Bobby's head, an arrow was stuck through an apple into the pole. I remember how Billy Conley, our class bully, ate this apple after the play was over. When the bow-string twanged (of course a real arrow was not shot), the stage-hand twirled the pole to make it look like the apple was split in half on top of Bobby's head. I remember that once my father said Bobby Gordon was a sissy.

I work on the tongue for a bit. The felt is too rosy, not scarlet enough. But it will have to do. I have cut it out (there is a huge fork at the end, of course), but I must still sew it into the green mouth of the dragon. Amanda will look so cute in the costume. She has lost a bottom tooth recently, and I can just imagine how she'll look when she gives her roar. I had just lost a tooth when I was the wind. When the ominous storm started in the overture, three other girls and I had to spin around wildly and twirl across the stage to show the commotion. We wore strips of white crepe paper tucked into our skirts. I almost became nauseous from dizziness. My mouth got wet, and my skin got clammy. Five of the tallest boys played trees and waved their arms to suggest the effects of the storm. The mothers of the kids in the play got to sit in the front. All of them, including my mother, sat primly with their pocketbooks on their laps. There was one man in the audience. I remember he had on a string neck-tie with a large turquoise clasp. As I was spinning, I focused on his tie intermittently to keep my bearings and to keep from falling down. I saw the curtains, the wall, the mothers, the turquoise clasp, the exit sign, the curtains, the wall, the mothers, the turquoise clasp. Like that, around and around, a regular spell of vertigo. I am amazed how everything reminds me of everything else. We had to spin for almost three minutes.

I guess when the bowstring twanged, Bobby Gordon thought he was really going to be shot. That's when he peed his pants. He had on tan pants, and you could easily see the growing spot it made. One mother tittered, and another whispered, *Oh, that's too bad, what a shame.*

At dinner that night (we had beef stew), my mother told my father that I made a grand wind. That's what she said. *Grand.* My father was chewing beef stew. I felt proud that I had not vomited on stage. My father just grunted (*"Hmmph"*) and kept on chewing.

Bobby Gordon's sister got pregnant during her sophomore year. She had to quit school and was taught at home. The boy who made her pregnant became her husband after high school. He is our electrician now. I hear they are still happily married. Isn't it interesting that I keep my spare buttons in a Mason jar? Just like my mother did. So much of this costume keeps coming back to Bobby Gordon for some reason. I attach large green buttons to the front of Amanda's costume. The green of the thread does not quite match, but I'm sure no one will notice. As I push my needle in and out through the button holes, I think of the newscaster explaining that the dead wife had been a local high school track star, a cross-country runner. As I stab and stab the button, hitting the thimble carefully every time, I find myself wishing she could have run away, far away, away from her murderous husband. I notice that I am counting my stitches. I never get to thirty-seven. I force myself to think of William Tell to keep from getting to thirty-seven.

Sewing the scales onto the back is the easy part. The hangers make them rigid, and they are easy to handle. There are seventeen of them. They are largest in the middle of the back, and then they get smaller as they move down the tail. Both thirty-seven and seventeen are prime numbers.

As I swallow the last of my cold tea, I think of how next week I will be sitting near the front of the stage, in a row with the other mothers. There will not be many men in the audience, perhaps only those who work the night shift, or maybe one who is unemployed. I will stare at the stage, wondering when Amanda will come out to do her roaring. My mind will wander. Perhaps I will imagine George staring at his computer screen, or calling his secretary to have some copies made. My friend Elaine Sutter will be sitting next to me, trying to still her squirming son. She will nudge my elbow with hers. I will look up and see a little girl lying on the stage, dressed in white, moaning in fright. She is the maiden that the knight will save. To my left, at the wing of the stage, the knight waits. He has on white gym shoes, silver armor made out of cut-up cardboard boxes, and he holds a small sword, also silver, made out of two laths nailed together. The middle of the high purple stage curtain will rustle. I will take out my camera, look through the view-finder, and adjust the settings. Amanda and June, the little girl who plays the tail of the dragon, will shuffle onto the stage. They have to walk back to back, so that June can work the tail. Amanda walks too fast, and the fabric of the dragon stretches. When Amanda suddenly stops, June bumps into her. My heart is racing. I see Amanda's small face inside the mouth of the dragon costume. I lift the camera for the shot. Amanda roars once, but it is barely audible. The audience laughs indulgently. When my flash goes off, I think of the secretary making copies for George, and of the little flash inside the copying machine. The maiden cries out, much louder than Amanda's roar, *Save me! Help! Save me!*

    Somehow I know that, at some time in the future, I will show this photograph to a friend of mine. *That's my daughter,* I will say*, the dragon in the photograph.* I know that years later I will look at the photograph, and I will think of Bobby Gordon, who wet his pants on stage because of an arrow that was never shot. I will think of the woman who was stabbed so

VOLUME II

many times by her husband. I will see the flash of my camera, and the yellow spots I sewed onto the green felt one October morning. Thirty-seven times. I will see the small dark "O" of Amanda's open mouth with its missing bottom tooth. I will remember how she roared just once, too faintly, and how she was never a dragon again. That's too bad. What a shame.

Back Roads

by Annamaria Formichella Elsden

What my mother doesn't realize is that I am driving the car. Her auburn head faces forward in that way she has, like she fears and trusts the world at the same time, and she keeps both hands carefully perched on the steering wheel of our wood-paneled station wagon. Vigilantly obeying the speed limit, my mother believes she is shepherding us through all manner of neighborhood, first past houses solitary like ours and then two—and three-family homes and then high-rise apartment buildings with boarded windows like black eyes, as we approach the city by the back way. We avoid the freeway, the unabashed elevated beeline of the central artery, when making our frequent downtown pilgrimages. Instead we creep into Boston at sea level, through stoplights and past donut shops, and surprise the city circuitously, at the last minute, like a snake coming around from behind a wall to confront a towering gardener.

My brother sits in the front seat next to her, his head resting directly on the cold glass of the passenger-side window. He looks small on that long Oldsmobile bench seat, his neck bent like it's broken. I know my mother thinks she is taking extreme care of both of us. That's why I keep my secret from her, as I sit in the back seat methodically angling my stick shift in the direction the car needs to go.

It's an ice scraper, actually, one of those long plastic jobs with a scraper at one end and a brush at the other. Miraculously, a red brush on a wooden handle is all I need to both power and steer the car. I hold it upright between my spindly eight-year-old legs, close enough to the seat in front of me that my mother can't see it. She probably wouldn't notice anyway. She always gets distracted when we make these trips into the city: smoking more than usual, darting her eyes to the rear-view mirror frequently and so quickly I'm sure she can't really be able to see what's behind us. Luckily I have my magical navigation system at my command. Using a combination of the gear-shifting I have seen my father do in his sports car and the large arcs my mother makes with her power-steering-wheel, I keep us on track to downtown Boston. Occasionally I check my mother's expression in the rearview mirror, frowning when her eyes frown.

The last time we made this trip it was raining so hard that the drops bounced back up off the pavement in a blinding mist and only my thorough knowledge of the streets got us to our destination. That was the time I fainted when the nurse came to draw my blood. She took out a lot, filled maybe six test tubes or so, siphoned so much life from me that in the end I leaked out of myself entirely. A fluttery tingle blurred the sides of my head as I watched the needle slide out, and then I dribbled onto the floor. In my mind, I removed myself to a fantasy in which I was driving in a car with Mickey Mouse, motoring skyward into a bank of white, puffy cartoon-clouds. In reality, my mother tells me, my eyes rolled upward until they were all white and I slid like a waterfall off the orange plastic chair and onto the floor. My sister apparently called for me from her bed in fright. But, as I said, I was soaring with Mickey into the blue beyond and knew nothing of the efforts made by the hospital staff to revive me, or of my sister's alarm. When I came to I was disappointed to see the blank white walls around me. I bragged to my mother, "I was driving with Mickey Mouse." She looked concerned and dark around the eyes as she reminded me I hadn't had any breakfast and my blood sugar was low. That was why I had passed out.

    As we wait at a light and I keep my stick in neutral, I am thinking about my mother's explanation, about my blood sugar. It seems to me that toast and jelly wouldn't have helped any. Something about seeing my life's force on the *outside* of my body had sent me into a downward spiral, like when you pull the plug on a fan and the blades coast ever more slowly to a stop. Without enough juice to power me, I was left all weak and flimsy, like I am starting to feel now in the car just remembering.

    I have to resist the urge to turn us around and speed back home. I tell myself it is my responsibility to maintain control of the car and to deliver my mother and my brother safely, that it is my duty to pay this visit. But I fear that I am hurtling toward disaster, that the world has gone crazy and if I look away from the road *for one second* we will careen into an oncoming bus, and even the hefty bulk of our Vista Cruiser will be unable to save us. I want to stop and go the other way, put the images that pass my window like film frames into reverse order, want it so powerfully that it might as well happen, does happen. This is what I think the priest meant when he told us that wanting a sin in your mind is the same thing as committing it. Wanting and doing collapse into each other. My thoughts fly to the safe spot in my mother's bedroom at home where there are no needles, only pictures of three little children lined up on an ironing board by a professional photographer, smiling faces that look healthy and can't ever be scared. I want to go home so badly that I feel guilty.

The guilt plagues me all the way to the hospital, sits with me in the waiting room with its sad old blocks and children's toys that no one wants, climbs back up into the car beside me for our return voyage. On the way home all I can see is the wooden cart they wheeled her toward me in, and the bruises on her arms from too many IV tubes. She looked so small, like they were shrinking her in there. I wonder whether the IV tubes drip fluid in or take fluid out. I think maybe they've taken too much of her blood, like they did to me. It makes my throat ache, so I concentrate on my stick shift and the outside landmarks, turning left at the run-down package store, right at the church that will burn down a few years later, and hugging the wall along the cemetery.

My mother's hands are trembling and her head seems shaky, which may explain why she takes the right fork in front of the nursery school we used to go to, instead of the left. I push and push at my control stick, but there is no response. The car stubbornly continues on its misguided path, away from the direction of our house, away from the roads that I know, toward some mysterious destination. Outside the trees look enormous and menacing, like the monsters that line the path at the haunted house on Halloween. I know they're fake, just local kids dressed up, but they frighten me anyway.

The farther we go the stranger everything looks until I start yelling at my mother and crying, lying down along the length of the back seat so I can throw my feet up and down in high kicks. "No!" I scream, unable to tell her exactly why it all feels so wrong. "No, no, no," I shout like a brat, beating the ice scraper against the floor and trying to make something that would seem like a difference in this car that blithely continues on its wrong way.

The cold green vinyl of the seat makes me shiver and my mother asks what is wrong, her concerned voice like a bucket of water on my flaming agenda. When I sit up again I don't know where we are and my sister's face hovers above the road, pale and yet bright and smiling at me like I sparkle, like I could have just leaned over and picked her up and carried her out of there into the March sunlight.

The Greatest

by Ron Sheasby

There's a old joke goes like this.
—Whaddya think Babe Ruth woulda hit if he coulda played today?
—Maybe .280, .290.
—Is that all?!
—Yeah. well. you gotta remember if Babe Ruth was playin today, he'd be well over 90 years old!

A good joke but a lie. Babe Ruth in his prime couldn't of hit .200 in any league which had black pitchers in it and I know because I seen the game where the Babe batted against Satchel Paige in Wrigley Field in July of 1932 when I was 10 years old and it like to break my heart. You won't never read or hear nothing about that game because of what happened but I'm here to tell you what DID happen because I saw every pitch from the owner's box.

I remember the date because it was my birthday 5 July, the day before the first All Star game in Comiskey

Park. You could look it up if you don't believe me. I'm selling the old Chicago American from the corner of Irving and Western and smoking a Phillip Morris when this mean looking old biddy all of 30 or 50 or something fisheyes me and says

—How old are you, young man? and just then a Checker cab pulls up, rear window going down and Babe Ruth is grinning out at me wearing that same cap all the kids is wearing only this one is Camels Hair and ours are cotton, mine has holes in it for crissake, and the old bitch is saying something but I can't hear because the Babe's handing me a sawbuck and saying

—Gimme a paper Keed and keep the change! so I do and blurt out around my coffin nail

—Geeziz Babe what're YOU doin here?! and his grin gets bigger and I can smell just a touch of whiskey on his breath, not a lot, just a little like Dad when he's just getting started but not like later when the beatings come, as he says

—Goin ta Wrigley Field, Keed, ta the game! and a bald little guy which I don't recognize next to the Babe pipes up

—No game today kid, the Babe is mistaken! and a bigger guy on the other side who looks an awful lot like Lefty Grove has the paper open to the sports and says

—Nothin not a word! and the baldy says

—Thass the way it's supposta be, hey! and the light goes green and the Checker roars east on Irving towards Clark.

I don't know how long I stand there but it must of been a while because my fag is almost burning my lip, so I spit it out and look at the old bag who says

—Well, are you going to sell me a newspaper OR ARE YOU NOT?!! and I say

—Lady stick yer money up yer ass! and she looks just like Maggie when she is pissed off at Jiggs but I don't hang around to talk and drop the papers taking it on the Arthur Duffy straight east after that cab just as fast my legs can carry me.

VOLUME II

After a while them legs give out and my lungs ain't all that great with so much smoking so I'm walking sweaty in that July heat, hell, it must have been 90 that afternoon, looking for a Red Rocket which I can easy afford since with Babe's sawbuck I got enough to ride and still buy Dad his halfpint. Shit, I could get a fifth but what he don't know won't hurt him, I'm thinking, when I see Skinny Williams pop out of a doorway by St. Bennys. He's probably the only kid I know is a bigger and better booster than me, my Dad not approving of him, not because of boosting but because he's colored, which don't bother me none. In fact I kind of like it because he don't have no dad to beat him, only his mom, which is too busy scrubbing homes out in Winnetka and Wilmette for the rich to pay much attention, so he does what he wants which is the way I'd like to be. He is probably my best, maybe my only friend.

—Where da fire, Bags? and he filches a coffin nail out of my shirt pocket but I don't care.

—Remember how the Cubs bought Babe Herman?

—Yeah and they supposta be buyin Chuck Klein too, but they too cheap so they ain't gonna!

—I tink dey just bought da Babe instead! and the Phillip Morris falls from his lower lip while his eyes look like saucers so I tell him what happened and before long a streetcar clangs along and we are off to Clark and Addison.

Wiggely Field is crawling with coppers and Andy Frains only instead of helping people in, they're turning them out, not that there are many and when me and Skinny try to buy a ticket since I can easy afford the couple dimes it takes, a cop which resembles W. C. Fields with a pot belly slaps his palm with a billy stick and looks daggers.

—No game today, move on!

—But . . .

—Move on an take da little nigger witcha!

   Skinny got his name because he likes to say there's more ways than one to skin a cat so we go over the left field wall when nobody's looking, me making a stirrup with my hands for him first, then him pulling me up and we both drop to our feet onto the grass in left. Inside the field is filled with ballplayers in different uniforms but more to the point a couple of red face Andy Frains see us and we take off towards center with half a dozen ushers in light blue and gold and cops in dark blue puffing along behind with pretty soon a bunch more in front so we cut for right but that don't do no good because there's a small army waiting for us and before long we are being hauled kicking and screaming and dragging our heels by the W. C. Fields cop who has appeared like magic and has a hammerlock on me. I can see uniformed ballplayers out of the corner of my eye, including Babe Ruth with his pinstripes and hat too small for that big head, grinning like the big ape he is though I kind of doubt he recognizes me when a voice comes from a box just behind third

   —Bring those young men over here! and W.C. snaps to without never letting go of me

   —Yessir, Mr. Wrigley! and pretty soon I am facing this clean shaven man with slick back hair beneath his homburg and grey eyes which look like money. He's the new owner, his father died earlier in the year, and when he did, I seen his picture in the Trib, kind of pudgy and smiley, but this guy looks like he don't never smile. He tells them to release us and looks at me.

   —You won't run, will you, boy? and I shake my head no, so W. C. lets me go and I am held in place by those eyes. I hear another voice say kind of weak like and coughing

   —One of KAFF KAFF them is a KAFF negro. How KAFF KAFF KAFF appropriate! and I realize this is President William Veeck not him which in a few years would plant the vines for the Cubs then later hire a midget for the Browns, but his dad which don't look too healthy hisself, and besides him there's 4 or 5 other guys in the box—fedoras and a Camels Hair like Babe's plus one boater with a long face and a short smile and a tie knotted just so below this wrinkly old face out of which hardly comes nothing the whole time we are there, but also never loses the smile . . . and even a silk high hat like the guy in Monopoly but Mr. Wrigley is the only one can hold my attention.

—What's your name, boy?
—Bags sir I mean Rudy uh RUDOLPH sir!
—Very good, boy. Now can you tell me your full name?
—Rudolph Bagwell sir!
—Excellent! And your friend? and I start to answer but Skinny pipes up.
—Ah kin answer fer myself, Mistuh. Mah name Skinny Williams! and squirms out of the grasp of this pimple face usher to stand tall for Mr. Wrigley.

Well, he gives us a regular third degree but what it boils down to is me and Skinny promise to never tell nobody, even our parents, about the game so we can stay and watch. While talking we been looking around and not only is Babe Ruth on that field but what seems like both squads from the first All Star game to be played in Comiskey the next day plus a bunch of coloreds among which is Satchel Paige! So of course we promise on our momma's souls, mine having special meaning because my Mom's dead, but as much as that means there is something about Mr. Wrigley's eyes make me want to keep that secret, and I have from that day til now.

—Say Mr. Wrigley, how'd you get all dese players fer one game?
—Same way you get any ballplayer to do anything today, Son, I paid them handsomely! and they all laugh not the sort of hearty HAW! HAW! HAW! like Dad and his buddies do down at Schuliens when somebody tells a Rufus joke but more polite and refined like they was afraid their mustaches

would fall off if they laugh too hard. And then somebody asks Mr. Wrigley ain't The Bambino, just like that, The Bambino, a little past his prime and Mr. Wrigley says maybe so but he's still the biggest name in the game, it having been a choice between him and Lou Gehrig which is why Gehrig ain't there and they all laugh that fruity little laugh again. And it is true. This is the first year Ruth don't lead the majors in homers since the Big Tummyache even though he did hit the first All Star homer the next day, but none of that matters.

What happens that day would have happened if he'd of been in his prime.

Then Mr. Wrigley allows as how a few of the stars couldn't come on account of the short notice, but when I look around I can't see many which missed—Lefty Gomez and the Babe, plus Jimmy Foxx, Al Simmons, Joe Cronin, Ducky Medwick, Paul Waner, Lefty ODoul, Mel Ott, Mickey Cochrane, Pepper Martin, Leo Durocher, Red Ruffing, Schoolboy Rowe, Lefty Grove, Rip Collins, Gabby Hartnett, Lon Warneke, and Frankie Frisch. The whites is mostly on the infield and in right and center where there's no big scoreboard like they put in a few years later and no vines neither, the walls just brick, and if you bounce off of the wall, tough shit. Off by themselves in left field playing catch away from the whites is them coloreds most of which I don't recognize but of course that long tall drink of water Paige and a chunky and muscular guy name of Josh Gibson, and Skinny later on points out Buck Leonard, Cool Papa Bell, Judy Johnson, and Double Duty Radcliffe, which is not only the manager but the backup pitcher and catcher, plus some others I don't recall, Skinny knowing because he goes out to Comiskey Park on days when the Sox ain't playing to see colored teams like the Chicago American Giants and Pittsburgh Crawdads or something. The white manager is Charley Grimm which is kinda odd because he's only the first baseman on the Cubs, Rogers Hornsby's the manager, but Rajah ain't nowhere to be seen.

VOLUME II

I don't really care to talk much about that game but I suppose I got to. It is like racing your milkman's horse against a thorobred, that's how much faster them coloreds is. They can't swing the bat no better than the whites, maybe just a little, but speed? Don't make me laugh. First pitch of the game Cool Papa Bell dumps Lefty Grove's fastball down the third base line and beats the throw, then steals second, third, and home on Mickey Cochrane! Next guy up hits a Texas Leaguer into right and takes second when Babe is a bit slow and breaks for third to get caught in a rundown but scores when Leo Durocher panics and throws one into the third base boxes just over our heads. Me and Skinny is both scrambling for the ball when we realize ain't nobody else going to go for it, unless it is Mr. Wrigley and his pals, which don't seem likely so we both grin and I say

—Skinny, I'll flip yah fer it! and Skinny throws that big smile from cheekbone to cheekbone, come to think a it he musta been part Indian like me and Dad, and says

—Nah nah Bags... Aftuh YOU mah man! so I get my first and so far only souvenir baseball.

Lefty Grove actually got good stuff, although Gibson clips one into Waveland in the third and tears around the bases like a greyhound, but compared to Satchel Paige, Lefty's pitching batting practice.

Paige pumps once, twice, 3 times, maybe 4, with bench jockeys like Babe Ruth going

—C'mon, you big spook, throw the damn thing! and never says nothing but rears back back back until you think he will fall, left foot climbing, climbing, climbing until it is over his head and for a second that white ball is dangling in his brown hand next to his right kneecap with the trouser leg puffed over it and then the shoe starts down and BOOM!! the ball is kicking dust out of the catcher's mitt as Pepper Martin waits to swing.

Or comes right at Ducky Medwick's head while he hits the dirt and then the ball snaps over the outside corner low but high enough for a called strike.

Or floats lazy over the plate with Ruth hisself already wrapped into his follow through.

Gabby Hartnett comes over to our box after pinch hitting for Grove with 3 bad swings and taking out a big red handkerchief and mopping his forehead apologizes but Mr. Wrigley says

—That's all right, Gabby. How would some of these big black bucks look in blue and white? but Hartnett don't hear nothing, being still busy wiping that kind of fat red Mick face of his, which is funny because the rest of him is all lean.

—It starts out like a baseball but what gets to the plate looks like a marble! And when I told him that, you know what he said? He said, "You all mus be talkin bout mah slow ball, Mistuh Gabby, mah fas ball look like a fish egg!" but Mr. Wrigley don't hear him as York hits a can of corn to center, Waner goes down on 4 pitches and Gabby has to trudge back to catch Lon Warneck's warmups, his sore arm not allowing him to do much more all season long, while Mr. Wrigley is explaining to the other swells.

—After all, we employ Irish and Jews! Is there really that much difference? and Mr. Veeck says

—The Cubs KAFF KAFF employ no Jews!

—Is it not the principle of the thing?!

—I am more KAFF KAFF than just a little bit concerned KAFF about how the rest of baseball will react KAFF KAFF KAFF! and them grey eyes flash thunder and lightning as Mr. Wrigley says

—There speaks the voice of my dear departed father! The Cubs haven't won the World's Championship since 1908!! How long must we wait?! and nobody says nothing.

No white man that day hits the ball very hard in spite of very generous calls from the white umpire, shit, they get only get maybe 3 or 4 scratch hits all game, but Paige seems to specially enjoy humiliating Ruth which don't hit a foul or take a ball just 1-2-3 OUT 1-2-3 OUT 1-2-3 OUT until his last at bat, which is still real painful to talk about even after all these years.

It starts before the Babe comes to bat in the 9th. Warneke and Lefty Gomez actually hold the score down pretty good so them coloreds is only leading 4 to 0 with Pepper Martin leading off by nailing a liner which Judy Johnson runs down in center. Then Paige fans Mickey Cochrane on a 3 and 2 hesitation pitch that Mickey swings so hard at he falls down. Now Paige calls out his catcher Josh Gibson and entire infield and they talk until Buck Leonard gets angry and Mr. Veeck says

—They want that KAFF KAFF two thousand dollars! and Mr. Monopoly says

—There's a two thousand dollar pot? and Mr. Wrigley says

—Two thousand apiece, winner take all!

—Lord, more than those colored boys make in a year! and then Double Duty Radcliffe comes out and starts arguing with Paige who just shakes his head no and smiles. Pretty soon the umpire steps over the plate and takes off his mask and blue serge cap and you can see his bald head shining in the late afternoon sun, rolls of fat round the neck, and says something sharp and they all go back shaking their heads, Radcliffe to the dugout, Buck Leonard to first talking to himself, only Gibson don't go back to squat behind the plate but stands 6 feet outside while Paige grinning like a lunatic lobs up 4 wide ones for an intentional pass to Frankie Frisch! You can tell none of them like it with Gibson cussing under his breath as he tosses it back to Satchel, and the rest standing around in the field almost in shock like they been told it was against the law for blacks to beat whites, and they would all be arrested after the game if they did. Ducky Joe Medwick steps in and Paige tosses 4 wide of the plate and with 2 on and 2 out damned if he don't give Foot in the Bucket Al Simmons ANOTHER intentional base on balls and them bags is full with Babe Ruth digging in with a look on his red face like he is planning on killing both the ball and Mr. Satchel Paige and he don't much care which comes first.

Paige steps back off of the mound and takes off his cap to wipe his brown face with the back of his hand, white inside just like yours and mine. He studies the Babe a while then says in a voice loud enough to be heard all over the park

—Mistuh Babe all Ah been done hearin about since Ah wuz a tadpole wuz about how great you is . . . the greates ballplayer evuh wuz!

Paige studies the ground for a while then continues

—An evuh since Ah been growed Ah done heard stuff lak "Ain't it a shame he black, ol Satchel woulda bin the greates ballplayer evuh lived iff'n he hadn't had the bad taste to be born cullid!"

Then he looks Ruth right square in the eye.

—Well, you know, Mistuh Babe, Ah bin wonderin lately which one a us actual IS bettuh. Leavin the race question outta it, that is. Now Ah know that ain't somethin bin concernin you very much, whut wif bein rich and white and famous an all but it sho do puzzle mah poor ol black haid . . . . so Ah aims to find out the answuh to that question. Right now! You ready, Mistuh Babe? and Ruth says

—Pitch the ball, nigger! and Paige just smiles and says

—All right, Mistuh Babe, this here first pitch gonna be a fast ball bout knee high onna outside! and WHAP! the ball is right where he says it would be and by before Ruth can move.

—Now this nex pitch, Mistuh Babe, gonna be anothuh fast ball only shoulduh high an onna inside . . . and even fastuh! and it ain't only faster but exactly where Satchel calls it, and Babe's eyes get big in his head until they look like milk saucers and Satchel's grow small and slitty like a big black cat about to pounce on a Baltimore Oriole, but his voice remains southern drawly.

 —Mistuh Babe, iffn you thought them las two pitches wuz fast, jes wait til you see this one! So to make up foah it bein so fast, Ah'm gonna throw it right smack dab down the middle a the plate!! Ready, Mistuh Babe Ruth? Here it come! and I never see that pitch, hell, I don't think the umpire sees that pitch but he knows it is in Gibson's glove and that glove is belt high and in back of the plate so he chokes out

 —Strike three . . . kinda squeaky and Ruth drops his bat to the ground and stares at it while Satchel is strolling off the hill towards the first base dugout singing

> If it hadn't been
> For the referee
> Jack Johnson woulda killed
> JI'm Jefferee.
> Free beer!

and in the owner's box behind third base there is absolute silence. Finally the smiley guy breaks it but no longer smiling.

 —My Gawd, can you picture that happening in front of fifty thousand white men? and somebody else says

 —They'd lynch him! and someone else says

 —They'd lynch us! and Mr. Wrigley says

 —Gentlemen, they would lynch us all, but I can assure you that this is never going to happen! and turning to me and Skinny

 —Young sirs, did you enjoy the game? and I can see Skinny did since he is grinning from ear to ear so I lie and say I did too and then we all go home.

 I can see why he did it. For that one game he was King of the Hill and what he rightfully should of been if his ancestors wasn't slaves. And after the game and a shower in a real big league locker for maybe the first time in his life, he left out the park and had to say "Yes Sir Nossir!" and get out of the way of that white cop which resembled W. C. Fields or some asshole just like him. In other words after having just proved beyond doubt that he was a better ballplayer than the best the white world had to offer, he became a nigger again.

I would of done it, too.

I would of stuck that ball so far up Babe Ruth's ass it would of come out of his ear!

Mr. Veeck kicked the bucket before the season was up which didn't surprise me none and Charlie Grimm replaced Rogers Hornsby as manager which surprised me even less. And while he won the pennant, the Yankees took 4 straight in the Series with that big gorilla Ruth supposedly calling his shot but I doubt it—ain't nobody that good and like I said he wasn't as good as he was cracked up to be anyway.

My Dad drunk hisself to death in '35 and I become a ward of the state which I definitely don't wanta talk about. Skinny was dead the following year after getting stuck late at night in a transom he wasn't suppose to be in and a white cop drew on him from behind and I caught a midnight freight to Texas shortly after because I couldn't stand living in a city like that no more. Skinny was 2 weeks dying and I was with him most of the time. I never cried so much in my life, not before or since, even for my Mom or when I was on The Canal and most of my platoon bought the farm.

That first night I was in my foxhole feeling none too comfortable when some Nip screamed

—Brood for the Emperor! and one of our jokers shouted

—Blood fer Eleanor! and we all laughed.

Then another Jap shouted

—Babe Ruth stinks! and I couldn't hear the answer because all I could think of was "You donno the half a it little man, not the half!"

VOLUME II

I'm a crabby old man now living in Dallas and got to get up 8 or 9 times a night to take a leak, and them kid docs down at the VA been up my ass more often than a Kansas City fairy. I suspect Skinny and them dead Gyrenes got the best of it checking out when they was still young and good looking. Saw this special on TV the other night about how good them coloreds was and how it was racism keeping them out of the Hall of Fame and I imagine that's true, but don't know for sure because I don't follow baseball as much as I did when I was a kid. In fact the only thing I am sure of is what happened the day before the first All Star game in 1932 when Satchel Paige struck out Babe Ruth 4 times on 3 pitches in Wrigley Field, and now you know as much as I do.

[SIGNED] M/Sgt Rudolph A. Bagwell USMC (ret'd)

The Atlantic Ocean and Other Things

by Chris Reed

On my answering machine was a message from Fran. Spain was still treating her well; she had just arrived in Seville, where, later, she was going to visit Christopher Columbus' tomb. Every day, it was becoming easier to converse with the locals as her grasp of the language matured. She wished she had paid more attention to Señora Beck in high school. She told me this on the answering machine. There was a picture of us next to the phone, and in it we looked in love—amorous sparkles twinkling in our eyes, selfless lopsided smiles pressed on our lips. She'd be back in June, at the end of the quarter.

Fran and I had been dating for two solid years, years of contentment and warmth, ease and quiet respect, and we shared an apartment a few miles away from OSU, where we both attended school. When she left I gave her a note that said I'd miss her as a tulip misses its plucked neighboring rose. Those words, I figured, sounded full, and I meant them. Sure they're cheesy, but it's a cute kind of cheesy.

It had been about four hours since my dog had last been out, so I leashed him and brought him out into the breezy spring afternoon. His name is Jay. Somehow, Jay had recently learned the strange ability of nodding back when nodded to. I had taken a liking to us sitting across the room from each other and nodding back and forth. I'd nod, he'd nod, I'd nod, et cetera. This could go on for some time.

After Jay did his business—the fruits of which I left lying there, stinking, in the grass—I went inside and made a pot of coffee. Ever since I'd had trouble sleeping, I'd been drinking decaf. At that point in my life sleep had become an obstacle, something to do and get out of the way as soon as possible—no time for jittery late nights followed by lazy oversleeping. On average, we spend twenty-six years of our lives asleep. And that's if you manage not to get killed by a ridiculous accident or a murderer. Sleeping: talk about a waste of time. I poured the coffee into my favorite mug, one of those silly "I heart NY" ones, with a chip on the rim and oval spoon scrapes in the bottom of it.

I walked in the steamy trail of my coffee to the kitchen table and took a seat. I don't smoke, but Helen, a girl I'd met on the bus a couple weeks ago, does, and she'd left her pack of Camel Lights and a lighter on my table. Why was she at my kitchen table? Because she'd come over whenever she was in the mood—about twice a week. Yes, I still loved Fran. No, I hadn't told her, nor did I plan on it. Those physical relationships usually lose their pizzazz in a couple of months, depending on the frequency of intimate contact. So I took out and lit one of her cigarettes, holding it awkwardly between my first two fingers, sneering the chemical taste on my tongue. From the corner, Jay eyed me with disapproval. I said to him, "What do you know about being human?"

That night Fran called again. I wondered how much her phone bills were.

"I love hearing your voice," she said.

"You too," I said. "Hey, you're starting to develop an accent."

"Really? Gosh." I could tell by her voice she was smiling. I knew it would make her smile, me saying that. "You should come here and visit me," she said. "You'd love all the huge cathedrals. Yesterday we went to this one called the Gothic cathedral, this insanely gorgeous one. And if you came I could introduce you to my new friends. Hey, are you cheating on me?"

After these Gatling-gun bursts of thought, her words took a few seconds to register in my mind. When her question finally did, my head sunk in disbelief. My dog, who was looking at me from his corner, took this for a nod, and nodded back.

"Am I what?"

"Cheating on me. Messing around with other women."

She would've had to have an immaculate international web of information to have found out about Helen and me. Because of the fuzzy morals of the situation, I had decided to tell not even my closest friends. The only people who could possibly know would be eyewitnesses, and since we only did our business in Fran's and my apartment, that limited it to my neighbors, and I knew nobody around here cared what I did or with whom.

"Cheating on you?" I said. Then I remembered seeing some detective movie in which a cool detective had laid out the signs of someone lying, one of them being repeating the question to buy time. "Of course not. Why would you ask me that? Are you cheating on me?" For some reason, accusing her back seemed like a super idea at the time.

"I had this dream-that-wasn't-a-dream last night," she said. "It felt like a premonition. Wait, that means predicting the future, doesn't it?"

"I believe so."

"It was like it had already happened. ESP? Anyway, you were sleeping with some bouncy redhead in our bed."

The words bouncy redhead described Helen to a T.

"Don't be ridiculous. It's just your subconscious anxieties surfacing in your dream-life. I know about these things; I read a book on Freudian dream analysis." My dog, from across the room, was throwing me a "you're a feeble, immoral idiot" look.

"Just figured I'd ask. The dream seemed like more than a dream is why I bring it up."

"You know what else it could be . . ." Like a fool, I went on.

"What?"

"It could be you're seeing all kinds of good-looking Spaniards, and that makes you feel guilty, so your subconscious is showing you images to help you come to terms with your guilt." See, I tend to blabber around the subject when I lie. It always ends up sounding cardboard and pathetic, but I can't help doing it. I should practice lying more, to get better at it.

I kept on talking. "You see, if you're having carnal feelings you feel guilty about, your brain, when you sleep, shows you that I'm probably having the same carnal feelings too, so you can get by without beating yourself up. It's natural."

Carnal feelings?

"So you're saying that you want to sleep with other women."

"No. You think I do. That's what I'm saying."

She sucked in a deep breath, blew it out. "Anyway," she said. "Be good."

Before bed, I was writing in my journal when Helen called and insisted on coming over. She was crying. When she got here, she took me by the thumb and tugged me into Fran's and my room. We got in bed, and her body felt like melting wax in my hands, malleable and syrupy. It was the first time she spent the night—she slept on my side while I slept on Fran's. We woke up the next morning in a mingled-limbed position.

"I gotta brush my teeth," she said. Already, at six a.m. she was cocked, loaded, and ready to go. I rubbed some crusties out of the corners of my eyes. "How about I use your toothbrush?" she said. "Or are you not prepared for that level of intimacy?"

"No, go ahead." We had practically turned our mouths inside out into each other's seven hours ago. What harm could it do? I lifted an arm and took a whiff of my odoriferous armpit. I joined her in the bathroom.

"Tell me about Fran," she said. She squeezed the toothpaste tube right next to the opening.

"She's in Spain. What do you care about Fran?"

"Tell me something else."

"You've seen her picture." Last night, before we fell asleep, she had plucked the picture of Fran and me off the nightstand and analyzed it in the square of moonlight that fell through the window onto the bed.

"I didn't think she'd be so beautiful."

"What's that supposed to mean?"

Kneeling, Helen slid my boxers down to my ankles and dragged her little fingers along my legs as she stood up again. Her hands came to rest on my hips. "Can I get in the shower with you? I'm stinky."

I set two towels on the toilet and ran the water over my fingertips until it was warm as tea. We got in the shower.

"Hey," I said. I believe my using "hey" to begin sentences is something I picked up from Fran. "How come you were crying last night?"

"I wasn't crying."

"Sure you were, on the phone."

"I don't remember," she said. "Something stupid, probably."

The hot water sprayed on my face, dripped down me, coated my skin. Helen was behind me arranging her various hygiene products on the porcelain ledge.

"Did you dream last night?" she asked me. "You weren't sleeping very soundly."

Right then I remembered that I did dream; the images came back to me with the force of a blow to the gut. I dreamt of a hazy, bright scene in which Fran was making love to a handsome, muscular Spaniard in a sea of maroon sheets, her hands clamped together behind his masculine neck, white-knuckled; his arms bent around the small of her back, scooping her into him. Funny how your brain takes things from the day, messes them up, and sticks them in your dreams.

"Did I dream?" I said. "Not that I recall."

"You kept stealing the covers, and I kept pulling them back. Like tug-of-war."

Briefly, I wondered how I could steal *my* covers, but didn't bring it up. And anyway, Helen started rubbing me all over with the soap, so I turned around to face her and forgot all about everything for a good while.

For breakfast I began making some eggs, but Helen bumped me aside with her tiny hip, claiming she could make the best scrambled eggs in the tri-state area. She could crack them open with one hand. I set the table; she hummed a tune I didn't recognize.

"I'll make toast," I said.

"Already being made. You can pour some orange juice."

I stood at the table and watched her. The bread crisping in the toaster, her scraping Fran's spatula through the milky eggs in the skillet. It was right about then I realized she was overstepping the bounds of a physical relationship. Making me breakfast was something Fran did, something that implied caring and affection in a more overt way than our amateurish lovemaking did. Her standing in the stove's heat, red hair still wet, wearing my old Hard Rock Café Boston T-shirt, her with an air of comfortable authority, preparing eggs for the two of us—a couple—it made me dizzy.

My knees gently buckled and I fell into a chair and rested my head on a cold plate on the table. Suddenly my stomach felt heavily unsettled.

"Are you all right?" I heard her say, then felt her little fingers comb through my hair. "Honey, what's wrong?"

I believe she helped me dry-heave into the toilet. I don't remember clearly.

Four hours and a vivid dream later I woke up in my bed to find my mouth parched and Jay's warm, furry body lying snuggled up next to me under the sheet. The closed blinds smartly shut out the sun. I felt viscous, disoriented. Helen was sitting in the recliner next to me, reading my journal by lamplight. After a moment of smiling at me, she leaned forward and closed my journal, saving her place with an index finger. A relatively ornate leather-bound book, my journal was a gift to me about five years ago, and I'd been writing in it in sporadic bursts ever since. Occasionally I'd pen a sappy poem in it or display my childishly whimsical artistic talent by doodling in it, but most of the time I'd just spill my mind onto the page. Last night, for instance, I had written about Helen, and our stumbling upon each other on the bus.

"Feel like soup?" she said.

I lifted myself onto my elbows and looked around. Jay's head rose, his mouth crackled with saliva as he opened and shut it. Helen pressed a warm hand to my forehead and brushed my hair back in a way that reminded me of my mother. My mouth tasted like I had squirreled rotten fruit in my cheeks two months ago and was now bearing the brunt of the stench.

"Has Jay been out?" I said.

"At ten. Don't worry. I'm on top of everything."

"Is that my journal?" She now held it snugly against her belly.

"You're a pretty deep guy, you know that? And when I first met you I took you for an average Joe."

I sat up, rousing my dog again. "Look," I said, "I have to get to class at one."

"No soup?"

Again, I had dreamt of Fran and the dark Spaniard. Him and her rippling rhythmically in each other's hot breath, enveloped in the bright fog and maroon sheets. Steamy Spanish air surrounded their sweating bodies. A vase full of the moist, blossoming flowers he had given her sat absorbing sunlight on the windowsill. It seemed more solid than a dream, like an experience. Like I was there, bodiless, observing the scene with no emotion. And Fran's newly purchased pink floral-print dress crumpled on the floor like a torn wrapper.

"You know what?" I said. I maneuvered so my legs were hanging over the edge of the bed. "I'm going to skip class, and let's go get some lunch."

A coy smile on her face, Helen set my journal on the nightstand, put her hands on my knees, kissed my mouth. She said, "Where do you want to go?"

I said, "It doesn't matter."

Denny's is where we went, the smoking section to suit Helen's vice. We were placed in an uncomfortable corner booth, so that we had to sit cattycorner from one another. Our knees bumped. Helen smiled at me like we were in on some secret the rest of the world didn't know. I didn't know it either, but I smiled back.

"What do you think of club sandwiches?" she said. She held the laminated menu loosely in her hands, so that it swayed.

"I think they're good sandwiches," I said. My menu was sticky. "But I always get breakfast when I come here. I love breakfast food."

She considered this, then said, "How come you're always alone, not doing anything, every time I call?"

I kept my gaze fixed on my menu, on the crisp, clear pictures of the various meals one could order. "I have Jay. He keeps me sort of busy."

"Do you miss Fran much?"

I looked at her to see if she was looking at me. She wasn't. "Why don't we talk about something else?"

"I just want to know."

She put her hand on my arm to comfort me, an action I found strange, since she was the one making me uncomfortable.

I said, "Not as much as I would have thought."

She rubbed my arm a little, and then removed her hand. This made me consider that someone I know might come in and see me with this other attractive girl who wasn't Fran. Someone might wonder what I was doing here with this other attractive girl and someone might spread the word around. But that train of thought seemed paranoid and irrational, so I quelled it.

The waitress, a tall, solid woman, came and took our orders: French toast and sausage patties for me; and Helen got a tuna salad sandwich, apparently abandoning the club idea.

When the waitress left, Helen said, "There's something I want to ask you."

"What's that?" I said.

She leaned in conspiratorially, looking at me intently with her busy green eyes. "Are you afraid of death?" She said it quietly, almost whispering, in a low, serious tone.

I wasn't sure what she wanted out of this question, though it occurred to me that I had written several passages in my journal on the subject. I said, "Yes."

"Me too," she said. "I think about it a lot. I wonder, is fear of death natural, or is it a human construct?"

"I don't know," I said.

"Or is it mostly an American thing?"

"I'm sure other cultures are afraid of death. It's really scary."

It was apparent that this was, in fact, a real concern for her—at least as much as it was for me, and it was not something I took lightly.

"How does one come to terms with death? It's, like, the one definite in all the world. Whatever our differences, we all know we're going to die."

"You're right."

Her eyebrows bunched down contemplatively for a moment, and she said, "We start rotting the second we're born." This was followed by several blank seconds of us staring into space, blinking.

But then the waitress came back, with a tray bearing my orange juice and Helen's Pepsi. I thanked her as she set my glass on the table. She tossed a couple of straws between Helen and me, and vanished.

Helen shifted closer to me, so that her knees pressed gently into my left thigh. We sipped our drinks.

"I'm not so sad when I'm with you," she said.

Looking back, I would think that her saying this would have had an effect similar to when she stood over the scrambled eggs in my kitchen and I got sick, that it would have reminded me of Fran and how much I loved her and made me question what I was doing with this strange other girl—but for some reason it didn't. Helen scooted closer and rested her head against my shoulder. And I kissed her hair and told her everything was okay. Everything would be fine.

On the ride home, Helen and I were sharing humorous stories about our past significant others when, from under my car's hood, a loud grinding squeal began, and continued with increasing volume. The noise sustained for several seconds, its pitch rising, until, with a few slapping sounds like a card in a kid's bicycle spokes, it stopped and my engine cut out and left us gliding down the road, powerless. I pushed the accelerator pedal all the way down to no avail. Still rolling forward in the car, I turned the key in the ignition, but was rewarded with only the wheezy rasps of a dead engine. Luckily we had enough forward motion to pull into the parking lot of a nearby Giant Eagle without further incident.

"That didn't sound good," Helen said.

"This thing's an old piece of crap," I told her.

"Do you know anything about cars?"

"Not even the first thing. Let me pop the hood and have a look."

It was a useless gesture. The mass of wires and metals and plastics and tubes and belts made about as much sense to me as advanced astrophysics. "All right," I said. "Hey, let me use your cell phone to call my friend Mark. He'll pick us up. He should be done with classes by now."

Mark was probably my best friend. We often went drinking together. On the phone he sounded as though I had woken him up, groggy, but he agreed to come. Helen and I leaned against my car in the cool breeze, our shoulders touching, and waited.

"Um," I said. "I sort of haven't told Mark about us, so when he comes could you pretend we're just friends?"

Helen turned to me, pursed her lips, squinted her eyes. She kissed my cheek and grinned. "Of course. I mean, that's what we are, isn't it?"

"You know what I mean." I nudged her playfully with an elbow.

"I think before this happened," she said, "I was telling you about the time my aunt walked in on Scott and me."

"By all means, continue."

Mark arrived and kindly brought us back to my apartment, where, to assure him that nothing was going on between us, Helen left in her car while I invited Mark in for a cup of coffee and maybe a whirl at a video game. He said, "Sure."

Jay, light-hearted pup that he is, jumped all over Mark as he sat on the couch, tail wagging wildly.

"So how come you're not getting with this girl?" Mark asked me. "I mean, she's hot, and Fran's halfway across the world."

Carefully, I handed him his swirling cup of coffee. "You know I'm not like that."

We played a racing game for a while—he won repeatedly—and he left.

I sat on the couch; Jay sat across the room, staring at me. I nodded to him. This time he didn't nod back. He sat there on the pale linoleum floor and stared at me as the sun slid down the sky outside. Then he yawned. Then I yawned.

I broke it off with Helen a few days later. She sobbed and pleaded at first until she realized my mind was made up, I was obstinate. Then she called me an obscene word and hung up without saying good-bye.

Turns out that when I dialed Mark's number on her phone after my car broke down, her phone saved the number. Mark told me she called him that weekend and sheepishly asked him out. I knew that sheepish wasn't a trait that Helen would ever wear sincerely, but I didn't say anything. He thanked me for introducing them. He tells me it's getting serious.

Fran comes back tomorrow. I'm going to the airport with her parents to meet her. Fran and I will take them out to a fancy restaurant in the evening, then we'll bid them goodnight and come home to our apartment and our bed, where we'll pick up all the old rituals right where we left off in January.

Maybe eventually I'll ask her about her dark Spaniard, and she'll tell me the truth about him. His name is Juan or Pedro. He likes motorcycles. And she'll ask me about my girl. And I'll tell her everything except the name. Or maybe I'll say her name was Alison or Kate. Then we'll hold each other and forgive each other, whispering our love to one another, and everything will be mostly back to normal, at least on the surface.

And maybe Fran and I will go on double dates with Mark and Helen, and Helen will shoot me surreptitious looks, eyes gleaming with malice. And I'll give her back friendly grins. Our malignant shared past will be a secret between the two of us, Helen and I. Oh, and Jay. But he'll just glare at me from his corner with his knowing, inky eyes, forever holding his grudge because he doesn't have the healing outlet of speech. His grudge like Helen's grudge, like the nuggets of distrust between Fran and me, hiding just under the surface, festering, manifesting themselves in subtle actions. Subtle little passive-aggressive actions like the dozens I probably do daily without even realizing it, each one of them with a gritty root, something buried I don't speak of for some ridiculous reason or other, but should.

It's stupid, but that's exactly what we'll do.

A Red Bicycle

by Kathryn Hamilton

Me and Rex liked to ride out to the old mill most afternoons after the bus brought me home from school. Well, I would ride and Rex would follow, or sometimes I'd follow him cause he knew by now where we were going. Just a place to go to and mess around after school. By mess around, I mean ride my bike through the open grounds and maybe hunt for any old tools or other good stuff left behind, although I'd pretty much cleaned the place out after going there nearly every day since late September.

See, I didn't much like hanging around my house in those days. My dad, being a preacher, worked at home a lot, always wanting me to be playing football instead of whatever else I wanted to do, and my best friend, well, my only real friend if you want to know, Barney Harris, lived out in the country and rode another bus home so we only saw each other at school. My old man didn't much like me being friends with Barney anyway. Meanwhile I'd discovered the old mill was just about as good as any place to go.

Rex liked it too. Sometimes he'd find rats hiding out in some of the boxes the mill folks had left behind, especially if I'd get them going by throwing rocks at the boxes so the rats would scurry out. Boy, Rex would sure get excited over those rats. Some of them looked big, maybe big as cats. I know my mama would've had a heart attack if she'd known what me and Rex were doing.

Course I didn't tell her or my old man either where I went. They thought I spent afternoons at friends' houses or at the park down the street, I guess. Dad knew I wasn't practicing football, that's for sure. They never asked me anyway. Which was fine with me.

You'd think I'd get sick of riding my bike, but I never did. Even though it was a second-hand one; well, actually it had been remade from several old bikes. Dad had gotten a man who worked at the hardware store—Mr. McReynolds, who was sure lucky they had cash registers at Harrison's and that his name was McReynolds in this town, or he'd probably have been sent to that place in Milledgeville a long time ago (except he could work with his hands fairly well)—to fix it for me when I got my paper route that fall. Dad said he couldn't afford another new bike so soon after getting Bobby his, so I'd have to use this one for a while. I had already kind of figured out Santa was your folks, but that pretty much gave it away since Bobby had gotten his bike—a Schwinn—from Santa the Christmas before. This one rode okay, except the seat kind of stuck up funny in front, so I learned to go slower and be more careful on rough streets. Sometimes it felt kind of good, but too many bumps and I'd sure be sore. I knew whackers were used for something more than peeing but I hadn't figured out exactly what yet, so I thought I'd better play it safe.

I guess it sounds like I lived in a dumb, boring place if all I had to do every afternoon was to ride out to an old abandoned mill with my dog and mess around, which is just about right. Murray back then was just a hole in the wall in south Georgia down near Waycross where the gnats are out twelve months of the year, Main Street being one long street like an uphill bowling alley with the courthouse—ugly with peeling white showing green underneath—at the end. Old men would gather like birds on a fence most fine days to sit on the bench right outside the courthouse and talk. Me and Rex would pass them on our way to the mill and I'd wave just to be nice. Only one of them I knew was old Mr. Sumners who had been janitor in our church until he got too old to bend over and come up easy, so he let John Rogers take over and went to the bench.

Our church was around the corner at the end of Downy Street, a big, old red brick building that had been there since the 1800s, probably looking just the same as now. Of course, we'd painted it a few times on the inside and probably put in electricity and stuff like that. See, it kind of really was our church since my old man was the preacher there, had been since before I came around. My brother Bobby remembers living somewhere else; at least he says he does. He's older by two years and says he remembers when they lived in Macon, but that's before I arrived on the scene. And Bobby never let me forget that he'd lived somewhere else besides plain old Murray, Georgia, even though he was only two years old when they moved here, and I sure can't remember a thing that happened when I was two. Bobby always said he had a superlative memory, but he said he was superlative in everything, and he believed it too.

Not that he wasn't pretty good at a lot of stuff. He was real good at football. Baseball too. He didn't play basketball yet, but I knew we just had to give him time. See, Murray didn't have a kids' league for basketball in those days, so you couldn't play for real until the eighth grade back then.

Every so often I got kind of glad Bobby was my brother, like when Roy and Leon Calder got to messing with me before school. One of them, usually Roy, the older one who probably should have been in about eighth grade but was only in fifth, would come up and grab a button on my shirt and say, "Want that?" I found out real fast you lose, no matter what. If I said, "Yeah," he'd jerk it off and hand it to me; if I said "No," he'd jerk it off and throw it away. Geez, I hated it when Roy did that. I knew Mama would ask me a thousand questions about that missing button and then Dad would get in on it. And Leon thought he was hot stuff too. He'd come up and grab me on the chest, right on the ninny, and say, "What's up, dipshit?" Man, that hurt. They'd laugh and laugh, and I'd want to bash those snotty faces in, but I knew I couldn't. See, they were tough; both Roy and Leon had the biggest arm muscles I'd ever seen. And they must have liked for everyone to see those muscles, too, because seems like they were always—even in winter—wearing short-sleeved shirts. And they walked with their arms away from their sides, almost like their arms were too big to fit right or something. Kind of like Popeye or Bluto (while I probably looked more like Olive Oyl back then).

Even more than me, though, they really liked going after my friend Barney. He's even smaller than me. They'd do the same button-pulling or ninny-pinching thing on him as they did on me—whatever struck their mood—but Barney'd always mess up and start to cry. Man, I knew it was hard to keep from sniveling, especially when it hurt, but so far I hadn't cried yet. Of course, with me they didn't yell "Jew boy" or "Jesus killer" either.

They learned fast, though, not to mess with me when Bobby was around. Bobby, even though he was younger than Roy, was bigger, and Roy just never tried to bother me after that one time Bobby socked him. That was after the second button incident. I felt a lot of pleasure seeing Roy's nose gushing blood all over his shirt, not as much pleasure as if I'd socked him myself of course, but pretty darn good, I'll tell you. Course Dad wasn't too happy when he found out Bobby had been fighting, Dad being a preacher and all. We both had to listen to his sermon about "Love thy neighbor" and "Turn the other cheek," not that we hadn't heard it all before.

Of course, Bobby couldn't be with me all the time.

See, I guess I was kind of a nerd then. I hadn't grown much in the last couple of years, kind of got stunted, Dad said, because I'd been sick a whole bunch, mostly flu and colds, but when I had chicken pox, they had a time with my fever getting so high, even had to put me in the tub with ice cubes once. Anyway, I guess I was kind of runty and I liked to read, so maybe I did act a little nerdy. Encyclopedias were my favorite thing to read. Dad had just bought us a new set of World Books that year and I read the two S volumes from front to back. One book even opened automatically to snake cause I read that part so much. I made a hundred on the test the World Book lady gave at school that fall, only she didn't give me a hundred, said I missed one on flying squirrel being a rodent, but I took the book up to her and showed her where I got it right and she said she'd change my grade, but she didn't. I think she thought I cheated or something. She wouldn't know I read that part already on flying squirrels when I read the S volumes all the way through.

This was the year Joe DiMaggio married Marilyn Monroe, the year of Brown v the Board of Education, the year my brother won the Best Camper Award at Boy Scout camp, and the year I discovered I would soon have a little sister. I was nine years old, and all these events affected my life, or at least at the time I thought they did, even though one other event actually became the one I remember most vividly.

See, first off, I was a Yankees fan in a house where it was thought to be a sin to be a Yankees fan. Both Bobby and my old man, well, practically the whole town for that matter, rooted for the Cardinals since St. Louis seemed the closest to being a southern team in those days. Whatever team you were for in Murray, though, it probably wasn't the Yankees. In fact, quite often during World Series time, my dad would harangue the Yankees from the First Presbyterian pulpit. It was almost like God was against me too, so I had to secretly chortle when Mantle would hit one out, or Whitey would throw another shutout. I'd hoard my Yankees baseball cards, trading carefully with foolish classmates who, hating all Yankees players, would fall into my trap and trade a Berra for an Alex Grammas.

Geez, it hurt when Joe went and married Marilyn. Plus, I had to listen to my dad and Bobby discuss how stupid he must have been to get caught up with someone like her. Oh, our supper conversations became dominated for what seemed like years with that event, I can tell you. Man, I was sure glad when Joe finally smarted up.

The Yankees weren't the only team my dad hated either. Sometimes it seemed he felt more animosity toward Notre Dame football than he did toward the Yanks. He'd yell at the radio when they'd be announcing scores, sputtering stuff like "Papists! Papists playing football!" My mama used to get mad at Dad, but it didn't do any good. She'd say, "Robert, hold your tongue, now," but he wouldn't. Bobby hated Notre Dame too, though he couldn't get away with yelling at the radio. Like two peas in a pod, my mama would say about my dad and Bobby, or Pete and Repeat. Personally, I didn't care one way or the other about Notre Dame since they didn't play Georgia or Florida either for that matter. They could sit up there in Indiana and beat whoever they wanted for all I cared. Dad never harangued Notre Dame in his sermons, though, like he did the Yanks. Maybe he was a little scared of the Pope.

As for Brown and the Board of Education, well, I guess all I remember of that was one afternoon my mama asking me if I'd mind going to school with the coloreds. She wore her frowny expression that day, and made sure she asked me after Bertha who cleaned for us on Thursdays had already caught her ride and gone home. I shrugged and said I didn't care and went on reading the encyclopedia I'd been reading, but I did pause to think after Mama had gone back to the kitchen. I didn't know many colored boys and girls, not really. Bertha's kids had grown up and left Murray for Detroit, and, according to Bertha, were just raking it in up there and begging her to come too. But she kept telling my folks, "Law, I'd be scared to go that far from Georgia." Anyhow, I found it hard picturing myself seated in Murray Elementary Mrs. Henderson's fourth grade next to colored boys and girls cause I couldn't put faces on them. I bet Roy and Leon would give colored kids a hard time, though. I wondered if this new law meant they would have to come to our Sunday school classes and church too. I guess everybody in Murray knew folks at the colored church made more noise, at least more than we First Presbyterians. You could be riding by with your car windows just barely cracked and hear the shouting and singing coming from their little building on Bell Street Sundays. I wondered how my old man would handle that; he liked his services orderly, all the hymns smooth and calm. I mean, we didn't even do "Amazing Grace" for Pete's sake—too emotional, my dad said. I kind of smiled to myself to think of Dad trying to preach with folks hollering out A-men and Yeah in the middle of his sermon. But then, maybe old Mr. Wallace would stay awake better with some audience participation.

 Boy Scout camp usually came at the end of summer right before Labor Day, since we shared our campsite with other kids' groups, like Girl Scouts and the Salvation Army Camp for Underprivileged, to name a few, and for some reason they all got to go earlier than we did. The end of August might be cool in some parts of the country, but in South Georgia, summer heat has not yet left. In fact, it's probably the worst part of summer since all the bugs have had a good three months to multiply, so by late August, you're lucky if you can see through the swarming fog of gnats and mosquitoes. I kept welts on my legs and arms from their bites, plus some frequent patches of poison ivy—all pinkly coated with calamine and all heavily scratched. In fact, my legs had probably completely recovered themselves with new skin several times over before we left for camp.

    Now, I wasn't yet a scout that year, just a cub who wasn't really supposed to go to camp, but since my dad was scoutmaster, I was privileged. I think, too, that my mama had something to do with my going. And Dad wanted to help me get tougher, I bet. Anyhow, I went along, with one other kid who wasn't old enough either whose dad helped mine, but he was a real baby and I sure didn't want to hang out with him. He had the bunk over mine at first, just had to have the upper deck, and one night I woke up with pee dripping onto my face. We swapped bunks fast, even the mattresses.

    Camp Mooney looked a hundred years old. When I got to eighth grade and read the poem that starts, "This is the forest primeval," I thought right away about Camp Mooney: all those huge, ancient pine trees surrounding a few old broken-down, unpainted cabins, with stilt-like legs that were beginning to crumble so that some tilted noticeably. If you put a marble on the floor of any one of them, I bet it would roll right out the door.

    It's probably a good thing there were plenty of air holes in those cabins too; first, because of the heat even at night, and second, because of the farting contests after lights out. Not really contests; someone, probably that Butch Jones, cause it always came from his side of the cabin, would start it off and intermittent farts would explode in the night silence for what seemed like forever. Even I got in on it. Of course, it wouldn't really last that long. My old man would let us go for a while, then he'd holler, "That's enough, boys!" There'd usually be one or two more, but everyone knew my dad meant business, and we'd settle down.

    We did all the usual camp things, like hiking, canoeing, swimming. I wasn't good at much of those; however, when we got to crafts, I excelled. Funny thing, Bobby did all the other stuff great—as you'd expect—but he never was so good at crafts.

We were making leather belts. Oh, they came from some kind of kit, of course. But we had to put them together, then burn designs in with some special tool, then paint Indian-like pictures on them. Mine was shaping up just fine too, with just enough triangles and circles burned in; next I would paint maybe some trees and teepees on it. I really looked forward to that hour or so of crafts every afternoon. I even had a lot of older guys coming to me for help and advice on making theirs once they took a look at my belt.

That was the funny part. See, Bobby, from the first day we got to camp, was in contention for the Best Camper Award. Actually, he started getting ready for it before we left, asking Dad for advice—like refreshers on canoeing maneuvers and such. Shoot, I just felt good if I could get the canoe going without tipping it over much less think about fancy maneuvers. But not Bobby. He was a born competitor, and he was doing great, getting more points than any of us—except for Harold Dean.

Harold was the son of another Murray scoutmaster, and Harold was a competitor too. As a matter of fact, I think both the dads were pretty competitive. I know my dad sure wanted Bobby to win and beat Harold. Besides, the Deans were Baptists.

Anyway, day by day, points began to pile up, and Bobby led Harold in just about every category, but just by a little. One night after Vespers—a little earlier than usual as Dad hadn't been as wound up as on other nights—Bobby came up behind me while we walked back to the cabins and whispered, "Meet me at Mossyback—11:00."

I knew it had to be important. See, Bobby hadn't even looked my way the whole week so far; I guess he still resented Dad's letting me tag along when I really wasn't old enough.

Not that I blamed him much. He didn't come to camp to be saddled with a nerdy little Cub Scout brother; that's for sure.

So at 11:00, or thereabouts (I had to keep checking my watch with my flashlight under the cover while hoping that the fart contest wouldn't be prolonged this particular night), I slipped from my bunk, out the doorway (no doors on these cabins), and through the woods to Mossyback's Grave.

Now don't get the idea that Mossyback's Grave is any big, scary thing. I mean, it's really just a mound of dirt with moss growing on top that someone decided to stick a tombstone on and say a hunchback got buried there is all. At least that's what my old man told me. He said someone probably wanted to get some scary stories going at camp. I figure Dad probably had it right. After all, even Girl Scouts camp here, for Pete's sake.

So I followed the path through the woods with my flashlight—it wasn't far—and waited for Bobby, hoping he wouldn't be too late, cause even if you know it's not a hunchback's grave, just being out in the woods at night by a tombstone can give you goosebumps. The light from my flashlight, along with that of the moon, turned Mossyback a kind of sickly gray-green, and the wind blew a little bit so I kept seeing a spooky shadow of a branch moving slowly back and forth across the grave. Lightning bugs blinked all around me while my flashlight beam tried to follow any strange sound that came from deep in the woods.

So while I waited there with the familiar noises of chirping crickets and mosquitoes buzzing in my ears, trying not to think about where I was and feeling each minute's full length, I considered what Bobby might be needing me for. I came up blank, but I knew he probably wanted me to do something for him; that's the way it usually worked with my big brother.

I had it right, at least about him wanting me to do something for him. See, Bobby had heard about my belt—

we didn't have crafts at the same time—and he wanted me to help him with his. "Otherwise, Ben, that little snotnose nerd Dean'll beat me out of my award. Ben, you gotta help me."

He had it all planned. He'd just slip me his belt when he left the crafts cabin, and I'd work on his instead of mine.

Of course I agreed. I mean, he's my brother, right? I figured I could get my belt done later.

Man, did I have to work on that belt. First off, Bobby had messed up putting it together, and I had to take it apart and start again, and then he'd burned these crooked triangles and circles—they looked kind of like wopsided water balloons—and I had to burn them again to even them out. I had to be real careful not to let anyone see me, so I took to sitting in another area, but that didn't really matter since the guys probably didn't even know I wasn't there. I kept itching to get to the painting part on my own belt, but ran out of time, it took so long to repair Bobby's. But I got it done. Looked pretty good too, considering what I'd started out with.

Bobby won the award. He stood up there and grinned and grinned at everyone while Dad—who was trying hard to look like he didn't care—handed the plaque to him. Bobby had made me promise never to tell about the belt, said he'd really get me good if I told. He didn't have to worry. I wouldn't have.

Once school got going, camp and the summer that in June had seemed to stretch before us like an endless highway became a distant memory as I busied myself with regular life, first having to straighten out my paper route that Billy Brookes had messed up while I'd been gone. See, he'd overslept a couple of mornings, and that's all it takes to get some of my old customers going. I mean, these guys get up at 5:30 or 6:00 every morning just waiting on their paper, and it's a major flub if they don't get it on time. So I had to go by and assure them I wouldn't let it happen again. Then

Mama announced her news. I suspected my old man already knew, but even though I had noticed my mama getting a little pudgy, I had no idea she kept such a secret. Sure enough, she told us at supper one night that we'd get a baby brother or sister before Valentine's Day. Of course, both me and Bobby held out for a brother, but as you already know, we got a little sister instead. Which was okay, I guess. I mean a baby is a baby.

Then along about Thanksgiving time, I noticed Rex didn't seem to be feeling so good. Me and Rex had been heading out to the old mill nearly every afternoon for over two months; then one day he just wouldn't go. He'd gone running with me that morning while I delivered papers, even though days had become short and we had to leave in a darkness that had a nip to it now, and I sure found it harder and harder to get up. I mean, Rex loved to run, especially now that cooler weather had arrived. He was a hound, a Heinz-57 Dad called him, solid black except for a brown spot over one eye. Pretty smart as dogs go too. I taught him to fetch before he was six months old and to sit and speak not long after that. Although Mama complained that my instruction fell short since I hadn't taught him not to smear snot on the kitchen window when he begged to come inside (only she didn't say it that way, of course). But I couldn't believe it when he stayed on the porch instead of following me that day. I came back right quick, didn't even go all the way down the street as a matter of fact; I just messed around the yard that afternoon and checked on Rex periodically.

By the next morning, though, I knew something was wrong. Rex had begun to shiver, didn't even try to get up anymore. And when I went out to go on my delivery, he didn't look my way. I got a sick feeling in my stomach and kept it all that day. I felt even worse when I got off the bus that afternoon and Rex wasn't waiting there like usual. I walked home and found Dad ready for us to take Rex out to see Dr. Webber.

Dr. Webber—the best we had around these parts for a vet—looked Rex over pretty good, then gave him a shot and a bunch of pills and said he thought it might be distemper. That made Dad frown, though it didn't sound so bad to me, not like rabies or something.

But that shot and all those pills Dr. Webber gave us for Rex didn't seem to be working. Nothing worked.

I stayed with him as much as I could, kept him covered up with an old blanket so he wouldn't shiver so much. I mean, I even talked Mama into letting us move his bed inside to the kitchen at night.

And I said a lot of prayers. Now, just because my dad's a preacher doesn't mean I talk to God a lot. Probably I kind of take it easy there if you know what I mean. Since Dad does so much praying already, I must have figured anything extra was redundant. So praying for Rex was kind of special for me. I promised God just about everything I knew to promise—all the general stuff, like I'd be a better brother, son, student, you name it. Then I even got to specifics like promising to never say damn or hell or even sonofabitch again. I figured God couldn't turn me down.

But Rex just wouldn't get better.

That Saturday morning, Dad said he wanted us all to go with him to the hardware store in town to look for our Christmas presents. See, it was getting close to the big day, only a couple of weeks left, although I sure hadn't begun to feel the Christmas spirit. However, Dad insisted, so I tucked Rex's blanket around him in his bed on the back steps, told him I'd be right back, and off we went.

As soon as we got to Harrison's I saw what I wanted. Old Mr. Harrison had lined up five or six Schwinns in his front window, but I could only look at one of them: a red ten-speed with the thinnest, smoothest, sweetest tires you ever saw. I could almost feel myself whizzing through the streets of Murray riding that thing, know the splendor of having a million jealous eyes watching me. I could hardly walk through the door; I didn't want to take my eyes off of that bike.

Bobby wanted a special knife, and he and Dad went to the back of the store to look at those. Mama walked over to the window and stood by me. I hadn't uttered a word since the moment we'd pulled up and parked in front; I could only stare. Mama reached out and touched my shoulder softly; she whispered, "Don't set your heart on that, Ben." I looked up and felt all those sweet, red bicycle dreams evaporate at once. Her face told me more than her words.

I knew. The new baby would put a strain on a budget already stretched. Dad had already warned us. Oh, man, it hurt to turn my back on that bike. I swallowed hard. "Okay, Mama," I said, knowing it wasn't okay, hating the world's unfairness, wanting to scream and yell and hit someone.

"Maybe next year, son." Mama patted me again and I walked slowly over to the knife counter to look with Dad and Bobby. I could use a knife, I guess.

When we got back to the house, I immediately remembered Rex and felt guilty for having forgotten him for the hour or so we'd been gone. I jumped out as soon as Dad stopped the car and ran around to the back.

At first I couldn't find him. The blanket I'd wrapped around him had fallen to the ground near the steps and I had a vision of Rex having a sudden recovery. My heart fluttered quickly as I looked around, believing I'd see him running toward me, tongue hanging pink from his mouth, ready to give me his welcoming licks.

Didn't I know better? I felt my heart drop heavily only seconds later when I saw a black lump lying at the base of the big Blackjack oak that loomed at the edge of our yard.

Whistling softly and calling, "Here, Rex, here, boy," I walked over there. I heard Dad behind me saying something; I caught a phrase of "Oh, I told him," then "Don't, Ben," but, though I think I realized what I might face, I kept on.

Rex still felt warm to my touch, though I had no question he was gone. A hole the size of a quarter in his temple, flies already gathered near the coagulated blood there, left me no doubts. Tears poured down my face as I sat next to Rex and stroked his smooth, sleek coat.

I felt Dad trying to pull me away, but I wouldn't get up. I heard him trying to explain, but didn't absorb his words. I felt so guilty for having gone away, so guilty for wanting that bicycle, for forgetting him for all that time. What did it matter if Mr. McReynolds hadn't finished the job and carried him away? Who cared?

We buried Rex right there, me and Dad, right next to the Blackjack. Bobby helped too, though I think I could have done it alone. Mama had to make me leave the grave and come in that night after dark, but I didn't cry again after that.

I never went back to the old mill, though I started to a couple of times. I just couldn't think of what I'd do out there anymore, so I always turned around and came back. Eventually, I ended up going to the park down the street and shooting hoops. I'd gotten a basketball along with a new knife for Christmas, and I actually got to be pretty good at hoops, believe it or not. My old man even walked down a few times and showed me the right form for shooting free throws. He got to calling me "Deadeye" after that cause I hardly ever missed.

You know, it's kind of funny that Bobby never did get interested in basketball, but I didn't really mind.

Bi-Coastal

by J. R. Carpenter

I'm still at work, stuck in a conference call, tied to my desk with a phone wedged between my shoulder and my ear. It's 5:40 on a Friday afternoon. Eastern Standard Time. Everyone else on the call is in California. Pacific Time. It's still the middle of the afternoon for them. They're all running full tilt on the premise that they will accomplish Many Other Things today. People keep joining the call and then leaving again. I can't keep track of who is on the line. We should have had this call last week but people kept canceling. Each time it got put off, I came to dread it more. Now it's finally unfolding—sloppy and mistrustful—just as I had feared.

It is the end of the day for me. The end of the week. I've been at work for three more hours than anyone else on the call. I am wilted and done for, and worst of all, I have an echo on my line. We've all experienced this kind of conference call echo before. Sometimes everyone can hear it; today it's just me. I sound like I'm two inches tall and stuck in a tin can. Hearing my own voice distorted in this way makes me feel edgy and inadequate: no matter what I say I feel as though my words lose weight and come out sounding hollow. I tried hanging up and calling back in but it didn't help. It's a continent issue—there's nothing to be done.

Don't even ask me what this meeting is about. Really, don't get me started. Everyday is like one big giant meeting only interrupted by the occasional change of scenery or the introduction of new characters. It's hard to get anything done with so many people panicking about how much stuff they have to get done. Now people are actually calling meetings to discuss previous and impending meetings.

Hank and I had our own meeting before we went into this conference call. We agreed that we would not be able to build the brand new on-line event registration system that marketing's been asking us for. We figured we had a perfectly acceptable contingency plan, but no. Liz still wants the whole shebang and will not be thwarted by technicalities. She says she doesn't want to know about the back-end. She says it's too late for a work-around. Liz loves buzzwords. Anthony, calling in from his cell phone, is furious that no one told him about any of this earlier, even though we had been trying to arrange this meeting for ages now. The buck-passing is escalating. Micro-management emerges as a form of denial. Things are decidedly out of control. As the issues overlap and become exaggerated people start taking things personally.

"This is NOT personal," I insist to a woman named Sylvia, who I've spoken to often but never actually met. I don't know how I got off on the wrong foot with this woman but I'm not doing a very good job of reassuring her now and it's making everyone on the call anxious. I wish everybody would just calm down. I am so distracted by the echo on the line that I lose track of what I'm saying. I am getting ahead of myself as I speak. I am getting into trouble.

"All I'm saying is that we *already have* an on-line registration form for this type of event. We don't *need* to build a new one."

"Yeah," Hank pipes up. "We can't keep re-inventing the wheel."

"Look, if you guys think I'm doing such a crap job here . . ." Sylvia is up a tree again. Thanks a lot Hank, I think to myself, thanks a lot. He's right of course, but I wish he wouldn't say it quite like that cause now Sylvia is telling us all over again how hard she's been working. She has been, but the same also goes for everyone else too. Now, sure enough, Liz is talking about how little bandwidth any of us has, which drives me crazy. Technically speaking, we have lots of bandwidth. We have a dual T3 for crying out loud, but no one would get that kind of humor at this point, so I keep my mouth shut.

I don't know how such a non-technical bunch came to be working for a software company. No one wants to hear why something doesn't work, they just want you to make it happen for them. Plus, it's politics. Some things may very well be technically possible, but that doesn't make it a good idea. The more I try to come up with a solution that works for everyone, the more complicated everything seems. The more I try to simplify, the more muddled I feel. The empty sound of my voice on the phone line taunts me. To hell with technology, the phone doesn't even work. Hank keeps agreeing with everything I say, which, for some reason, is making things worse. An echo in triplicate. I take off my glasses and put them on my desk. I am trying to convince Liz that even if my department had the time to build a whole new system, it wouldn't exactly work the way Sylvia wants it too. When Anthony cuts in and starts talking about a completely different issue, I put my head in my hands. Who called this meeting anyway? It's hard to reconcile the continent between us and the interdepartmental conflict of interests at hand. I can't shake the hollow sound of my own voice mocking me somewhere in the distance. I want to shout at the phone—"You're twisting my words!"

This feeling of tele-alienation is symptomatic of a work-related condition now known as Bi-Coastal Complex. Bi-Coastal Complex is common to employees of global corporations. I swear I type and talk on the phone for a living. Email is the glue that holds us all together. When I get to the office in the morning there are endless messages from San Francisco from the night before. When they get to work they will have endless responses from Chicago, Montréal and New York. I know not to expect responses from emails I send off to Tokyo until the next day but I might catch Munich on the phone if I get to work early enough. The hours in which we all overlap are so few.

And then there is the travel. Sometimes you feel lost—everything looks familiar but you are not sure which office you're in. Or which city. Sometimes you feel very tired but you're not sure just how tired because you can't remember which time zone you're in. Sometimes you think you've stayed in this hotel before but you haven't. You have to keep reminding yourself of the little things like a dozen different passwords. And always save your receipts. Other symptoms of Bi-Coastal Complex include knowing exactly how many air miles you have at any given moment, keeping a suitcase half packed, and stocking your filing cabinet and your laptop carry-on bag with bottles of hotel moisturizer.

Partly in order to remind myself where I am every day, I have acquired an intimate knowledge of the view outside my window. My eyes focus on the same buildings and trees and patches of grass hour after hour while my mind is in meetings in Petaluma, Paris, London or LA. Even without my glasses on, the amorphous physical world is sometimes more concrete to me than the intricacies of the arguments, the delicacies of the negotiations taking place over the phone. Today it is partly cloudy. I follow the movement of one very white cloud as it passes in front a much darker cloud while our ill-fated conference call bumbles on. Liz is tearing into Hank now. Sylvia seems to be talking to someone else in the background. Somewhere someone's cell phone keeps ringing and ringing. Suddenly I feel a pair of hands, calm and cool on my shoulders. They rest on my neck and upper back for a brief moment, more gently than a massage, and I feel a light kiss on the side of my head, just above my telephone ear. I reach up behind me. My hand finds her hair briefly, and then she is gone.

Her name is June. June sits three feet away from me. In an ocean of work the desks form rows like waves. Every day June and I sit back to back, bobbing and floating on the same tides of work, gossip, frustration and change. We hear each other's phone calls. We steal each other's envelopes. We help each other with the little things—filling out expense reports, recovering disc space, booking hotels. This is a work-related intimacy born of proximity. We are on the same coast. We speak the same language. Email washes over us in tides and gradually we are worn down: smooth and weary from weathering the storms. We used to eat lunch together; we hardly ever have time anymore. Especially not during the Tradeshow season. The tradeshows are upon us right now, like monsoons. They are vital to growth, but they flood us regularly with work. Thankfully, June's light touch just now interrupted my clouded thoughts. I smile. That was her intention. She knows what I'm going through. I've done the same for her—a ritual laying on of hands when someone is in danger of going bi-coastal during an international conference call.

Our call is still dragging on. Mercifully, I have stopped talking. I can see the situation clearly now in my mind's eye where I couldn't before. I envision the terrain of our call:

we are all messing around in the waves as they break near the shore of a nameless beach, coast unknown. The play has become frantic. General splashing about has given way to fear, a loss of footing, flailing and shoving each other away while grabbing each other for support. Sylvia, as it turns out, is ever so slightly afraid of the water. I'm not the strongest swimmer either. I struggle to make my way toward her, to try and coax her to come ashore with me. She is afraid I will drag her down somehow. She panics. She kicks; her foot gets me just below the knee. I lose my footing, sink slightly, and suddenly, I feel the undertow. I don't fight it. I go limp. It drags me down. I refuse to panic. The current carries me as far as it has to go and then unceremoniously releases me. I rise to the surface. I am much further from the beach now then I had been before. It is calmer here and I begin to tread water, breathing more easily. I shake my head like a wet dog and a salty pinwheel of water whirls from my hair, a spectacle captured briefly by the sun.

Instantly I am back at my desk. I raise the height of my swivel chair. I put my glasses back on. I remind myself—I am three hours ahead. I speak from the future. I must go back in time to help get this call on track. Sylvia is still fighting for a unique on-line event registration process. I think I've finally figured out why she thinks she needs one and how we could convince her that we can give her the same results given the technology we currently have. Explaining that to her is outside of the scope of this meeting. I want to talk to her about it in person.

Everyone is talking at once and no one is listening to each other. I think Anthony hung up a while ago. "Sylvia," I interrupt—"Sylvia, I am going to be in San Francisco next week. Can we take this discussion 'off-line' until then?" She responds to Hank instead. "You know, I don't even know what you guys do, I mean besides post stuff on the web." She means Hank and I. What a jerk. I bite my tongue and secretly will Hank not to respond to this comment. Later I will email him. We will bitch about this on our own time, but please dear God, let's not go into it now.

"Sylvia, what about Tuesday afternoon, what are you doing Tuesday afternoon? Can we meet?" She blocks that attempt too. "I'm working like a dog non-stop all day on Tuesday," she replies. I sigh. Silently. I take a look around my office. For as far as the eye can see people are working like dogs, for whatever that is worth. I mean, how hard do most urban dogs work anyway? My mental image of this conference call taking place in the waves of an unknown beach is suddenly interrupted by an exuberant golden retriever streaking past to catch a Frisbee in mid air. He trots back to show us and shakes himself in manic, doggy joy. If only he were a sheep dog. If only the issues we are trying to settle were a wide roaming flock of sheep, they could be herded together and driven toward the pen.

"So what about Wednesday afternoon?" Everyone is talking at once again and no one hears me. "Sylvia." My voice is calm. I am the only one who hears the echo when it bounces back at me as the other voices fall suddenly silent. "Sylvia, I would really like get some face-time while I'm in San Francisco. Even if it's only for half an hour. I think it will make communication easier for us going forward." I can't believe I've had to resort to such corporate-speak. Oh well, whatever it takes to calm Sylvia down. She sighs audibly, unaware of how much she's telling me with that sigh—she's going to make a date with me to get me off her back and then she's going to blow me off at the last minute. I'm so bi-coastal by now that I know this, but I don't care any more. I'll deal with that eventuality if and when the time comes. In the interests of tying up the call, I take her at her word.

"So Wednesday, say three or four in the afternoon, can you make some time?"

"OK, which do you want, three or four?"

She is still vaguely suspicious of me. Who can blame her? It's part of the bi-coastal condition—to mistrust, underestimate and fear your counterparts in other offices. Put a few frazzled strangers working for different departments of the same company on either ends of the continent confusing the hell out of each other and accidents will happen. I feel so helpless against the tide of the call that I focus on a face-to-face meeting like a beacon in the storm. Things will be more normal after that. The logistical details fall away and I remember that we are just people after all—people doing jobs. There will be endless more conference calls and thousands of emails propagating misinformation and confusion. Maybe we'll never really understand each other, or the task at hand, but I will have a face in my mind at least. Knowing what the person on the other end of the phone looks like and what they do with their hands while they talk, these details are like guiding stars in a clear night sky. "Let's say four," I tell her, "and I'll confirm with you when I look at my flight information."

Liz is suddenly cheerful. "So we can all be friends now?" She hates it when there is discord, especially when she's not one hundred per cent sure what it's about. I know Hank is still smoldering mad, but he's decided to let things ride for now. Anthony is long gone. It's hard to say if we're even ever so slightly further along than we were before this meeting, but Liz takes this minute agreement between Sylvia and I as some kind of point of closure and they all rush off to the rest of their day. I hang up the phone with a grim satisfaction at a seven fifteen on Friday afternoon. It rings again almost immediately. I cringe but the call display tells me it's just my co-worker calling from downstairs. He's offering me a ride home. I gratefully accept. I remind myself that my day is over and I force myself to resist the temptation to read any of the thirty-seven emails that have found their way to me during the time of the call. There will be more before the west coast day is done. I'll download them all on Monday morning and read them on the plane.

While my computer is shutting down for the weekend, I stand up, raise my arms straight up in the air and twist my torso side to side. The waters seem calmer now. We have weathered yet another storm. Weary from the struggle to stay afloat, I survey the sea of desks, rowboats in an ocean of work, some of them still manned at this late hour in the week. Engineers mostly. They come in late and work late. They don't spend so much time talking on the phone. June left over an hour ago with some girls from marketing. All of accounting is long gone. "I'm going home," I announce, to no one in particular. No one takes this statement personally. No one even looks up. Maybe no one heard me. After trying so hard to keep my tongue in check all week I speak whatever comes to my mind just to hear my own thoughts again. I note that now that my call is over my voice is clear and definitive. It does not echo without another coast on the line.

Dedicated in loving memory to Julie Gagné,
who helped me with the little things.

Hot Mango Chutney

by Theresa Martin

    Mango chutney, heavy in fruit, sugar and spices brings to mind the Indian women who make it for their husbands in cloistered kitchens, disrobing in the heat of a cook fire. Royal cooks of the Rajahs combine ingredients to make the perfect chutneys, seeking a perfect balance. By Ayurvedic tradition, Indian cooking respects the yin/yang, the masculine and feminine aspects present in every living thing.
    I have a friend who makes mango chutney. She sometimes offers it in barter for things she wants me to do. I remember when she needed a truck, my truck, to pick up some boxes she had stored in her father's barn. On an unseasonably warm day in late April, Kristen and I drove north among Indiana farm fields dotted with dandelions. We picked up around twenty boxes containing house wares, books, and pictures. Kristen assured me that her chutney recipe was buried in one of those boxes and she was in the mood to make it.

About a week later, I found three jars of chutney in front of my apartment door. She left them when I wasn't home. When I saw the jars stacked like a tripod on my welcome mat, I knew from experience that the payment was well worth the time I had given.

When my supply of mango chutney runs out, I sometimes pray for the phone to ring. I might even call Kristen if I'm feeling desperate, steeling my nerves for the feeling I get when I hear her voice and old memories seize my mind like the first heavy frost stealing the late autumn landscape. I've tried store-bought chutney, but it just isn't the same.

When we were lovers, Kristen called to invite me over one swollen evening in August, saying mangoes were on special at the market and she was going to make chutney. She asked if I had ever tasted it.

"No," I said, "what's it like?"

"You'll just have to wait and see," she tempted.

Kristen was a taste tester of sorts. She dabbled in anything and everything that sounded interesting to her. For the past five years, she had lived in and out of three different communes. Although she was raised in the Catholic faith, she sampled other religions as a matter of course, saying she liked to consider new ways of thinking. When I took her to a Cantonese restaurant, she ordered three entrees, claiming, "Don't you just love it—there's so much to choose from." That was Kristen's philosophy of life. Her lust for life was also the key ingredient in my attraction to her.

When I arrived at her house, she was sitting outside on a crooked porch bench smoking a cigarette. The air was so heavy with moisture that the exhaled smoke hung in the air like a blanket spread out over a nearby field of soybeans. I lowered myself into a lawn chair with a broken strap, careful not to break the others. She handed me her cigarette.

"Hot enough?" she asked, wiping the back of her neck with a damp rag.

I breathed a sigh and wiped the sweat from my face with the end of my shirt, saying, "Won't be able to sleep tonight anyway. Might as well be here watching you sweat over a hot stove."

I hoisted myself onto the counter in her cramped kitchen while Kristen dumped the bag of mangoes out before her. She chose the four that were the ripest and set them on a wooden cutting board, grooved from years of hard use. Sweat trickled down my back and into my jean shorts as we listened to jazz on the radio and chatted about Alanis Morissette's latest CD.

The recipe card, splattered with gold flecks, was propped against the back of the blue tile counter. I never saw her look at it. As I studied the scribbled words, my taste buds cringed: salt, brown sugar, vinegar—a full two cups of vinegar! It sounded hideous, but I kept my opinion to myself.

"Where did you learn to make this?" I asked "from your grandma or something?" I swept my arm across my forehead and then across my already damp shorts. Kristen's furrowed forehead informed me my question wasn't well thought out.

"No, my family isn't Indian." She rolled her eyes. "It's a recipe from a cookbook, you know." She answered as if she were an authority on cuisine, although she wasn't. In my experience, Kristen only liked to cook what she wanted to cook, when she wanted to cook; which often didn't include breakfast, lunch or dinner, especially when the weather was hot and humid and sleep was impossible no matter how tired we were. Every time we lay down on the bed, we would sweat until the sheets were wet and we had to get up and change them which made us sweat even more. During August, in Indiana, it isn't even worth going to bed. So we made chutney instead.

Kristen arranged the ingredients in a row on the counter. Right in front of me, she placed a step stool so she could reach up above the cabinets for two blue speckled bowls. I noticed how her long rust-colored hair clung to her shoulders, glued in place by her sweat. With one finger, I hooked and pulled a strand from under her arm before she lowered herself to the floor.

Perched on a stool, she wrestled with the mango, cutting away the pit to release its pungently sweet flesh. She chopped the fruit into one-inch cubes and placed them in one of the bowls with two heaping tablespoons of salt. I winced. Kristen eyed me apologetically, then laughed at me while stirring the mangoes around with the salt. She covered the bowl with a towel and got up to go out for another smoke.

We took the one leftover ripe mango and a knife outside to wait for the chopped mangoes to marinate in the salt. I sliced the fruit in half without peeling it, only separating it from the pit. We sucked on the sticky sweet flesh, sitting cross-legged in the grass, juice dripping down our elbows onto our thighs. The ants grew drunk cleaning up our mess. The air was still, yet vibrant with trilling cicadas and bullfrogs bellowing their ripened lust across the amber glass surface of the pond. Although the moon was full, clouds curtained its glow, except for momentary intervals when they would open up spreading light onto the grass like a giant scroll bearing stories of the Gods. She licked her fingers clean. I wiped mine on the grass.

Hindu legend tells that the mango tree grew from the ashes of the sun princess after she was incinerated by a wicked sorceress. Because the Emperor fell in love with the mango flower and its fruit, he would sit by the tree for hours each day. A mango ripened and fell to the ground at his feet and from the seed emerged the sun princess in all her beauty. Thus, in India, the mango became a symbol of love.

Kristen rinsed the mangoes in the sink and drained them on a clean white towel. Into a large stainless soup pot, inherited from her grandmother, she deposited each ingredient in turn: the rinsed mangoes, tamarind pulp, cider vinegar, brown sugar, raisins, crushed red pepper and allspice.

On the wooden cutting board, she transformed a six-inch piece of fresh ginger into a small pile of tiny white chunks no bigger than radish seeds.

"Have you ever tasted fresh ginger?" she asked, offering me a small piece with a wicked smile. I sniffed it before placing it on my tongue.

"Whoa," I spat it back into my hand.

"Don't you like it?"

"It's really hot," I said, reaching for a glass to get a drink of water. "Are you going to put all of that in?" I pointed to the growing pile of minced root.

"Of course, it gives the chutney the best flavor."

Within a half hour, the air in her trailer filled with the biting odors of vinegar and ginger. Kristen handed me the spoon and left me to stir the pot while she washed some dishes in the sink. The fumes were so strong I had to squint as I stood over the bubbling concoction. My eyes watered.

Stirring the pot was a meditation. I sat on the stool sliding an old wooden spoon, with a hole in its center, back and forth, back and forth. Kristen informed me that constant stirring is crucial to keep the chutney from burning. There's no rushing the process. It's just a simple exercise in letting go of time and agenda, giving them over to the chutney.

Making chutney requires a commitment—four hours at least. I never minded all the time we spent sitting in Kristen's kitchen talking philosophy, religion and food while I watched the glistening muscles in her arms and neck pulse as she stirred, with faithfulness, the emerging chutney. I can only liken it to a weird sense of foreplay.

"It's done," she said, hoisting the pot to the counter where seven jeweled jelly jars waited. After filling the jars, she scraped the last bits of chutney into a bowl and set the pot in the sink to soak. She reached into a cabinet and brought down a box of wheat crackers and set them on the counter.

"Now for the test," she said, scooping some chutney onto a cracker and handing it to me.

"Aren't you going to try it first to see if it's okay?" I asked, afraid to subject my lips to her eccentric cooking.

"No, you go first," she said, waving her hand at me, disregarding my concern. I lifted the cracker to my lips. The chutney smelled like liquor and made my head swim. But what I tasted that midnight would haunt me for the rest of my life.

All of my taste buds hummed at the same time. It was sweet like caramel, as hot as a fire ant's sting, sour like properly aged wine, with just a hint of saline, the amount you might detect in a single tear.

"What do you think?" she asked, scooping up her own golden glob.

I reached in the box for another cracker, "Wow, this is incredible! I could get addicted to this stuff."

"Yeah, the trick with chutney is to create a balance, you know, the way love ought to be." She picked up another cracker and dipped it into the bowl. "The flavors should, you know, complement each other perfectly." She said this smiling as if she had won an award for her culinary skills.

"Just like us?" I jested, attempting humor, but feeling serious all the same.

"No," she said, "not like us—not like anyone I know." Her head turned, refusing to face my surprise. "That kind of love just doesn't exist."

I didn't ask her why she said what she said. Maybe I didn't really want to know. Instead, I sank my attention into her chutney, knowing we would never really be lovers, but just friends.

Uncle John

by Tom Henighan

When I was a kid, although we weren't rich, I never lacked for toys. My memory is selective and doesn't always stretch back to those significant incidents that some people seem to be able to fetch from the past, but I remember the toys all right.

There was a small metal bi-plane, with a spring door and mysterious spaces inside the cabin to hide figures—Lindbergh or Wiley Post perhaps; a delivery wagon with a horse, a driver, leather reins and milk cans that looked exactly like the real thing. There was a World War I German helmet with a spike, a wooden Springfield rifle complete with a sliding bolt, a real blackjack, decoders and cipher sets. Endless things, in fact, all quite marvelous, including a collection of comics—any one of which in mint condition would enable me to retire right now. There was even a doll carriage.

Well, the doll carriage, I didn't quite get, but I remember how much I wanted it. I recall standing in a toy shop the size of Grand Central and picking it out from among the thousands of tempting things crammed in there. I remember how much I liked the feel of the steering bar and how, wheeling it back and forth, I could imagine a baby's big eyes staring up at me.

My parents, taken by surprise, put up with this perverse ecstasy for about two minutes and half. Then my father leapt forward and pulled me away from the thing. Horror dissolved into embarrassed laughter as they tried to pass off my vagary as a joke. They shook me a little and slapped me on the shoulders, as if I had a poisoned apple stuck in my throat. Then they turned sheepishly to the salesman, shrugged their shoulders, and said I probably wanted a little sister or brother.

I didn't. I wanted the doll carriage. But when I saw my Uncle John shake his head disapprovingly, when I saw his half-distant look, his teeth-gritting attempt at a smile, I knew it was hopeless.

My mother, who looked alarmed, took me aside and told me rather briskly: "Don't be silly, Paul. Baby carriages are for little girls. Uncle John doesn't want to buy you one! And he won't buy you anything at all if you keep it up."

I guess that calmed me down, even though my need for the doll carriage was very real and I might have shed a few tears of resignation and loss. They soon consoled me with a bright red racing car, the kind you sit in and pedal, or some such thing. Uncle John would have paid for that, I'm sure. Uncle John paid for a lot of my presents, and he was pleased to be around when I danced my joyful thanks. He liked my boyish enthusiasm and was always encouraging me to play sports and war games, and not to be so ready to help my mother in the kitchen.

My father and Uncle John had come over to New York from Scotland together. They were nearly the same age, and were recognizably brothers—both well-made but very short and compact, dark and smoothly handsome, with thick hair, strong faces and deep-set thoughtful eyes.

There were differences, of course. Although my uncle was a couple of years younger than my father, he was much more sophisticated. When Uncle John came to New York he went to work for a famous hotel, the Barbizon-Plaza, and soon became a manager of some kind, making a good salary. He stuck at this and climbed fairly rapidly. In the end he was almost the family plutocrat. That came out in the way he dressed—good suits, white shoes and spats, expensive, with just a touch of gangster glamour. It also came out in the way he smoked.

My father rolled his cigarettes with cheap tobacco, while Uncle John displayed his imported cigarettes in a fancy holder. With his broad confident face and that ivory holder set between his teeth, Uncle John even bore a faint resemblance to FDR, an image he cultivated quite assiduously.

My father, by contrast, was a shy, moody fellow, who lacked all small talk and social style. His chief party gambit was likely to be a terribly awkward joke, delivered with the worst timing, a joke his listeners had already heard many times and wished they hadn't.

While Uncle John had run away from home early, Dad stayed around and pleased his mother by going to work in the coal mines in Scotland. As a result he had acquired a hangdog attitude toward employers and developed a fear and loathing of money and the moneyed world. His one gift was his athletic skill. Before long, he had made a name for himself as a soccer player, coming close to international status. He soon moved to the States on the strength of promises from the soccer clubs in the old Pennsylvania league.

Dad was quite the hero in that setting, and although there wasn't much money in it, he was showered with gifts, free meals and trips, while dozens of women, including my mother, hovered around, trying to snare his attention. Of course it was a very parochial sphere in which to shine, and my Dad had no idea how to exploit it. Those old soccer leagues were very shaky, the teams were always going bankrupt, and when my father suffered a serious groin injury he had to retire, with no savings, and no compensating skills

For years he found nothing to do with his athlete's body, never even playing pickup with the kids on weekends. Instead, he sat smoking in the kitchen, reminiscing about the good old days with the Heidelberg or Scranton side, and persecuting me and my sisters until we began to hate and avoid him.

My mother, who thought she had married a local hero, was very disappointed, but settled down to steer the growing family through these trials. She took in washing, scrubbed floors, or baby-sat, while my father floated from one temporary job to the next, becoming, in succession, a night-watchman, an elevator operator, a warehouse hand.

Uncle John, of course, was a great support during these hard times. He had been interested in my mother, and had dated her a few times, but he had to give way when she opted to marry the soccer star. This caused no hard feelings between the brothers.

John took the whole business rather lightly, it was said, and since he never lacked for women his rejection by my mother had caused no more than a slight detour in his social life, or so it seemed.

He handled the situation so well that, before he married, he even came to live with Mom and Dad, renting the extra bedroom in our small apartment near Grand Concourse, a sensible arrangement that ended up saving money for all of them.

Uncle John was a very busy man. He worked long hours, whereas my father was often on part-time, or actually unemployed. Despite this, my mother felt it her duty on most nights to hold dinner for John, which caused my father, at a minimum, to sit around and grumble. When my uncle did appear, sometimes a couple of hours late, he would soothe my father's ruffled feelings with small presents, or even with the promise of a job. John often got tips on job openings, and if they were suitable, he would pass them on to my father. He'd explain to us how he'd run into some old soccer crony who remembered Dad as "the great Pat Walsh." According to John, to get "fixed up," all my father had to do was to go and see him, which of course Dad never did. Even before this message was delivered, John would have produced a bouquet of flowers or a box of chocolates for my mother, while she, all smiles, would be mixing the highball she'd been waiting so long to make for Uncle John.

When I was in my twenties one of my aunts told me about these times, twisting her lips a little scornfully at my youthful naiveté, for I made nothing of it, and remembered only with gratitude all the times Uncle John had led the way to some fabulous toy store, how he turned up at the apartment with a box of toy soldiers, a bag of comic books, or some treasure that he correctly divined would move my young heart to real ecstasy.

How I admired the man, with his tweed suits and silk ties, his polished brogans, his fedora and pigskin gloves. He would sit by the big Zenith radio, the cigarette holder pressed between his teeth, saying very little, yet mouthing—in his polished way—opinions that seemed the very essence of wisdom. Now and then, with amazing poise and timing, he would get up and make a drink for my mother, or pay her some compliment on the dinner, or on her dress or decor, and once again urge my father, in a kindly way, to go to night school, to get himself a car, to take some driving lessons, always trying to push him away from the ruts of depression that seemed constantly to trap him.

I could never understand how my father could resist these pleas directed toward his improvement; why he refused to learn to drive, why he paid no attention to his clothes, why he opted out of job training, and resisted every chance to exploit his former stardom.

Uncle John, as I got to know him, seemed more and more unlike my father, different from any of the adults I knew at that time. He made me think of a magical visitor, some Captain Midnight or Daddy Warbucks from the serials or comics. To me he seemed more like a politician or a diplomat than a member of our family, and I felt ashamed of my father for sitting glumly by and never acting on John's sensible advice.

Year by year my father's jokes grew fewer and more labored, dropped in among the endless cigarettes, as my mother gritted her teeth and wondered if Uncle John might come for Saturday dinner.

When I was about seven or eight, I guess, everything changed. Uncle John finally got married. His new wife was a tall gaunt woman, with thin lips and cold blue eyes. Her name was Marcie, and it was a while before I noticed how much she hated my mother.

I'll never forget the way Marcie used to sit in our living room, a bored look on her face, while Uncle John told one of his stories, and my mother came in carrying a tray of appetizers and a drink. Marcie was a teetotaler, and mother never seemed to have the right drink to please her.

"I'll take water," was her most common phrase, and my sisters and I, when we got old enough to notice, named her "the water buffalo." She used to sit there and eye me coldly, or if she did talk to me, she would correct some fault of manners or speech or posture, asking me, for example, if my back hurt—was that why I didn't stand up straight? Or didn't I think it was time I earned some money of my own and helped my parents (I think she first raised this issue when I was about nine years old). After she came along I hardly ever got any presents from Uncle John.

The years passed and she and John had no children, and I overheard my mother saying how it must embitter the poor woman, how it made her sour (by this time I had four sisters, none of whom looked or acted much like me). My father got on with Marcie all right (she rolled cigarettes and even laughed at his jokes), but after an evening with her my mother would shake her head and sigh, lamenting the terrible fate of poor John who'd been collared by such a person—"a good woman in her own way, but not for him," as Mom discreetly put it.

Then there was the incident at the wedding. It was a memorable moment, the first time I really had proof of how much Aunt Marcie disliked my mother. I might have been about eleven. The wedding was a huge one, held in somebody's roomy house; there was a large tent outside and possibly a barn. I remember eating myself into a state of bliss with several plates of chocolate cake and then suddenly going into near shock when I got my first kiss (in a clothes closet) from a beautiful cousin named Hillary.

I guess Mom and Marcie had somehow managed to avoid each other through most of that reception. I was feeling great and just happened to walk into the refreshment tent. We kids were supposed to keep out, but it was irresistible, because inside was a long table crowded with punch bowls, beer kegs and bottles of wine standing up together like rows of organ pipes.

My mother was serving punch with a long silver ladle, presiding over three or four bowls, chatting and laughing with the guests. I ran up to her and began to babble about how Uncle John was going to give me a ride in the rumble seat of his new Ford coupe, when all of sudden Marcie, white-faced and trembling, came marching through the entrance.

"Oh hello, Marcie," my mother said brightly, greeting her with a big smile and waving the ladle over one of the bowls.

"That boy!" Marcie said, and pointed to me. I shivered, though all I had done was to try out the rumble seat, jumping in and sitting there, smelling the leather, hardly able to wait for the real ride.

Marcie stood still in her tracks, glared at me and at my mother, then reached down and with both her hands seized one of the bowls and sent it spinning across the table in my mother's direction.

The liquid slopped and splashed, my mother gave a little cry, and the bowl rattled and finally came to rest just on the edge of the table.

Mother stood astonished, staring down at her dripping apron, as Marcie turned on her heels and stormed out of the room.

I was horrified and I guess I babbled out something like: "What's wrong, Mom? What's the matter with Aunt Marcie?" and waited for her to explain.

I expected Mom to be upset, but she just smiled, a smile that puzzled me then, though later I might have recognized it as the one a woman wears who has just forced her rival to show her hand, to reveal her worst side in the worst possible light.

At the time, of course, I had no such thoughts. It was just a moment, more puzzling than scary, because my mother hardly seemed upset, and everything was somehow accounted for by the fact that Aunt Marcie was such a touchy bird.

It stuck in my mind, though, that scene. I could never figure out why I was a villain; only later did I realize that that ride in the rumble seat was the first (and last) treat in a long time I had had from my Uncle John.

As my aunts explained it later, that incident marked a turning point. Things had come to such a pass between Mom and Marcie that everyone decided to pull their horns in a little, "for the sake of the family."

Years followed, full of polite exchanges, and marked by infrequent and carefully orchestrated visits.

All the same, my uncle appeared again in my life at some critical moments. He got me my first summer job, and part-time work to see me through college. When I left New York for a government job in Washington at age twenty-one he arranged for me to buy various expensive evening clothes at a discount, and booked my hotel in Georgetown.

He even gave me some advice, quite solemn and Polonius-like, explaining how to get to the Washington hotel and what to do when I got there. I remember how he shifted his cigarette holder, squinted through his glasses, leaned over and said to me:

"Take care of yourself, Paul. Don't stand on street corners, and always keep your hands out of your pockets."

I found it puzzling advice, though maybe he was still thinking of the doll carriage.

I didn't see him again until many years later, when I returned home from overseas to go to my father's funeral. By then I had learned something about the world, and even a few things about myself. Uncle John, though he had aged, looked as distinguished as ever. Marcie wasn't with him.

He took my mother to dinner. No doubt they had a lot to talk about. He had moved away to Pennsylvania and was about to retire.

And so he did, nor is he dead yet. In fact, Uncle John turned eighty-five last year. When I visited mother recently on her eighty-fourth birthday his name came up for the first time in a long while. She explained to me that Uncle John had recently written her.

"You should have seen the terrible scrawl!" she said. "I was sure the poor fellow had lost his wits. I couldn't read a word of it and just put it by. And then he called me. Oh yes, he called me all the way from Pennsylvania. And you know what? Marcie's left him."

"Really? Isn't it a little late?"

My mother ignored this reference to the age of the parties concerned. "What a bizzum she is!" she cried. "You know why she left him? She was afraid he'd get sick and they'd spend all his pension money on doctors. She decided to take her share of it and get out. I always knew she'd leave him."

My mother's outrage was tempered by a smile of triumph. "Of course I know why he called me," she explained with calm conviction. "He probably thinks he can pack up and move in with me. I wouldn't put it past him. You should have heard him whining over the telephone. It's sad! When I think what a fine man he was. When I think of the good times we had with him when your father and I were first together. Oh, we lived such a cheery life, the three of us! John always bucked your father up and encouraged him. But that woman, she certainly didn't like a good time. I could never understand why he married her."

"Maybe he was disappointed at not getting you," I said.

My mother looked at me sharply.

"Well, he had his chance," she continued in her usual blithe vein. "Nobody could ever say he didn't have his chance. It's twenty years now since your father's death and this is the first time I've heard from him. That woman had him tied up in knots, you know . . . Poor John, I always loved the way he smoked his cigarettes."

"I liked the presents," I said.

"Wasn't he generous? He never forgot your birthday. And don't forget the jobs he got you later on. And that tuxedo! Why, he treated you as if you were his own son."

"He didn't like the baby carriage though."

My mother stared at me.

"Baby carriage—what baby carriage?"

"You don't remember it? I once asked him to buy me a baby carriage."

My mother seemed outraged. "I've never heard of such a thing! I wouldn't go around bragging about it if I were you."

I quickly changed the subject to Aunt Marcie. "She seems to have resented Uncle John's interest in me," I said.

Here, my mother was on surer ground.

"Of course, what can you expect? She never had any of her own. She must have tortured him all those years . . . Still, I don't want him down here. I'm not going to cook and clean up for that old man! I like my life just the way it is, thank you!"

Later I called my lover, Stacey, and told him the whole story. "I wouldn't go around talking about the baby carriage," he warned me.

I was discreet, I kept my mouth shut, but thinking out the implications of everything, for the first time in my life I began to feel a little sorry for my Uncle John.

Brunch

by Dawn Ladds

It's Sunday morning and Paul and I aren't going out for breakfast. Morris knows something is wrong. He's a very smart dog and he *knows* it's Sunday. He also knows that if I don't go out for breakfast, he's not going to get any leftover sausages. He's thumping his fat, black tail against the hardwood floor just to let me know how supremely pissed off he is. I feel bad for him—I want sausages too.

My crutches are leaning against the phone on the wall, I can make it to the coffee maker without them though. As I lean against the counter with the coffeepot in my hand, I can see Mrs. Cramer out the window. She wants to know why I never go to church. She hasn't come right out and asked me yet, but I can tell that's what she's thinking. She's standing out on her driveway in that frumpy blue dress she wears every Sunday. She's got the matching purse out this weekend too—nice touch—extra frumpy. I pour a cup of coffee. The people around here are really something. "Even you know what she's thinking, don't you, Morris?" I say to him.

Yesterday, a man and a little boy came to my door to tell me that they had an exciting message from the Lord, and would I mind if they came in to share it? I opened the door a little wider so Morris could see them. Morris loves people, he just doesn't know how to react when he sees them. He came racing down the hall, jumped on the boy, and knocked him down. Morris didn't mean anything by it—he's a lab, he jumps up on people—but it was enough to send them away. Maybe I should open the front door and let Morris jump up on Mrs. Cramer.

My buddy Paul and I used to go out for brunch every Sunday. If you get to the restaurant while everyone else is at church, you never have to wait in line. It's perfect: no screaming kids, no crayons. Last Sunday, Paul was late. He was supposed to show up at my place by nine a.m. Instead, he showed up at 9:02. I could hear that nasty old Buick coming from a mile away. It was ridiculously old and the brake lights hadn't worked in over a month, but it got us to brunch and back. Paul made just as much money as I did, but he was one of those weirdos who likes shitty cars. If you ask me, it made him feel like a badass.

I had just let Morris out for one last pee when I heard the Buick's rattling chug coming down the road. That day, it sounded like woodpeckers caught in a fan. Dying, screwed-up woodpeckers. He pulled into my driveway just as Morris lifted his leg. "Good piss, Morris?" he asked, getting out of the car.

"I was wondering when you were going to get here," I said, grabbing Morris by the collar.

"Oh, no, Viv! Is it 9:02 already? What the hell was I thinking?" I stuck my tongue out at him and led Morris into the house.

"You be good while Mommy's gone, Morris. I'll bring you some sausages, I promise." I pushed Morris away with my leg, so I could shut the door.

"You still feeding that poor creature leftover sausages? He's going to fart himself into oblivion one of these days and it's going to be all your fault," Paul said. How was I supposed to respond to that? He was probably right. One of these days, Morris is just going to let out the fart from hell and be blown into outer space. That's where people and dogs go when they die—outer space. And once you're in outer space, boy, you just don't come back. All the karma in the world won't save you once you start floating around in that inhospitable crap-hole. "You're sure you don't want to go to church, now?" Paul asked as we backed out of the driveway.

"Yes, very sure."

"Would Madame prefer IHOP?" he asked, putting the car in drive.

"Madame would greatly prefer IHOP." I felt around inside my pockets, for my lighter. I guess I had forgotten it. I looked around the car for the pull-out lighter, "Where the hell's your lighter?" I asked.

"There isn't one," he said.

"You mean to tell me that this car's so old, it doesn't have a lighter?"

"Yup."

They had better have matches at IHOP, I thought. We pulled into the parking lot and walked into the restaurant.

"Two for smoking?" the hostess asked.

"Depends on whether you've got matches or not," I said.

"Here, have this," she said and flipped me her lighter. She seated us in a booth in that crappy, glassed-in smoking section that Paul and I had gotten so used to. If I had told her we were atheists instead of smokers, she would have put us in the same section. Glass keeps smoke and atheism out of people's hair.

"You folks having your usual, or do you need to see the menu?" Crystal, our usual big, husky waitress asked, bringing the coffeepot over.

"The usual, please, Crystal," Paul said.

Crystal looked at me, "You want me to just wrap the sausages up, or are you pretending like you're going to eat them this week?" Paul laughed.

"Yeah, what the heck," I said, "wrap them up, Crystal." Crystal nodded and trotted off to the kitchen.

I stared quietly into my coffee cup for a couple of seconds. Paul seemed to know what I was thinking. He got this funny look on his face and asked, "How many Sundays without church are we at now?"

"48."

"You're keeping track?"

"It's been almost a year, Paul. Fifty-two weeks in a year, minus one month—it's not brain surgery. We haven't been since Dad's funeral."

"Right," he said, dumping three packets of sugar into his coffee all at once.

I could tell he didn't want to bring it up. I didn't blame him really. Paul came over for Christmas dinner last year because he had nowhere else to go. He never really got along with his parents all that well. I'm not *entirely* certain why. He was a really handsome guy—tall, built, well-manicured nails, perfect hair—but he never had girlfriends. As far as he and I went, I never even considered dating him after two weeks of being his friend. We just got too close too fast. There was something unsettling, almost incestuous, about the idea of dating Paul. Anyway, part of me always knew he was gay. I never knew how to bring it up, though, so we never talked about it. Part of me thinks his parents knew it too and it made them uncomfortable and that's why they didn't get along. I'm rambling now but the point is, Paul was there when Dad had a heart attack during Christmas dinner. It was one of those freak accidents: one minute, turkey—next minute, life support. We stayed at the hospital with Dad as long as we could, and then Paul drove me home.

When we got home from the hospital, the house felt ten degrees colder. I put another log on the fire, but it didn't help. So I threw the family Bible in, leather binding, gold edging and all. I got a good five degrees' worth of heat out of that. And I'm talking Celsius, not Fahrenheit. It was Mom's Bible anyway. I guess she and Dr. Asswipe couldn't find room for it in the penthouse of the Manulife Center.

Paul's my family now. Moving here was a big adjustment and if Paul hadn't moved down here with me, I'd have slit my wrists six months ago. I think Paul handled the change better than I did. I'm not sure what my problem is. After all, it's not like I have any family back home to miss. Maybe I just miss Martini Night at Outer Mongolia—who's to say? Anyway, he liked to shop and he never tried to get into my pants. What more could I ask for?

"You think you'll ever go back?" Paul asked.

"Huh?"

"Church, dumbass. Do you think you'll ever try going back to church again?"

"Not bloody likely," I said, chewing on my stir-stick. "Want to go play mini-golf after this?"

"Yeah, we can do that."

"Come to think of it, I'm really not that hungry. Are you?"

"No," Paul said, "not at all."

"Wanna just take it home?"

Paul called out waitress over. "Sorry to do this to you, but can we just get our meals in takeout boxes?" Our waitress said that would be fine and hustled back to the kitchen.

"Morris will fart like a king today," I said to him, just as the waitress brought over our boxes. She gave me a dirty look.

"Mini-golf, then?" Paul asked, getting out of his chair.

"Mini-golf," I said. He offered me his arm, just to be silly. Just to be silly, I took it and together we strutted out of the Cyber-Glass Smoking Atheist Containment Chamber. I let my cigarette dangle from the corner of my mouth so I could leave a wisp of smoke behind for the non-smokers. Screw them.

We got into Paul's pimp-wagon and pulled out of the parking lot. "You think you're actually going to beat me today?" I asked him.

"Yup, I think today's the day," he said, surfing one hand out the window and turning the radio on with the other. We pulled up to a stoplight. It gave me a chance to light another smoke. I guess I forgot to give the hostess's lighter back. "You and your damned cigarettes," he said and stuck his neck up so he could lean his face out the half-opened window.

"Light's green," I said to him. He took another deep breath of air. I don't think he heard me. "Hey, dumbass! Light's green." I gave his sleeve a little tug.

That's when it happened. Paul's head slammed forward into the window frame. I didn't see what happened next because my head slammed into the glove compartment. When I looked up, the Buick had been pushed into the oncoming traffic lane, somehow we were on an angle. Again. My side, this time. Hard enough to dent the door into my leg. I saw the blood, and then I must have passed out.

When I woke up, I was in a hospital bed. I asked a nurse where Paul was and if Morris was okay. She gave me a sympathetic look and said she'd find a doctor for me. I lifted the sheets and saw my leg. I had a cast up to my knee and there were cuts and bruises everywhere.

"It took us a long time to get the glass out of your leg," someone said. I peered out from under the sheets. A woman of about fifty in a doctor's coat was standing next to my bed with a clipboard.

"Where's Paul?" I asked.

The doctor looked solemn. She started talking medical mumbo-jumbo, which I drowned out, and then said, "Miss Lunsford, I am so sorry. We did all we could." I went quiet. "I'll leave you for a bit, you just push the button on the side of your bed, if you need anything. Do you need anything right now, before I leave?" I stared at my leg under the sheets and said nothing. "Just push the button then, Miss Lunsford," and with that, the doctor left.

I didn't want to talk, but I didn't want to be alone either. I pushed the button on the side of the bed. A fat nurse with blonde curls appeared. "Is everything alright, Miss?" she asked. I stared at her. "You just lost your friend, didn't you?" She sat down on the edge of my bed and held my hand. "Our Father works in mysterious ways, my dear. Try to remember that Paul's in a better place now." Paul? Better place? Paul's in outer space. Outer space is not a "better place." Who the fuck did this woman think she was? I stared at her for a while. Then she got up from my bed and turned to leave.

"You stupid ass!" I screamed at the nurse. "He was important! What the fuck am I supposed to do now? Huh? What the fuck am I supposed to do now?" I had to get out of there. "And where is my fucking dog?" I said, red-faced. I pulled back the sheets and tried to get out of bed.

"I know you're upset, but you can't leave," the nurse said. I screamed a few choice words at her and she left. Five minutes later, she came to my bedside with a needle—a tranquilizer, I guess.

The next morning, I took a cab home. The cab driver helped me out of the car and up the front steps. Morris had shit all over the house. I wasn't sure how I was going to clean it up with this stupid cast on, so I left it there. It sat there for a few days, adding a certain *je ne sai quoi* to my living room, until Stacey, my secretary, came to bring me a fruit basket.

She cleaned up Morris's poop and we had a couple of drinks. We chatted for a while until she gave me the whole God-has-work-for-Paul-to-do-in-Heaven speech. I kicked her out after that.

There is a knock at my door. I grab my crutches off the wall and hobble over. Morris just about knocks me to the ground as I open the door. He wants me to let Paul in. Instead, Mrs. Cramer is standing there with a pie in one hand and a Bible in the other. Morris jumps on her and tries to get his nose into the pie. She puts her things down for a second and pets Morris's ears. "Hello, Vivian," she says sweetly, "how are you doing?"
"Peachy," I say, "come on in."
"Shall I set this on the kitchen counter for you?" she asks, smiling.
"Yeah, that's great. Thanks, Mrs. Cramer."
"Evelyn, dear. You should call me Evelyn." I couldn't care less. "I decided that instead of going to church today, I would come over and worship with you," she says, making herself quite at home. She walks over to the coffeepot and looks around.
"The cups are in the second cupboard to the left," I tell her, "the cream's in the fridge. I think the sugar's still sitting on the counter." She reaches into the cupboard and grabs Paul's favorite Bart Simpson mug. I want her to put it back.
"What an odd little fellow," she says, pointing to the picture on the mug. "'Don't have a cow, man!' What an interesting piece of advice. Who is this, Vivian?" I roll my eyes.
"It's Bart Simpson," I say into my coffee. Mrs. Cramer chuckles about "Don't have a cow, man!" and pours some cream. I watch her nails curl around Paul's cup. "You just sit down over there, dear, and I'll read to you." She pulls out a chair at the kitchen table. I'm too dumbfounded to say anything. Most people know better than to come over to my

place to get their Jesus-fix. For some reason, though, I can't bring myself to tell her to leave. It's kind of nice to have some company on my first Sunday alone.

Staring at the ceiling, I notice there's a light bulb burnt out. That doesn't stop Mrs. Cramer, though. "Not to worry, dearie," she says, "there's plenty of sunlight." She tilts her Bible toward the sun and reads a few passages. I stare at my leg and think about Paul.

"Thanks, Mrs. Cramer," I say politely, when she closes her Bible.

"Do you have questions about the Lord's teachings?" she asks. I pick at a scab on my knee and think for a minute.

"Yeah," I say, "my best friend was gay. Is that OK with God?"

"Well, dear, the Bible says that—"

"And where are my fucking parents? God's a bit of a cheap bastard, isn't he?" I light a cigarette while Mrs. Cramer stares at the ground and fidgets with her wedding band. "Why don't you tell me what it's like to have a family, Mrs. Cramer? Tell me. I wouldn't fucking know." I lean in and stare at her, waiting for a response. She pretends to pick some fuzz off her dress.

"You just enjoy your pie, dear," she says, getting up, "and here, have some reading material. The Lord will answer all your questions." She hands me her Bible and walks towards the front door.

"Don't have a cow, man!" I scream after her. When I hear the door shut behind her, I hobble over to the counter. It's an apple pie—the good kind—with the crumbly stuff on top. I shove forkfuls into my mouth and look at her stupid book. "The Lord will answer all my questions, indeed!" Just as I take one last drag on my cigarette, there is another knock at the door.

"For crying out loud," I say, shuffling to grab my crutches. Luckily, Mrs. Cramer's husband lets himself in. He's still in his church clothes when his kind, old face appears in the kitchen doorway. He has a light bulb in his hand. It looks so tiny in his gigantic fingers.

"Heard you had a light bulb burnt out," he says.

"Yeah, that one over the table," I say, pointing to it. He gets up on a chair and changes it for me. I thank him.

"Anything else I can do for you while I'm here? Would you like to talk about anything?" He sits down at the table next to me. His big, bushy eyebrows furrow sympathetically and then he looks at my hands. I think he wants to hold them and tell me everything's going to be okay. His dirty fingernails are about the size of my fist. His fingers have little cuts all over them from pruning his rose bushes without gloves. His eyes have that wise look about them, like he knows about people and life, or something. "I know you miss your friend," he says.

"Do you?" I ask with tears welling up in my eyes. I bite my tongue to try to stop them from coming. "Do you, really?"

He stares at my hands and is silent for a couple of minutes. "Can I do anything else for you before I go?"

"Actually, would you please put a fire on for me?" I ask.

"No problem," he says, getting up, "sure did get cold in an awful hurry this week, didn't it?" He walks into the living room. I can hear him crinkling paper into balls and throwing them into the fireplace. He comes back into the kitchen. "Got some matches or something around here?"

"Yeah." I hand him the hostess's lighter, it's been sitting on the table all week. He walks back into the living room and lights the kindling. "You going to be okay?" he asks.

"Just fine," I say, looking for my cigarettes, "I'm sorry I was rude to your wife."

"Oh, Evie's a tough old girl. She'll bounce back," he says. "Well, I'll be going then. You just give us a call if you need anything, okay? Oh, here's your lighter," he tosses it to me.

"Okay, Mr. Cramer, thanks."

"You take good care of your mommy, okay, Morris?" He gives Morris a kiss on the nose and lets himself out. Morris always takes good care of his mommy. I play with his ears for a bit and look into those big brown eyes of his. No book could ever make me feel better the way that black, furry face does. He sniffs the lighter in my hands. It probably smells like sausages, like brunch—like Paul. Morris looks me square in the face and then jogs off to the corner of the living room. He comes back with a tennis ball that Paul had written on one day when we were bored. It said, "I'm Morris and I'll fuck you up if you steal my tennis ball." I smile weakly and throw it down the hallway. Morris chases after it.

"Enough," I say to myself. I put the Bible between my teeth and the pie under my arm and hobble them into the living room. I sit down on the couch with Mrs. Cramer's Bible. It's obvious she loves her book. The leather is as pristine as it was the day someone with a shaky hand wrote "Dearest Evie, may the Lord always light your path" inside the cover. I run my finger down the spine and wonder if I should give God another chance.

If it wasn't so cold in here, maybe I would give God another chance. Morris returns with the tennis ball and stares at me expectantly. He needs to go to the park, poor guy. "Not right now, Morris," I tell him. I grab the brown, wool blanket off the back of the couch and draw it around my shoulders. I sigh and then I throw the Bible into the fireplace. "This one's for you, Paul," I say. I watch the navy blue leather shrivel and burn. I eat another forkful and then, just to be an asshole, I throw Mrs. Cramer's pie in too. I put my feet up on the couch and swallow my last mouthful. It's a good pie, kind of a pity to waste it, really. But hey, it's five degrees warmer in here already.

I hobble back into the kitchen and put the pie-plate in the sink. There's a big, shiny carving knife sitting there with pizza cheese on the blade. I turn on the tap and scrape the cheese off with my fingernail. I wonder what the weather's like in outer space.

Horseshoes

by Jason Ockert

Bud and Nadine are by the grill on the patio. A minister pronounced them husband and wife at the Baptist church a few hours ago and this barbecue is their reception. A neighbor ordered a champagne fountain but it hasn't arrived. She, the neighbor, couldn't make it herself. Emily and I are tossing horseshoes. I loosened my tie but Bud hasn't yet. He must be uncomfortably hot over the coals; he's cherishing the day, believing himself dapper in his little rented tuxedo. Hell, he does look good, I suppose. Nadine, my mother, has a new white dress with chiffon and lace. A *whisper of lace*, as Emily pointed out to me earlier when I asked what that shiny stuff was. Emily has been wonderful. She dressed Nadine and applied the makeup, wheeled her down the aisle right on cue. I stood next to Bud and swatted him when he got too fidgety. Then the vows. Bud said I do in his sing-song voice and Nadine, with great effort, mouthed I do when asked. She doesn't speak after the stroke. I don't know if a marriage is official if you don't say the words. She could have been saying, "I'm through" or "Not true" and nobody'd know. The truth is, you could see she meant forever in her face, those blue eyes said it clearly enough.

Summertime insects collide against the house with soft thuds. There are katydid husks on the trees outlining our property. Emily and I are down here next to the tomato garden. She's up a ring or two. I am in love with her, absolutely. First I fell in love with her mom, Ms. Hunter, she's dynamite, but I'm thinking now that was lust. With Emily I laugh all the time. Her minty breath lingers on my clothes in a way that makes me feel cleaner than I've ever felt before. She has suffered through bad relationships and is bright enough to know I'm the real thing. I'm gentle with her, I don't believe I'll ever make her cry.

Bud is standing on a cinder block so he can flip the burgers. He is too short to turn the patties without help. Nadine is smiling with her hands folded in her lap. The wedding ring looks super-gold against her white dress, her frail fingers, in the afternoon sunlight. Bud will be a spectacular husband, I believe now. The two of them are awkward, there's no doubt, Nadine has these spasms and throws her food across the room if she doesn't have a tight grip on her plate, and people think Bud's a midget. At first, I was overprotective of my mother. I didn't want to see her hurt again. Besides, I had committed myself to taking care of her. Then I discovered Emily. Somehow she helped me come to terms with the fact that Nadine and Bud needed me but wanted each other.

At the reception I told Bud I was proud of him and his eyes welled up with tears. He tried to choke them back. Then I told him that maybe once in a while I'd refer to him as Dad, and he wept like a child. I hugged him and he tried to throw his arms around my waist, which didn't work. He fastened his thumbs to the belt-loops in my slacks and gave me a squeeze. I nearly got mushy myself.

I've found money in the stock market, enough to support

us with the insurance Nadine gets from the accident and Bud's exterminator paychecks. The market is a cinch, newspapers tell you everything, I know when to hold 'em and when to fold 'em. I've earned enough to buy Emily dresses and lingerie. We've made love, I'm getting better at it, I've learned to pace myself by breathing slowly. The world is fine. Hell, I think everybody's happy. There's a summer breeze and I'm not sweating in this heat with my suit on. Emily kisses the back of my neck and tells me that it's my turn. She has a silver dress that breaks just above her knees with a slit moving up her leg exposing thigh when she leans forward.

"Yeah, it sure is my turn, I'll take it."

I look at the railroad spike sticking out of the lawn, swing my arm back, and release the horseshoe. It starts to climb, wavering slightly. Then the wind carries a smell I know immediately. Pabst Blue Ribbon and sweat. It is my father's scent.

He is standing in the side-yard, neither in the back nor in the front of the house. Nadine and Bud cannot see him from their position on the patio. I have not seen him in ten years or more, ever since I was eight. There is a cleft in his chin I don't remember. The one picture I have of him, one he sent for my sixteenth birthday, one I've studied and kept in a small teak frame in my room, didn't show him with a cleft in his chin. In the picture he has on a Cubs baseball cap that casts shadows over most of his face, blurring the details. He's wearing faded-gray overalls and it occurred to me that he might be a farmer. I didn't know what he did, at sixteen. Nadine told me as far as she knew he was a salesman.

Sold tractors? I'd asked.

No, bits and pieces of anything. He won sales awards selling fishing gear, I know that, Nadine said. He mentioned that.

Why didn't I get any gear for my birthday? I don't fish, but I'd have tried back then knowing the hooks were from him.

Now he is wearing a tan blazer and off-white corduroy slacks. The brown tie around his neck is too small; there's a grease stain on his left knee. He's got a gut and is nearly bald, his head is glistening in the balm. Still, he's handsome, perhaps the casual way his shoulders are thrown back and his feet planted to the ground. The stance says, *I'm here for you, come on.* At the same time it says, *I could give a shit about any of this.*

The horseshoe is ascending. My old man has a package in his hand wrapped in blue-and-white paper with champagne glasses floating around. Is it a wedding gift? What could my father possibly give Nadine now? He has not provided for her. Child support was a joke. I dropped out of school and found a job at a deli, then an animal hospital, a chicken restaurant, paper boy, pharmaceutical-runner; whatever I could fit around Nadine. I introduced her to Bud. The package doesn't look heavy in his hand. Wine glasses? Silverware? A tackle box? I think that's a wasp buzzing around his elbow. His eyes are gray-green and watery and the expression in his mouth tells me he is recollecting things; processing me, his son.

Taller than me, he thinks. *Thin, too thin, really, he'll need to broaden that chest before anyone takes him seriously. He's still got his hair, that's what mine looked like at his age, I'll need to tell him to forget about it, it'll never last.*

At eight, I remember my father taking me down to Byrd park, to the quarry where we sat on weathered stones and floated soda-can ships and Styrofoam sailboats with sipping-straw masts. He packed bologna sandwiches, mine without crusts and lettuce, his with extra mayonnaise. We talked about how ducks were the strangest animals in the park. We tossed rocks at our boats until they sank or sailed out of range. After a while he told me he would be leaving and to be a big boy about it. What I thought he meant was that he was going to the store for ice cream, or driving up to Langdon to see his father, grandpa, for the weekend, he did that sometimes, or over to Tritch's to fetch fresh ears of corn to go with supper. I said OK and found a friend on the swing-set. He left. I don't have any memory of his back fading into the twilight or of him saying *I love you, son* or any sharp pain he was trying to choke back that showed in his eyes. I was swinging, happily. I never thought he meant forever. A few weeks later I figured it out. Nadine gave me reasons I didn't buy.

    The horseshoe is still rising. It is rusted at its base, I have flecks of reddish steel under my fingernails. The smell of cut-grass mingles with my father's scent. I hear the whack of a wooden baseball bat against a ball somewhere up the block. The sound makes my teeth ache. Have those crickets been humming this loud all along?

    At twelve, after Nadine explained that my father was an alcoholic who ran off with a waitress, I gave her the silent treatment for nearly a year. My father wasn't the man Nadine thought he was. Once Dad took me for a drive in the country. We weren't going anywhere, just listening to music. A song came on that he told me to remember. It was April and dragonflies were everywhere. They zipped past the car. One fat fly smashed itself on the windshield. We both said, ouch. Then he said, *He won't have the guts to do that again!* I laughed and laughed. I tried to explain this to Nadine. She didn't think anything was funny. I refused to speak to her until I was thirteen when I accidentally asked her to pass the Fruities at breakfast. She passed them and wept. There was no reason for her to cry. I suppose I was becoming a man. I apologized. She'd suffered, obviously, no need to blame her. I wanted to get to the bottom of things. I wrote letters to my father: *Remember the time we flew a kite out in the field when there was no wind. You said it flew on Lindwall willpower. Remember that?* And, *Dad, I was trying to think of the title to that song you told me never to forget. Why did you want me to never forget it? Did you know you were leaving then? Didn't it go, "The leader of the band is tired and his eyes are growing old. But his blood runs through my instrument and his song is in my soul,"* isn't that how it went? I sent a half-dozen unanswered letters to return addresses on child-support checks he occasionally sent; Akron, Omaha, Jefferson City, Louisville, Cicero, Kankakee. Then I turned sixteen and got the picture. The return address was in a town called Bunny, Arizona. I figured I'd visit, took on night work at the morgue making sure nothing moved, earned half the money it took to buy an airline ticket out west, and Nadine had her stroke.

My father's face is framed in the up-turned horseshoe as it has found its peak and is heading down, spilling bad luck on him. Above a flock of blackbirds are passing. Their cries sound like hangers on racks of clothes at JCPenney's as undecided customers check out shirts, skirts, slacks, bathing-suits; not this one, not this one, not this one . . .

My father is thinking that there is still time to get to know me. I'm sure there's regret. He will ask for my forgiveness and if it were as simple as that I'd give it to him right off the bat. *I forgive you, no big deal, I'm not hurt anymore. Let's have a drink.* He'll try to understand how I've been. *What do you want to know? I can't tell you everything, you've been gone so long; nearly forever. It's like when you read a book and learn about a character for a few hundred pages. You put the book down and forget. I could be your Willy Wonka. Or was it Charlie working at the chocolate factory? What's that, you didn't read it? I'll bet you did, just don't remember now. What about Ishmael, remember him? Oh come on, you fish, you've got to know Ishmael. He never got seasick like I got the time Mom and I went on that cruise in Vero Beach. Yeah, I've been to Florida. Wanted to go to Disney but there wasn't time. Want to know why? Which moment do you want, Dad?*

Anything. What's new?

Hey, I finally learned how to ride a bike!

Yeah, good for you, son, I'm proud of you. I always had the darndest time getting you to straighten it out. You didn't want to let go of those training wheels.

I guess. Well, I learned now. You tried to teach me?

Yeah, I bought you that green dirt-bike with the frog-sticker on it.

No, no frog sticker. That waitress have a son?

What's your mother been telling you? Remember I'm still your father. A green frog, big smile. On the handlebars.

Whatever. Mrs. Huser taught me. Remember Joan?

Of course I remember Joan.

Of course he would remember Joan. She enlightened my mother, I've come to find out. Tried to nudge Nadine and Edward into couples therapy. When things turned to shit Mrs. Huser shouldered my mother's insecurities and gave Nadine a little spine of her own. AA. That could have been the breaking point for him.

I bought a ten speed.

Great. Maybe we could ride down to the quarry. I'll buy you a Dairy Queen.

Quarry's gone, Dad.

Oh.

Used-car lot.

Son, I'm trying here.

I know Dad.

What about with the ladies, you got that Lindwall-mojo working?

Mojo?

That charisma, that charm, that groove, you know.

Sure I do. Sure I've got it.

Your friend is quite a looker.

Don't look, Dad.

Perhaps he'd nudge my chin or pat me on the back or wink at me or say, *You know son, you've got to be careful about diseases* . . . or go inside the house that once held his life, into the kitchen he'd not remember like this, *There's something different in here . . . Are the doorframes wider somehow?* he'd think the space was unnecessary and maybe, finally when he realized, *Oh, right, they need to be extended so Nadine can wheel herself in and fix a bite,* maybe he'd feel a bit guilty about something, the excess fat in his own legs; anything. He'd palm a couple PBR's for us to drink out in the sunset-soaked lawn and catch up and catch up and catch up.

The horseshoe is dropping and I'm starting to think that it might have been a bad throw. What can I say, I was distracted.

Dad, I can do better.

I'll ask him where he has been, not because he owes me explanations, I'm beyond that now, I just missed him, missed who he could have been.

I've been working.

Doing what?

Sales mostly. I'm good at it, people trust me. When that doesn't pay the bills I've done carpentry, mining, laying railroad tracks, lawn mower; anything.

Swell.

Boy, I can still bend you over a knee if you keep patronizing me.

This after cocktails, after catching up.

I'm not.

Leaving your mother was the hardest thing I've ever done and leaving you was no picnic either. You can't understand this, but it's like I woke up one day and realized I had the perfect wife, a wonderful boy, a house, respect on the job, everything I'd always thought I wanted. That frightened me.

Then I'd wonder if he was drunk. Would he preach to me this way if he hadn't been drinking? *Do you believe this shit when you're sober?* I'd want to ask, but wouldn't. After all, here he is, on stage, finally. *Didn't that song that I've tried to forget that you told me to remember say, "I'm just a living legacy to the leader of the band?"*

You remember, huh? Son, I panicked, had to flee. Your mother was better off without me then.

VOLUME II

That song was about a father and son who were musicians. When the old man kicked it, the son played on out of love and respect for his Dad. How does that relate to us?

I don't know. It was just a sad song. I thought you should hear it. The music isn't always so good, son. The sweet song doesn't play forever. When it sours, my advice to you is to work. Get up in the morning, shake out your oats, square yourself up to the day. Day by day.

That's what you've done?

Yes, sir, I have. You'll do it to.

I'm interested in the stock market.

What for?

Money, support Mom. She can't do much, you know?

That's too bad. I'll have to talk to her, try to cheer her up.

She doesn't talk. I can't explain to you how she communicates. Ask Bud.

Horseshoe is plummeting. Mrs. Huser was the neighbor who ordered the champagne fountain. Maybe my father is delivering it? What coincidence, really, the old man is back in town working for the discount liquor store up on Kinzer Ave. I've been there a few times and never seen him. That's about perfect. Wonder how long he's been in town? Did it slip his mind that this was once his house? What's he going to do now? He knows I've seen him, his lip is twitching.

He'll ask where he should put the fountain.

Set it up there, on the patio. Thanks. No, you know what, I think it'd look better in the center of the lawn where we can all see it, like the centerpiece. Sorry to bother you. Actually, how about you drop it down here by the tomatoes that way we can all enjoy the splendor of the garden this evening with a nice alcohol spray, toast this new marriage. Sounds good, doesn't it Pop? You could stay for a quick one, couldn't you? On second thought, why don't you take it down the block and stick it in one of Tritch's cornfields with the wasting scarecrow? There's nothing like a sunset in the field. Put it there, Edward, we'll join you when the sun's ready. How about that? There'll be a tip in it for you, old man. Here it is: You've screwed us once, alcoholic, all you can do now is work yourself into oblivion; sell doorknobs or whatever someplace else. You can keep whatever change is left. I could say this. I might say this after horseshoes, god-damnit.

The horseshoe is starting to topple end over end as it descends.

The truth is that nothing my father does now will ever erase what he has already done. So be it. Let's not talk about the past. Let me look at you, see your smile. I've heard that I have your teeth, *Let me see your teeth, Dad.*

The horseshoe is way too far to the left. A terrible throw. Emily will beat me. How can I introduce my father to her? I don't want her to meet him.

Maybe that's not my father in the side-yard standing with the package. It's been so long. There could be some sort of spigot wrapped up nicely for looks. He might be a delivery man. This could be his uniform. I've never worked at a liquor joint, but if I did, I'd probably smell like this man, like my father too.

The horseshoe flops to the ground several feet away from the railroad spike. The man moves toward the patio. Two workers appear hefting the champagne fountain.

"Nice try," Emily says, placing her hand on my shoulder. She is patronizing me. I don't mind.

"Thanks, I'll do better," I say, slipping my hands into my pockets.

Emily tosses her hair and prepares to throw her horseshoe. I measure my steps carefully in the lawn as I walk toward the house to introduce myself and to put my thoughts behind me.

Snakes

by Mark Vogel

Leon caught Jack at the edge of the woods, in front of a tall milkweed, spacing out on nature once again. Leon watched, smiling, his feet dug into the pine needles as Jack used his broken pocketknife to slit the milkweed with an eight year olds surgical precision. Jack had no idea how long he'd been out here or how mad Dad would be. He had no idea Leon was openly cultivating his father's anger, that he was a pawn in this game.

When Jack threw the pod to the lake it floated crazily on the dark surface before being attacked by the ever-watchful bluegill. *If bluegill grew as large as carp, they'd bite your leg off.* That's what his father had said on every fishing trip for the last ten years. *Be patient and just about everything will come to you.* That was the weakness in his father; he loved the small things like bluegill. If this many bluegill lived in the lake, big bass rested somewhere close by waiting for darkness. His dad was content to fish for bluegill all day long. Leon wanted to hook on to the big monster bass. He and Jack would come back after supper when the shadows fell on the water.

Oblivious to the bluegills and their murky violence, Jack focused on the juice oozing from the stalk. After a proper deliberation he stuck his tongue tentatively to the liquid. As if all of nature existed to satisfy his kid's curiosity. That was the sign for Leon to move. He rose and in two long strides pounced, rolling Jack to the water's edge. Pinned in the stagnant muck, Jack twitched and thrashed as Leon stared into his rolling eyes, watching the terror turn into fury. Then he spoke in a calm, adult voice.

"Don't you know dummy . . . Milkweed juice is bad poison. It could kill you."

"But you told me . . ."

"Yeah . . . I've told you a lot of things. Rule Number One: Don't believe everything people tell you." Leon mussed Jack's hair lovingly, seeing with satisfaction his brother was already forgiving him.

Dad was winding across the hillside, a frown evident from two hundred feet. Leon wasn't surprised by the frown. He had been cranky from the beginning, like it was Leon's fault for not being bubbly and full of jokes just because they were going camping. Dad had been up at six, forcing them all to an obscenely early start. Leon had resisted from the beginning, as if now at fifteen he should decide for himself, and maybe even stay home—though that option had not been offered. He and his dad had quarreled early, and during the endless winding Ozark drive the tension grew in the hot air. After eight hours of driving at a snail's pace on winding roads listening to news programs, swap shops and country music Leon and Jack had run far and fast to the lake before Mom and Dad started unpacking, before they could detail the endless chores, and lay out plans for Sunday's drive to the church which they had called a week ago for times of services. Leon ran to avoid seeing the leaf blower, the flag, coolers, lanterns, mosquito candles, rakes, hoes, axes, hammers, fishing rods out the wazoo.

When his father stood in front of them, Leon saw the irritation etched on his brow.

"You know, your mother and I might want to have some fun too. Did you think there wasn't any work?"

Leon looked contrite, knowing it was best to stay out of his dad's way until after supper. He'd heard it before. Fun for his father meant roasting marshmallows, taking a shower at the bathhouse, building a fire, and talking with the neighbors. His father could find fun in peeling potatoes, or in greasing the cast iron skillet. Leon knew that during their run to the wilderness the entire campsite had been prepared. By now the station wagon was unloaded, the firewood bought, the campsite aesthetically arranged with assorted electric cords, an army shovel, eight or ten fishing rods, and lawn chairs. The gas stove was assembled, the water jugs filled, the clothesline hung from tree limbs, the Apache tent trailer erected, the awning tacked smartly with guide ropes, the bedding unrolled.

Was it his fault Dad worked too hard and long, whether in the office or the wilds as if there were rules dictating suffering before fun? Now his dad stood glaring, sweat on his forehead, wearing the threadbare sleeveless T-shirt that made him look like a refugee from a concentration camp. His look said it all—discipline and work, discipline and work—until it was all done. To Leon, that meant that half the time no time for fun ever existed. Leon was going to get his fun when he could.

"Your mother and I don't ask much."

"Right," Leon murmured.

"What did you say?"

"Nothing." Leon knew the message about order on camping trips, and clearly stated rules. *You may use my tools;*

just put them back where you found them. You have to be prepared, and that means thinking ahead.

They followed the trail back to the campground and found the tent-trailer secure, the water jugs full. Dad had expertly staked out the land and followed the game-plan. Mother was already messing at the stove, her supplies staking out her territory. They ate on the red vinyl tablecloth, with his mother pushing the celery and the green jello with embedded grapes as the epitome of health. By the time the ninety-nine cent Wal-Mart sandwich cookies were devoured his father had the firewood arranged and ready to light.

Leon and Jack knew that after supper Mom and Dad would scout out the territory searching for people to talk to. His mother's farm upbringing emerged each time she met an outsider—she acted like she hadn't talked to anyone in weeks. As if she was still sitting on the side of Highway 61 under the walnut tree, swatting at flies, waiting for some exotic urbanite to trail down from St. Louis to tell her about the world.

She had already made one exploratory visit to the neighbor's compound. Already she was cataloguing with delight the mundane details of their lives.

"That couple is from Rapid City, South Dakota. Did you know, people come from all over to be here. They have a daughter in the Navy . . . They drove all night."

After the meal his parents took off on their walk with orders to Leon about dinner dishes and bedding. Leon cringed as he glanced over at the neighbors, seeing the beer, two motorcycles, the air conditioner, and the flickering TV set, all wrong as wrong could be. That wasn't the way to live. *How could Mom and Dad be so undiscriminating, when my minute indiscretions are noted as soul threatening?* He angrily gouged at the skillet as a mosquito lit on his arm. *If they only knew what I think of doing with Susan, and what I've already done.*

In the trailer that night, Leon and Jack snuggled in their sleeping bags, listening to the cicadas talking in the trees, feeling that home was ten thousand miles away. Like most every night Leon was talking aloud in a half whisper making sense of the day, telling stories. Jack lay close, his head on Leon's arm, his eyes half-closed. Leon told Jack about Indians living without camping coolers of hamburgers, of pioneers harvesting milkweed, wild strawberries and grubs from stumps. He explained about seventeen year locusts, the medicinal properties of red dogwood berries, why mulberries stain the skin, and how mud turtles have sex. They discussed why earthworms came out on the pavement after a big rain.

At one time or another Leon had explained just about everything he knew to Jack. His brother's inclination was to believe. Leon knew he too had once been that way, up until the late night story time when he told Jack that pickles were alligator penises, carefully packed by old women from Chester, Illinois in an old factory down by the river. Jack believed for at least a day that those were the number one pickles in the country. He said something to his teacher at school, and she called home, and Leon had his mouth washed out with soap.

In the half-light Leon began the familiar story once again.

"They eat them in every bar, every diner. Look for them. They're right there next to the gallon jars of pink, pickled eggs."

Jack nodded as if he still believed, and Leon abruptly stopped.

"Do you believe everything anyone tells you?"

"But you told me a million times."

"I'm telling you now, you can't take anyone's word on anything."

They slept as the breeze ruffled the canvas, as the neighbors walked the gravel road that crunched and talked like it never did in the daytime. Leon woke once in the half-light, brushing the canvas wet with night air, sure he had heard a wildcat scream in a back hollow.

Susan had focused his agenda. Seeing her every day was more important than throwing the football with his Dad or going on family camping trips. Leon wanted to see her every minute. He feared if he didn't touch her each day she would drift off and disappear. So the thought of spending five days camping threw him into an immediate and prolonged panic. Six months before meeting Susan, Leon would have cleaned his tackle box, rearranged lures, and dreamed of fishing for a month before a camping trip. He would have badgered his Dad to buy new lures, to leave home early so they could fish at dusk. But instead of eagerness Leon had fought this trip at every step. He made no move even to pack his graphite rod. That look in his dad's eyes that said *no, there's no need for girls at your age* had caused it all to go to hell and left Leon with no choice but to say *yeah, it will happen no matter what you or anyone says*. If his dad couldn't understand Susan, Leon wasn't going to pretend that fishing could make them close. He was about to start high school in three weeks. He would see Susan if he wanted to. That's all. His dad would get it eventually.

Eight nights before in the last week in July, the big fight happened. All afternoon Leon and Susan played tennis. When they quit they rode their bikes the mile from the sycamore-lined park to her empty house. In her kitchen Leon drank the lemonade Susan offered, taking in her too quiet home. Curtains hung on every window keeping the heat outside. He didn't know how to act. Used to scrabbling for ten minutes alone here, a half an hour there this afternoon threatened to stretch on forever. For once they had a whole world to themselves in a place where time had died. He kissed her and her eyes closed. Ten minutes later they were in her bedroom. There was a moment with the air conditioner breeze making the room clean and fresh, when he took her in lying on the bed, her arms outstretched, smiling. Leon marveled that he was there—that he had done nothing to make it happen. Together they laid together, snuggling close, content to kiss and roll, fully clothed in smiles.

Later somehow he disentangled, and left in a daze. He rode his bike wildly down the hills, a wide smile on his face. How could he explain to his father it was okay to be mesmerized by the beauty of muted sun in a girl's bedroom? How could he explain that he was still innocent—that he and Susan could look and touch and kiss without exploding into pornography. *How could he explain that no sin existed between them?*

Though he should have gone straight home, he didn't. For once, just feeling himself free and alive was enough. He wanted to savor the afternoon. He ended up in the park to play fuzzball with Wilkening and Schwab. He got lost in the game, the whole day caught up in the magic of Susan. Mel Davis uncharacteristically hit a shot over the grandstand into the lagoon. Several times Leon told his team he should leave, but he was needed to keep the side alive.

When he got home at nine that night his father was waiting. Trying to brush aside the questions, Leon tried to make for his room. He'd stayed away too long. He knew they were worried. *But couldn't they for once let it go? Couldn't they see the innocence in his eyes?* Leon kept his eyes down, looking meek, and moved to turn his music on. His dad stood in the doorway.

"Your mother asked if you had eaten. You didn't answer. Where were you?"

"I'm sorry . . . I'm sorry. I was on my bike, playing ball. I told you I would be playing ball."

"You were playing ball since one this afternoon?"

"Yeah, Bill Wilkening, and Greg Schwab, and some others. Then we watched the college game."

"All we ask is courtesy and some consideration for others. Did you know your mother was worried about you?" His father grabbed at Leon's arm to make his point. "You just need to tell people where you are going to be."

Leon pulled away, twisting backward.

"Okay. I don't know where I'll be all the time."

His father reached for him again.

"Leave me alone," Leon cried out. Cornered, Leon crouched into a fighter's pose, his heart beating fast, his fists up. *I don't care, I don't care, he comes a step closer I'll hit him.* His father stopped, wary of this new phenomenon. The energy was all between their eyes. Some line had been passed, some message conveyed, and both of them were shocked by how fast the craziness had traveled. Then a flicker of sadness crossed his dad's face. And Leon, seeing that look, knew it was ludicrous to push his Dad this far. He saw the scene as if it was written in a book—a fifteen-year old son crouched defiantly in front of his father, his fists ready to strike—the kid so locked in his anger he was out of control. Yet, Leon kept his fists raised, his face rigid, until his father sighed and walked away. That scene had been the prelude for this camping trip.

Bright and early Leon and Jack were out on the dock, ready for swimming. They'd focused on swimming since they got up. Dad was pleased they were eager to plunge into recreation. Now that the stress of driving and setting up was over he was ready to move on to camping fun. After breakfast,

Leon and Jack grabbed towels and walked deliberately on the root strewn trail to the deserted mud beach. Leon knew the plunge into the deep forest lake with fog drifting off the water this early wouldn't be a piece of cake. Yet, there was no question about whether he was going in. The rule for vacations was you swam where you could, preferably as early as possible. Leon prided himself in rivers, streams, ponds, sloughs, and lakes. He knew ahead of time the depth of this lake, the aggressive underwater plant growth, the general eerie shadiness of the hills hunched over the far shore.

Leon pushed Jack's air mattress into the transparent water, Jack looking spindly, white, and sleepy, not too sure about swimming so soon after oatmeal and pancakes in this lake lying deep in the valley with trees bunched thickly on three banks.

Lying quietly on his mattress in the deep water to absorb heat and not the breeze Leon focused on the vine-like plants arching up from the underwater slime. Closer to shore a green mat of plants crawled over the surface. Leon felt the goose bumps rise as the water inched between plastic and flesh. The secret was to lie quietly until the sun gathered power. He dreamed of Susan brushing her hair before the mirror, he standing behind her holding her waist.

He replayed the night a week before in her father's car sitting close, reaching for each other's hand. The scene never far from the surface showed Susan in the movie theater magically out of the darkness lifting his hand to her breast. He replayed this scene over and over, the hand on the white blouse, the hard ridges of the bra, the promise of skin underneath. That night under those flickering lights in the midst of that quiet crowd the warm moving skin underneath the fabric sent the message—*This is me . . . Explore.*

When Leon turned over on the air mattress he was aroused, flushed at the imagined touch of fabric and skin. Fueled by the breeze Jack's mattress bumped gently against Leon's arm. Already Jack's back was pink.

"You're getting a burn. Keep your toes in the water and you won't get red."

Jack dutifully slid his legs into the cool water. A crow lazed from the pines, a signal the day was maturing, calling out his wilderness disdain for their presence. A bluegill slid tentatively from the depths. Leon watched the kid's closed eyes as the fish came closer, drawn to white hairs, and bit. Jack screamed excessively.

"Ooh. Something got me."

"Probably a horsefly. Get in the water and hang on."

Always the believer, Jack shivered as he entered the water where the vines seemed to reach for his legs. Within a minute he thrashed his way back onto the mattress.

"There's something down there."

Leon settled him, bringing the two mattresses together, talking softly, pointing out the vines, showing Jack the hiding places of lake snakes, of green darting madness. He explained why white bodies of loggers sat motionless in the depths protecting the lake's mysteries.

"Why do you think they call it Loggers' Lake?"

Leon talked until Jack's fish fear subsided and the heat began to regain its power. As Leon stared into Jack's vulnerable eyes, he thought about how he could eventually make his brother tough. If he didn't succeed, when Jack got to 8th grade, they'd eat him alive.

Leon contemplated the steps to opening the air valve on Jack's mattress. He reached out quietly and did his work as Jack dozed in the heat. Without an air mattress, confronting the deep green depths would be a challenge.

Back on the shore Mom was there to frown and soothe the kid. Under her watching eyes Leon explained it was nothing but a joke.

The next night with the lantern sending light over the water Leon and Jack sat with their dad on the dock, listening to the whippoorwill, fishing for catfish. When the taut lines tugged, his father yanked, Jack yelled, and they watched the struggle, the lake yielding to the frenzy within. Then the fish, all blue and white and trailing algae, emerged on the boards flopping, and his father cautioned both of them.

"Watch for the barbs, they can hurt bad."

At that moment the fish rolled, his dad grabbed, and his palm was stained with blood. The boys stared at the catfish, his mouth slapping open and shut. "Big enough, maybe two pounds," his dad said, as if the wound meant nothing. He wiped the blood on his pants, put the fish on the stringer and resumed his vigil. Leon and Jack laid on the boards, carefully keeping their legs on the safety of the dock.

Leon watched his father's attentive gaze on the water. The blood was still fresh on the pants. His comment was his usual fishing command.

"Be patient."

(*Do not let parts of the worm dangle off the hook. Jerk gently only when the fish is clearly on the line. Use a net to lift fish from the water. Watch for snakes.*)

Leon was still in no mood to listen. He wasn't remembering the fifty camping trips his father had organized. He wasn't remembering the endless days playing catch, or the day his dad fell off the roof putting up the basketball goal. He didn't focus on baseball trips to St. Louis, or the many times he'd seen pride in his father's eyes. Just four days before the fight that wasn't really a fight, Leon had seen something he'd rather forget. What he saw was his father in his summer Saturday frayed jeans crouched next to the tailpipe of the running Volvo, a garbage sack in his hand, bent on yet another project. His father bent on doing what he was going to do. Leon thought nothing of it. But then he heard the plaintive meow that meant Mollie's new kittens were in that bag, and his father was doing something that couldn't be made right later. Before his father could see him Leon ducked back down the steps to the safety of the back yard.

Mollie, searching for her offspring, had appeared at his window that night, bewildered.

Were those kittens carted away as trash, shuffled off without comment? Was it the time in the military that made him do it? Would he do it again? Adults were supposed to know what they were doing. And some adult actions just couldn't be forgiven.

That night in the trailer Leon lay awake next to Jack listening to the tree frogs and cicadas. Leon marveled at the depth of life moving in the darkness. Dead kittens were a part of life, as was Susan. Not ten feet away his father snored, oblivious. His dad's heart would stop dead if he saw him kissing Susan on the blanket as the air conditioners purred. If Leon was home, he'd pry the window open, slide to the ground, quiet the dog, and set his bike in motion into summer night air whipping his hair. Soaring toward Susan, like he'd done before.

Six weeks before, at two in the morning when even the dogs were quiet, he and Susan arranged a blanket on the lawn outside her bedroom. As the blanket grew wet with dew, when nothing mattered but their closeness, Susan's father's voice came straight out of dream, muffled by bushes and insects, but real enough to startle. Leon, drawn from his meditation on Susan's breathing, sprang to his feet and ran. Susan scurried to the front porch and back to the house. Leon made it all the way home that night without brakes.

In the trailer Leon listened to the thunderstorm rolling across the valley and wondered about the secrets his father kept mute. He couldn't see his father shirtless on a blanket in the summer night with a girl. His father as far as he knew had never been young. He couldn't see his dad making mistakes at all—whatever he had done had to be deliberate. Finally, when the dreams came, Leon saw the lake weeds growing from the mud, reaching toward the campsite, the lake monsters peering with reptile eyes from the water.

In the morning, in a fishing-fever Leon and Jack hunted worms in the overgrown, rock-strewn ravine. Uncovering the humus under rotting logs he found more than bargained for—night crawlers, sometimes ten inches long, thriving in the moist roots. Jack overturned a rock and four worms squirmed for darkness.

"Wow. Come here," he squealed in delight.

Together they threw boulders, lifted logs, plunged into the dark weeds, determined to unearth every worm. Covered in dirt and sweating, Leon lifted a great, half-eaten log, then heaved it to the side. In the moment of release his eyes replayed in slow motion the snake, fat and dry, falling into the soft dirt left by the rolling log. The snake was alive, and the rattles shook slow and quiet.

"Snake. Watch it."

Even then Jack didn't believe and stood stolidly, looking for confirmation.

The snake moved, on a flat rock, his triangular head hard, eyes focused on Leon's leg, the gray rattles shaking hypnotically. Leon motioned for Jack to come closer.

"Watch it, watch it. He can kill ya."

Leon raised a rock high above his head. He'd kill the snake dead as a door-nail. He'd see its guts splattered. As the rock came down the snake struck, and Leon saw the head reach fast, a demon on primitive power, a machine.

He screamed, stepped back, his feet dancing.

"He's got to die."

He hit the snake again and again, ten times. The snake jerked, tried to strike feebly, and then lay listless.

Movement in the entrails brought Leon and Jack closer. Leon probed with the stick, looking for the mechanics of death. Out of the murk six miniature snakes waggled in wetness onto the rock, little bits of dirt clinging to their fresh skin. Jack's eyes widened as he backed rapidly away.

"Wait. It's okay, wow, babies, can you believe that?"

With contagious panic Leon poked at the snake, flipped it over, leveraging the stick under the snake. When he lifted the stick with a jerk his strength was more than he realized, and the dead snake flew into the air big and heavy and seemingly moving in all directions. Leon ducked, scrambling for cover, turning to see where it would fall. In horror, he saw the snake draped across Jack's shoulder. Twisting in revulsion, Jack pawed at the snake, then tripped and the two were there—the snake and his brother trying his hardest to fly from slime and evil and snake and his brother.

Leon wanted to stop him, to make it better as Jack ran in panic. Leon felt a twitch, a cough of love as he stood and watched. The poor kid, how scared he must have been.

That night with Jack sleeping by his side Leon laid on his stomach, his face toward the wilderness, dreaming of Susan. His father's snores tried to drown out the noises of the night. Only the thin canvas walls kept his family world in place. In the trailer the air was thick and moist. Outside the winds blew in the treetops. A distant splash in the lake said the Big Life was going on without him. Leon wanted a world where he paid attention to the rules that really mattered. When he got home he and Susan would take their clothes off and just rub.

Jack shifted, murmuring in the fits of a dream, lingering just on the outskirts of the waking. He still lived in mom and dad land, with Santa Claus, and Jesus. Leon knew that he too, had lived in that world. Leon's favorite picture captured his father with his arm over his shoulders, the dog at their feet. His father's eyes in the picture looked straight ahead as if he was protecting Leon from danger. Leon still knew that feeling of rightness in his dad's arms. He was never going to fight him again. But he was going to have to protect himself, and to do that, he had to figure out just what was out there. He had to do the exploring alone. He and Susan would go to the county fair to see the livestock and the guys with tattoos. He'd show her the sixty-year old dwarf sitting in his half-pint lawn chair, the green boa wound round his neck. There would be cigarettes, danger, and darkness.

There was nothing to do but plunge on.

Jack stirred, in danger in his dreaming. Leon touched him on the arm.

"Hey," he whispered, "It's okay."

Leon vowed to teach him when he could.

All the Colors of the Rainbow

by Mike Hood

The Dean looked at the rolling green hills of the campus through his office window as he felt the rounded bulge below his rib cage. The truss kept it from showing, but it was there, about the size of an egg in relief. Unfortunately, the elastic noticeably flattened the rest of his abdomen. People would say, "Have you lost weight?" Or, "You must be working out." Or, "Aren't you looking well!" All of which grieved him even more because these comments were painful reminders of the growing distance between the appearance and the reality.

The reality, at least on some basic physical level, was what the doctor called pancreatic detachment. It was as if one organ (usually beginning with the pancreas) would declare its independence from the rest of the body and strike out on its own. Other organs, he was told, would eventually follow suit. Although there was no cure, he was advised to avoid heavy lifting and "relations that weren't routine." When the digestive tract started to go, there would be gastric distress. And near the end, as the body moved toward greater and greater disorder, there would be periods of uncontrollable weeping as the heart began to break loose from its moorings. It was all covered in a full-color brochure, *Pancreatic Detachment and You*, which the doctor had given him along with "Truss XL" scribbled on a prescription pad with a smiley face stamped in red at the bottom.

The Dean reflected on the coming chaos. Had the workings of his internal organs been like the great periods of Western culture, say fifth century Athens, or the high Middle Ages, or Elizabethan England, when all the complex cultural forces interacted and coalesced into a remarkable and recognizable pattern that became a point of reference, a bench mark, for all subsequent eras? He had eaten the produce of the earth, breathed the air, felt the fire against his face, and drank the water. He too had coalesced for a brief moment and now like Israel after the reign of Solomon, the Roman Empire in the days of Augustine, or the Church after Martin Luther, he was coming apart. The pattern was organic. He whispered to himself, "You can't mandate what matters."

At that moment, his secretary interrupted his reflections. "The consultant is here," she said in a soft voice that sounded like footsteps on the deep piles of his own carpet.

The consultant's hand shot across the desk. "William 'Bill' Williams from Garbus, Inc.," he said. "You certainly have a beautiful campus here with all these rolling hills!" Both arms were raised toward the Dean's window. Was he making a charismatic gesture?

The Dean nodded as he felt the lump shift a bit to the left.

"Looks like you've been staying fit! I'm on the road a lot, but I never miss an opportunity to stretch my legs, go for a good run." The Dean thought about his pancreas, free at last, sprinting down the interstate on a dark night being pursued by a swarm of state police. Did the runaway elude its captors, was it apprehended and brought back into the community of organs, were there fatalities? He would look for the story in the morning's paper among the suicide bombings and new slimming diets, but there would be nothing, as if it never happened.

"Upfront," the consultant said, with his hand resting on the Dean's forearm, "I want to dispense with all formality . . . . I want you to call me Mr. Bills."

When the two men were seated, Mr. Bills pressed the fingers of his hands together and stared at the floor for a moment. Was he going to pray? Then he looked at the Dean with great concern so that sincerity flooded the little pools of his eyes.

"I'm here on a mission," he said as his voice trailed off with deep emotion. He looked at the floor to regain his composure. "I'm here on a mission," he said with more strength in his voice, "to cut through whatever realities may be troubling your institution to help you shape an image, a vision as it were, that will capture the imagination and reinvent what you are."

The Dean attempted to respond, but Mr. Bills looked at the floor again and raised his right hand like a major league batter calling time to better prepare himself for the next pitch.

"At Garbus we're committed to one thing." His voice swelled with emotion. "We're committed to building community, to finding the harmony and making it prevail!"

There was a faint click, and the Dean heard music, the muffled, ethereal voices of an angelic choir coming from what seemed a great distance. Was this the music of the spheres? Mr. Bills had turned on a tiny tape recorder in the pocket of his coat.

"Permit me to analogize for a moment." There was a miniature crescendo in the chorus of voices. "A community is like the human body, and the body itself is framed by a harmony of sounds. Sometimes if we listen carefully we can hear them!" There was another crescendo in the music.

The Dean closed his eyes and listened. A portentous rumbling erupted in his gut. In panic he felt for the lump, but it dodged his prodding fingers.

"Each of us," Mr. Bills intoned, "is made in the image of that harmony. In the great metabolic dance of life, we all must harmonize together, listen to the music and follow where it leads us. Don't you agree?"

The Dean, nodding his ascent, bolted for the restroom, trailing clouds of yellow-tinged gas, which Mr. Bills saw as butterflies floating on the air, fluttering to the music as they thinned ascending heavenward.

When the Dean returned to the office, he no longer heard the music. Mr. Bills had removed his coat, rolled up his sleeves, loosened his tie, and held in his lap a legal notepad with "For Your Notes" printed in large black letters at the top of the page.

"Now it's time for me to hear your story," he said in the most comforting of tones.

Feeling much relieved and having once again located his rogue pancreas now clearly to the left of center, the Dean settled into his large administrative chair and narrated events which Mrs. Bills recorded as follows: "As a preface to my comments, let me point out that what drives the college is diversity. The mission statement says that we are 'committed to being open to all ideas, races, colors, creeds, and nationalities without making distinctions of value.' In the curriculum, for example, since we could not teach all foreign languages, we eliminated the language requirement entirely. To be consistent this meant getting rid of English composition as well. In literature, we try to offer a smattering of everything such as Professor Pretty's course in literature authored by emotionally troubled American-born non-Jews of Polish descent whose parents through mistaken identity became victims of the Holocaust."

At this point, a hoard of mostly one-armed, mentally-challenged Croatian grounds keepers on enormous riding lawn mowers came thundering over one ridge and then another of the rolling green hills. As they approached the administration building, they were joined by more Croatians wielding voracious weed eaters and powerful blowers. Because of the deafening noise and one or two minor accidents, the interview was brought to a halt for approximately twenty-five minutes.

When the interview continued, Mr. Bill's notes indicate that the Dean said something like the following: "It started shortly after the beginning of Fall Semester. A male student, a senior, majoring in Business Administration, with a minor in International Transportation Practices in Third World Countries, turned red. He goes to bed white and wakes up the next morning red. At first, everyone thought it was a joke, maybe part of a fraternity initiation. The student assured us he had not intentionally changed colors. However, in an age of green hair and multiple tattoos, no one seemed to pay much attention. But then there were others. A beige communications major, a pastel blue accounting major, an aquamarine biology major, and so on.

"President Amshay immediately recognized it for what it was, a potential public relations disaster. At an emergency session of the Executive Staff, he proposed makeup. All members of the staff concurred. Our decision represented a clear-cut application of the President's HAD policy (Hide, Abide, Denied), a policy which had endeared him to the Board of Trustees over his years at the college.

"So much for the short-term solution. We need a long-term strategy, for which we have turned, as you are aware, to Garbus. This is what we know: All color changes have occurred in white males, who expect to graduate in the spring and who will be going into highly competitive fields. Given the current laws regarding discrimination and sexual harassment in the workplace, which do not protect while males until they are forty, we believe these students without conscious intention have changed color to qualify as a protected class."

(Mr. Bills' account of the Dean's account ends here. Did he concur with the Dean's conclusion? As a kind of playful literary allusion, just to try on the perspective, Mr. Bills had scrawled across the bottom page of his notes, "Exterminate all the brutes!" With some reluctance, he had crossed it out. Then below, he carefully printed and double underlined the words, "embrace diversity," which, like a burnt offering, was held up, perhaps with too much confidence and without recognition of the nature of the offence, to the gods of harmony and order.)

Two weeks after his interview with Mr. Bills, the Dean stood by his office window gazing at the rolling green hills. He watched bands of wild-looking Albanian immigrants on a fleet of ancient tractors rumble over the crest of one hill, disappear, and then reappear on the crest of another. He had seen them the spring before. Now they were apparently "weeding" the grass with generous amounts of dark-colored herbicide, which looked similar to the fertilizer they had applied in the spring. The word "herpesite" had been clumsily scrawled on the side of each tank in oversized black letters. The liquid sloshed in translucent tanks from which it was pumped, leaving an iridescent residue on whatever it touched until it dried.

The cat-and-mouse game with his pancreas made him irritable and the gastric "episodes" had become more frequent. When he moved, he had begun to hear sloshing sounds like someone walking in galoshes filled with water. Nevertheless, he took great comfort in the view from his window. It was a reminder of and a link to the predictable patterns of nature. It occurred to the Dean that with a gilded frame his view might have been mistaken for a Constable, a Corot, or perhaps even a Turner on a rainy day. It might have been, that is, had not fire (some called it a conflagration) destroyed the building and most certainly the window through which the Dean spent the best moments of his day staring.

"The consultant's report just came in the mail," his secretary said, placing the thick, spiral-bound document on his desk.

After she left the room, he sloshed to his chair and began the report. It consisted of a title page, acknowledgments, a table of contents, the Garbus company philosophy, a history of discrimination and sexual harassment legislation in the U.S., an analysis of the college's mission statement as it informed hiring practices, the curriculum, campus life, etc., an extensive review of the problem, a list of the names and titles of those interviewed, an evaluation and discussion of the effectiveness of the short-term solution, and one underlined long-term strategy recommendation on page 526 (the last page of the report), which the Dean recognized as a haiku: "*Oh, lovely world! Hues of fading flowers color the arching rainbow.*"

Feeling an immediate rush of emotion, the Dean closed his eyes. Tears gathered, they hesitated, then raced full-throttle down his cheeks. When the vision came it was unbidden and utterly irresistible. A rainbow arched and circled all the way around the inside of his head. There was a mysterious fourth dimension that brought the colors to life. They vibrated, then danced to the harmonies of distant music. In that ecstatic moment, he raised his arms to embrace the radiance. As he did so, faces began to emerge from each of the colors. They grew larger and more distinct until they expanded beyond recognition. As they broke apart, the vision ended.

Three days later, after the Dean had proposed going public, the President and Executive Staff, following several stormy sessions of finger pointing, name calling, and disagreement over the PR fallout, finally consented. The Dean was selected to address the campus community because, as the President pointed out, the colors had sorted themselves by major, and thus, it was an academic issue. All agreed.

When the day came, the Dean believed it was going to be one of those definitive moments because his speech articulated a fundamental position on an important issue. It was comparable, he thought, to other foundational statements such as Paul's "Letter to the Romans," Lincoln's "Gettysburg Address," Kennedy's "Inaugural," and Martin Luther King's "I Have a Dream." Speaking from a podium on the left side of the auditorium stage and with the red velvet curtains of the proscenium arch drawn behind him, he delivered his "All the Colors of the Rainbow" speech.

He began by proclaiming his love for the college (especially his fondness for the rolling green hills), his affection for the students, his admiration of faculty, staff and administration, and his commitment to the mission of the college, the quintessence of which, he said, was embodied in just four words, "without distinction of value." He paused, feeling first the rising emotions which these words inspired in him, and then a sense of panic because of the growing discomfort in his abdomen. Like snake-in-a-can, when the lid came off, it was off to stay.

He took a deep breath and continued: "As many of you know, I am a private person and believe that it is imperative to keep the private person and the public person separate. In fact, that is my definition of what it means to be a professional. However, there are times when even I have to make an exception to this rule. This is one of those times."

What followed was the Dean's "personal" account of the student "transformations," then a heartfelt apology for the makeup cover-up, and finally a compelling description of his rainbow vision. This was the centerpiece of the speech, his triumph, as it were, which he presented in great detail. When he got to the climax of the vision, the part about the emerging faces, he said: "I was transfixed by each color and by all colors. I recognized that each color was constant, an entity unto itself, but it was, at the same time, changed by those on either side. I became aware on a felt, experiential level that the whole mysteriously transcends the sum of the parts. It was then that faces seemed to materialize from the colors."

He paused. The house lights dimmed, ethereal music hovered over the auditorium. The red velvet curtains parted as stage lights illuminated a row of male students, ordered by color from infrared to ultraviolet. Their arms were linked, forming a human color spectrum that went from one side of the stage to the other. People sucked in their breath, there were moans, small cries of wonder and astonishment.

"It was the faces of *these* students!" said the Dean with both arms held up in a hieratic gesture. "These faces, I tell you." His arms, now tracing the arc of an unseen rainbow, pointed to and swept across all those on stage beside him. "And when I saw *these* faces," he said, moved by his own words, "I knew them for the first time, and I spoke their names!" There was applause, people shouted cries of joy.

Tears welled up in the Dean's eyes. The lid was coming off. A deep rumble seemed to move the building. It was, as some later said, a sign of a new age. As the house lights slowly came back up, hundreds of butterflies circled above the stage. At this sight, the audience broke into loud cheering and wild applause. In the ecstasy of the moment, students came forward to embrace those on stage in an expression of solidarity and acceptance. The celebration continued long after the Dean (and the butterflies) left the building.

What happened next not even Mr. Bills could have predicted. Whether it was out of envy, or the fear of being different, or just the need to imitate others, students (both male and female, freshman through senior) began changing colors in large numbers. While this was not a problem in itself, the difficulty arose as students formed color cliques. The reds, yellows, and blues, because of their status as primary colors, assumed superiority by nature over others. All other colors, according to the primaries, were secondary, which, they said, made them second class, second hand, second rate. This didn't bother the secondaries because they knew they weren't tertiaries. Tertiaries were given all those phony lifestyle names like peaches 'n' cream, mood-glow fantasy, rosy-fingered dawn, etc. In reality, said the secondaries, tertiaries were the mongrels of the color world, definitely third class, steerage all the way. Tertiaries, in their own defense, insisted they were *neither* tints *nor* shades, but nobody listened.

In order to counter this thinking, the Dean, in spite of failing health and increasing sloshiness, issued a lengthy memo, "Not by Nature," in which he emphatically rejected the traditional Western belief in the existence of a human nature, labeling it "a destructive, outmoded fiction." The argument, bordering on incoherence, was reductive and sentimental having been composed mostly through a veil of tears. Those familiar with the Dean's work, however, recognized the memo as an adaptation of his controversial monograph, *Pelagius Revisited: Old Perfection for a New Age*. Unfortunately, the memo, because it either confused students or insulted their intelligence, was universally discarded. It filled the trash receptacles, tumbled over the rolling green hills, blew under shrubbery and stuck to the sides of buildings.

In addition to the issue of hierarchy, which the Dean's memo attempted to address, there was an added complication. Each color had a different "personality profile." Of the primaries, reds tended to be chain-smoking extroverts who passed out at parties. Most were business administration majors. Yellows were compulsive talkers who had a passion for decoupage. They were likely to be education majors. Blues were introverts with touches of genuine brilliance. They avoided the envy and hatred of others by talking quietly in dark bars on bright sunny days. Because they never declared a major, they rarely graduated. The secondaries were more conventional. Greens tended to be English majors, purples were inclined to political science, and most oranges ended up in recreational studies. Tertiaries (including tints and shades) were drawn to technical fields such as computer science, math, physics, electrical engineering, and so on. To the reds, all "terts" were mouth-breathing, bottom-feeding nerds!

Conflicts were inevitable. Anything negative that didn't have an obvious explanation was blamed on other color cliques. Every clique came under the suspicion of every other clique. Roving bands of color cliques armed with baseball bats, knives, and garden implements began "patrolling" the campus at night. There were scuffles and some reported injuries.

To prevent the violence from escalating and to help restore harmony to the campus community, President Amshay, in a flash of inspiration, called for a Day of Reconciliation. The day would begin with a noon cookout. The food would be served in front of the administration building, a symbolic gesture, to indicate the administration's willingness to work with students and help the community through this difficult time. The cookout would be followed by a short address from the President and then by community games such as egg rolling, three-legged races, tug-of-war with mixed teams, and softball. After the games, a rock band, Loitering Minors (Beach Boy imitators now in their fifties), would entertain students through the evening and, as the President hoped, toward the dawn of a new day. Faculty and staff were required to be present and instructed to mingle with students and participate in the games.

Late morning on the Day of Reconciliation, the Dean lay dozing on his office couch. When he awoke he was feeling particularly sloshy and weepy. He had given up trying to locate his pancreas. It seemed to have disappeared entirely. "*Pancreas absconditus,*" he muttered. It took all his strength to get to the window. Through tears, he saw lines of students ordered by the colors of the spectrum coming forward to load food on their plates. He thought he was having another vision, but then he remembered the day. As he scanned the rows of students from red to violet, his weeping intensified. He spoke the word "rainbow," and then said, "my rainbow." With the light being refracted through the tears in his eyes, the landscape became iridescent, and in that instant before the lash lines of his heart broke loose and he collapsed on the floor with both arms raised toward the window as a warning, he had come to know the awful truth.

It was best the Dean was beyond seeing what followed. A line of cigarette-smoking reds began taunting a line of pinks standing beside them. Reds hated pinks because they thought they were all wannabe reds and couldn't make it. In reality, pinks hated reds because they were smokers and because they were reds.

Blowing smoke at the pinks, the reds' leader, John "Johnny" Johnson, yelled, "Hey! Terts, maybe this'll put a little color in your cheeks." This sent his line into convulsive laughter, followed by an interval of deep, window-rattling coughing, up and down the line.

Because the pinks had turned their backs on the reds to protect themselves from secondary smoke, the reds, as soon as their coughing subsided, began flicking burning cigarette butts at the backs of the pinks. An errant butt landed in the folds of one of the Dean's discarded "Not by Nature" memos, which a few days before had come to rest under a juniper. It smoldered for a moment before bursting into bright orange flames. While Professor Pretty, who had come forward to investigate the disturbance, had no difficulty stamping out the burning memo, neither he, nor Johnny Johnson (along with his color clique), nor campus maintenance, nor the local fire department, nor the National Guard could stop the grass from burning. Water simply changed the color of the flames to a deeper orange, and ditching around buildings did not save them because the dirt burned as well. At the end of three days, the campus was a charred wasteland. Only a few smoldering shells of burned out buildings remained.

Fortunately, no one was injured. Most students later transferred to other colleges and universities and completed their degrees. Whether they did so or not, their "normal" color returned within weeks of their leaving campus. A disproportionate number went on to become consultants.

The Dean's body was never recovered. Some said that he had dematerialized like an evaporating rainbow, others that he had fluttered off like a butterfly. The fire marshal, who understood these matters only in a physical sense, said that the Dean "had been totally consumed" by the intense heat.

As for the campus, it was purchased by an international conglomerate, a leader in the fields of consulting and waste management, among others. The rolling hills were bulldozed for a mega mall. One section of the mall is called Shops on the Quad developed around a college theme. The "quad" is a small square of well-tended grass, surrounded by Study Hall (a bookstore), Student Life (trendy clothes for those under twenty-five), the Faculty Club (a gourmet restaurant), the Athletic Department (sports shoes and accessories), and *Brew*ster's (an upscale coffee house), which rests on the site of the Dean's old office. Just the other day, a regular at *Brew*ster's burned his mouth on a latte when he noticed that one of the baristas had turned purple.

The Painter

by Joseph M. Ditta

The worst of all possible things happened. He was fired from his job. He had now to go home and break that bad news to his termagant wife and to his three sons. He was, however, inured to bringing home bad news, having made a career of it.

Over the years, he had lost many jobs and left many others because he couldn't stand their drudgery. He would return home to the shame his wife heaped upon him and resignedly accept it. His wife, who worked loyally for the family, never restrained herself from shaming her husband in front of the boys when he was jobless. But worse, she would make their first son sit at the head of the table, opposite herself, at mealtimes, and set her husband's plate beside the youngest boy.

Then, in middle age, he went to college. Going to college was supposed to help him find a job without drudgery. He looked around at what to major in and found everything equally boring. He was not a student. He grew up in the streets, working in the fish market while going to school, then as a grocery clerk, a driver, a waiter. He finished high school, barely. He had, however, a flair for drawing. He always drew pictures for his sons, hanging them on the walls of their bedrooms—pictures of them doing ordinary things. When one of them was bad, he drew a picture of him doing that bad thing and hung it on the wall near his bed. More than anything, he liked to sign his name at the bottom of the picture. He always found imaginative ways of blending his name into the drawing. With a flourish, he would write: Ernest Christi, 2003.

This talent was untutored. It was natural and unsophisticated, blooming like a dandelion in the boot-stomped patch of mud that was his life. And the natural vision expressed by this talent was unspoiled by academic training, by which, of course, it would have been made to look like that of any number of thousands of others who went to the academy to become "educated."

But, to his good fortune, when Ernest decided to major in art, he proved uneducable. What the college did for him was to enlarge his notions. Whereas before college Ernest only knew pencil and paper, in college he discovered paint, canvas, printmaking, ceramics, sculpture—a dizzying array of expressive media he had never imagined as for himself. When he got his hands on these he went into a spell of creative activity that only ended now with his being fired from his job. It was a mighty spell, lasting seven years. But it was over.

On the dusty, drought stricken plains of the north Midwest, far, far away from where Ernest lived, there was a god-forsaken little college that educated annually about five hundred students. These came from the isolated regions of the northern prairie that were becoming increasingly more isolated as they lost population. The combination of long, hard winters, hot dry summers, wind, economic deprivation, and lack of every kind of opportunity kept the prairie, and therefore the college, from prospering. Having no realistic chance of hiring a genuine artist for their art department, the college was overwhelmed with gratitude when Ernest's application came wafting in, and so the Christi family left its urban existence for a new life. "Thank God," Ernest's wife said, when they arrived, "they have roads here."

At first, Ernest prospered. He had a place to work, a budget, though skimpy, to support that work, and a desire to work, to explore through every medium his own abilities, which he was still discovering. Ernest was very much like a middle teen in these activities, and his joy and enthusiasm were infectious, making devoted acolytes out of his students—all three of them. However, since he was the only person in the art department, he had to offer introductory art classes to all students. Running the art department kept him busier than he wanted to be, considering the feverish pitch at which he pursued his own work and his devotion to his three art majors.

After two years on the job, he had let so much of the administrative work go unattended that the department was in danger of losing its accreditation by the state department of education, and in spite of all warnings, Ernest couldn't tear himself away from his studios and from his teaching of his art majors. The result was the notice: his contract would not be renewed. He stared at it, and all the old familiar feelings returned. Already, he could hear his wife shaming him, see his sons' faces, the mixed look of anxiety and contempt that they were too natural to know how to disguise.

But to his surprise, when he broke the news at home that night, the whole family was joyous. "Don't feel bad, dear," his wife cajoled, with an expression of profound relief on her face. "Think of it as a new opportunity." He never realized how unhappy they were living away from the city, so immersed was he in his work. "We can go home to our friends, now," his boys said. They made him feel like they had been living in exile and that now those dry and barren paths were coming to an end.

He appreciated their feelings but was unhappy at the prospect of having once again to depend on his wife while he drifted from job to job. He despaired of finding another job teaching art. The only reason he had this one was because no one else applied. The college found him so inept an administrator that it would rather struggle with the problem of replacing him than continue to employ him. It was a damning judgment, and he felt it as such.

All the joys he had known drained from him. He stood on the street in front of his house, looking towards the setting sun. The street ended at an unplanted field in which cattle had been left to pasture. They were grazing, many of them turned in the same direction, towards the sun, which was making the sky brick red. Over the wide streak of redness, the sky was a pale aquamarine, and this faded into dusk overhead and around him. "Yes," he thought, "it is like exile." It felt like dying, too.

In the morning, he went to the campus to begin the tedious job of moving out his belongings. He had ambiguous feelings as he approached the doors to his department. He was affected by the family's excitement over going home. But he was down over the prospect of not working, for he had three canvases in progress, a block of marble that he was sculpting into a bust of his oldest son, and numerous pots, urns, vases, cups, platters, and other things awaiting firing. Would he ever get back to them? Were these, he thought, the detritus of a dead career?

He was getting on in years, and the unsuccessful stint at teaching left him demoralized. His wife readily found work and, glad to be back in familiar surroundings, left off harassing him. The boys prospered in school again. It was late November and he was still unemployed. Things were back to the way they used to be, except that in the interim

Ernest had found a calling, a deep and powerful urge to create, that was as useless to him and the family now as the picked-over bones of the Thanksgiving turkey.

When he was alone in the shabby apartment that was all they could afford, he worked on the three canvases he had started at the college. He set his easel in the parlor near the windows, and, his stomach feeling hollow and his self-esteem draping over the tops of his shoes, he painted—painted from memory, from instincts honed by his past painting, from a deftness acquired almost magically, and from desire to paint. The three finished, he started others. He painted quickly— roads on the prairie, lined on both sides with barbed-wire fences, hedged by corn or sunflowers, or covered with snow, or with the acid light of a prairie summer noon. He looked out the parlor windows and painted the street below. He painted the parlor. He painted himself. He painted the worn-out sofa with its bedraggled blanket cover, the lamp next to it, the floor, with its fake Persian carpet, even the door entering the apartment. He painted the leafless limbs of the trees hanging over the street right in front of his windows, giving them more reality on the canvas than they had outside. He painted his wife's portrait, his three sons playing in the snow outside, his neighbors coming and going, he painted until he couldn't see anymore. And still he painted.

The boys would come home from school and look at him and share in silence mournful expressions with each other. Their mother shushed them when they tried to talk about their father, though she shared their concern. She had given up harassing, but something new had entered their lives, and she didn't know how to understand it, no less how to deal with it. She looked at the canvases in wonder and said nothing. But she saw how he grew thin. He had stopped shaving, and she saw how his beard grew to his chest. He had even stopped changing clothes, and she would have to go to him and take off his shirt and undershirt and dress him herself with clean ones. The smell of the paints wore on her, though the boys never minded, taking this unpleasantness in stride. But she could hardly stand to lie in bed with him anymore, for he stank of sweat and paint and paint thinner.

One night she woke from a bad dream and looked over at the clock. It said three a.m. She turned on her side, snuggling, and suddenly sprung awake alarmed. Ernest was not there. She got up and put on her robe and went to look for him. But she found the apartment empty. Something was amiss, she knew it. She was overcome with fear when she saw the page of loose-leaf paper on the table in the kitchen:

> *Dear Miriam: I can make no further progress here. All the paintings I have done so far are yours. You have a right to them since you paid for all the materials. But you have a right to them for another reason, a spiritual one—namely, the claim of a wife to her husband's substance. They are all the substance I have. They are, in fact, more real than I am. I must go. Don't look for me to return. Tell the boys what suits you, only don't tell them I don't love them. I am no longer the person you married. I am not myself even to myself. I have grown so different, I don't know who I am. I think I have ceased to be anybody. I am only what I see and paint. I must go, because I don't have many years, and what I have to do is vast. I don't understand it, either. Goodbye.*

What did it mean? She couldn't comprehend it. She read it three times and then read it again. It sounded crazy, driven and crazy, and she didn't know what to think. Had he lost his mind? She called the police and told them that her husband was deranged and walking alone in the city. She gave them a detailed description and waited, sitting up alone in the parlor, wrapped in her robe. It was cold, so she pulled the blanket covering the sofa over her shoulder and rested back her head.

She dozed and woke several times, hoping for a knock at the door, for it to be the police with her husband in tow, and him all apologetic. She would care for him from now on, she thought, with more attention to his needs. But the knock never came. What came was a dim gray light against the shades of the parlor windows. So she got up to open one, feeling like looking out as the morning came. As the shade went up, however, she screamed in horror at what she saw—it was Ernest, floating in the air in front of the window. He had an expression of pleading on his face and was holding one hand out to her, palm up, and gesturing up the block with the other—as though he were telling her he was sorry he was going. She looked at him, floating in the air, and calmed herself. Opening the window, she shouted in a whiny, tearful voice, "Ernest, shame on you! You're acting like a little boy. Shame! Shame! You can't run away because life is hard. Think of me! Shame! Shame on you for not finding work and being a better father! Shame! Shame!"

She was still shouting "Shame!" out the window when her oldest son came into the parlor and shouted at her. She stopped and closed the window and pulled down the shade so he wouldn't see his father. But it was too late. He said,

"What's Dad doing outside the window?" and ran over to it and raised the shade and looked out. But no one was there.

His mother said nothing. She sniffed and wiped her nose and went back to bed.

The boy, now sixteen years old, stood by the window and looked out. He saw the sun lighten the sky and illuminate the houses across the street. As he stood by the window, he heard the apartment door open and turned to see his father enter. He saw his father then as one sees a stranger, unemotionally, objectively. Tall and thin and bony with broad shoulders and a stoop and a long graying beard and long graying hair. His father didn't look at him but turned towards the bedroom. Then, feeling a strange deadness he had no way of accounting for, he looked down at the street. A policeman was there getting into a police car. The door slammed and it pulled away, and as it did so, the driver turned off the headlights.

Power Play

by Evelyn Shakir

Selma

Pieter was almost everything Selma could hope for in a son-in-law. He was clean, he didn't come to her for money, and, when she told about the old days, he listened and didn't tap his foot. His manners were beautiful, in the style of her overseas cousins, though he was Dutch, not Lebanese, and was born in this country. But, as she explained to her sister, old world in his bones. Eunice grimaced. "Like you, I suppose."

Other things in his favor: he took second helpings, he turned his hand to the little repairs around the house that had defeated her husband, and once he bought her a microwave. "Mind you," she told Eunice that time over lunch, "it's not even my birthday."

"Ha!" Eunice opened her eyes very wide, then went back to stirring her coffee. Selma didn't like that in her, the little sarcastic ways, especially with her being younger. But Eunice was right, there was a problem. After a year or even longer of Pieter being just what he should be, something in him went haywire.

"It's like you throw a switch," Selma told her sister one Saturday, "and the lights cut out."

Eunice found an apron and tied it around her waist. With nothing better to do, she'd answered Selma's call to help with spinach turnovers and meat pies for Sunday. While Selma pummeled the dough, Eunice peered into the icebox, then pulled out the washed spinach and scallions and reached for a knife. Soon flecks of green were littering the floor that had been swept just that morning.

Selma frowned and tried again. "It's like the tide's been coming in, and now it's going out. Or like when you're a kid and you hold a balloon tight by the string, but, first thing you know, it's floating away anyway, over the trees."

"Your son-in-law's nuts," Eunice said.

Selma gave the dough a final punch for good measure. "That's what I mean."

Lorraine

So far, it had happened three times. Lorraine would come home to an empty house and know, from the feel of it, that her husband hadn't just run out to fill up with gas or buy a tool from the hardware. This last time, she was out early from work and came in the back way. Pieter was still in the kitchen with his scuffed leather suitcase at his feet and a down jacket under his arm. She begged him, actually went down on her knees and clung to his legs. "Why are you doing this?" He disentangled himself and sidled past toward the door. When she heard the engine catch, she rushed to the window and banged on the pane. His ten-year-old Honda pulled out of the driveway.

Lorraine racked her brain. Last night, he'd been tender. Too tender. She should have guessed he was saying good-bye. It hurt her to think he'd caressed her and his curly head nuzzled her breast while that secret lay coiled in his brain. But maybe not, it could have been later, something that came to him in the night and confused him, a panicky dream or a voice. She should have watched over him, held him tighter. Or something at breakfast that ate at his nerves. Pits in the orange juice, eggs too runny, toast too light. Had she prattled on like a teenager? Sometimes she did that. She remembered him across the table that morning, his back to the window; the early light, like a halo, tinting his hair a strawberry blonde. But his face was a blur.

"You live with the man," her mother would say. "You must have seen something was wrong."

But nothing, she'd noticed nothing at all.

Selma and Lorraine

The drip, plop of the kitchen faucet was getting on her nerves. But what made her head pound, that was her daughter. Dumb, hopeless, bound to take Pieter back when he showed his face in a month or two. Oh, she might pout for a couple of hours, but sex—of course, that was it—would bring her around. She'd telephone Selma. "He missed me so much."

Selma tried to talk sense to her daughter, to appeal to her pride. "You're a wife, but you live half the time like a widow." Lorraine heard her out, then made her statement. She would not file for divorce, she would not change the locks, and she didn't give a shit what her mother would not have put up with. Selma couldn't believe it, the tongue on her daughter. But in a few days they were on good enough terms again and settled into the life they led when Pieter was AWOL.

Monday through Friday Lorraine went to her job in the courthouse; evenings she did laundry, shampooed her hair, and paid bills or balanced her checkbook. On days she felt ambitious, she'd ride the exercise bike for thirty minutes while she watched *Wheel of Fortune*. She had a couple of friends from high school, married now, and once in a while, when one of them was home alone and bored, she'd dial Lorraine's number. At first, it gave her a lift to hear someone who wasn't her mother on the other end of the line. But the conversations were awkward, punctuated with long, breathing silences. After years of going their own ways, they'd lost track.

Selma kept busy as usual, vacuuming every day and scooting around—to doctors' appointments, to the Saharan bakery for bread and spices, to the butcher shop owned by an Armenian from Beirut. His was the only meat she trusted. At home, she sewed aprons and potholders to add to her supply. "You can never have too many," she told Lorraine. "I'm telling you so you'll remember."

Friday evenings now, she prepared dinner for two and had it on the table when Lorraine got off the bus at 6:45. Afterwards, in the den, they watched a video Lorraine had rented on her way from work. Anything with Doris Day or David Niven they both liked a lot. Saturday was free time. Lorraine could clean her apartment, shop for groceries, and mix enough tuna salad and boil enough eggs for five days of brown-bag lunches. Sunday after church, *gas tank full*, she and her mother visited great-aunts and cousins.

But Selma couldn't go long without stirring up the pot. "If I were you," she'd begin, and Lorraine would turn her face away. *Oh, if it were me,* Selma thought, *I'd take him to court, I'd hire a private eye, I'd put his clothes out for the Salvation Army.* One Friday evening she tried a new tack. After toying with the last bite of custard pie on her plate, she pulled her chair in closer.

"I'm not saying *divorce*, but at least give him a scare."

"How do you mean?" Lorraine asked politely. Selma noticed her eying the clock. *As if what I'm saying has nothing to do with her,* Selma thought. *As if I'm reading from Dear Abby.*

Selma sat up straight. "Turn the tables."

"Like?"

"Like him coming home some fine day and you're not there." She stabbed the last of her pie and popped it into her mouth.

Lorraine pushed her own plate to the side; but, Selma noticed, she didn't get up.

"How would I do that?"

Selma had always had to think for her husband, too. If it weren't for her pushing—"You can do better, Charlie"—he'd have died driving a bus instead of fitting ladies in a shoe store.

"It's simple. When he decides to honor you with his presence, he always calls to say he's on his way. Am I right?"

Lorraine shrugged. "I guess."

"Of course, I'm right," Selma insisted. "He wants a hot meal when he walks in the door. Now here's what." She spoke slowly so Lorraine would see the beauty of her plan. "When the phone rings, don't you answer. From now on, let the machine pick up. If it's someone else, all fine and good, you can talk. But if it's him, you grab a nightie and head out."

"Yeah, well," her daughter said.

But it was an idea.

Eunice

Eunice had her own ideas. Pieter was a bigamist, plain and simple. Of course, the family couldn't see it. *Not my Pete,* Lorraine had said when Eunice dropped a hint. Selma turned it over, but, in the end, she said the same. *Your imagination's working overtime.* Her sister and her niece, two peas in a pod. One day Eunice had been at Selma's when Pieter dropped by to mount a shelf for her jars of herbs and spices. After she set olives and cheese in front of him and poured him coffee, Selma had slipped upstairs to spritz herself with toilet water and smear on lipstick. *Don't you smell good*, Eunice announced, making a point of it, when Selma walked back in the kitchen.

Eunice admired Pieter's shenanigans. Not everyone could keep two sweethearts on a string, much less two wives. She still thought it was wives. One time, her tenth-grade chemistry teacher, Mr. Simms, gave her back a test with a C—on it. *I know you're smart,* he told her. *When you find what you love, you're going to shine.* Well, she loved making monkeys of the stupid boys she went to high school with, and later junior college. And she *was* good. Whatever fibs she told, they'd swallow whole. Especially, Mike Snowe. After he saw her cuddling up to Danny Fedo in the caf, she said that Danny was her cousin and in urgent need of TLC. His father—Mike mustn't pass this on, of course—worked for the CIA and was being held for ransom somewhere in the Middle East. When she touched Mike's cheek and rubbed her face against his sleeve, he bought it all. Anyone that dumb, she thought, shouldn't be allowed to cross the street without his mommy.

Not that Eunice didn't love her niece. She guessed she did. Why else did she plan to leave Lorraine the pearl earrings and mink collar she'd inherited from her mother and a few thousand on top of that? Why else did she keep telling her, "Don't be such a sap"?

Lorraine

At first, she didn't remember and would reach for the phone. If it was her mother, there'd be a juicy suck of tongue against teeth. *Lorraine,* she'd hear, *you're not cooperating.*

The first time that she caught herself and listened for the message, she heard her Aunt Eunice on the phone.

"Pick up, I know you're there," Eunice demanded.

"Fuck you!"

Lorraine clapped her hand over her mouth. Where had that word come from?

Selma

There was a word for people like her sister Eunice. *Trouble.* Never happy unless she was making it for others or was in hot water, herself. For instance, she was so pretty she could have had her pick of husbands, but she had to go for Elias Khouri. And for no other reason than he was the first guy who gave her a hard time instead of her doing it to him. Never mind he was a liar and a cheat, as Selma could have told her. In fact, did tell her. Maybe not in so many words, because Elias was Charlie's cousin and, in those early days, she didn't want it getting back to him. But she'd said enough. "Are you sure you know what you're doing?" and, another time, "Does this guy have a steady job?"

Selma had been in love with Charlie until she married him. Imagined all sorts of special things about him that turned out not to be there. She'd made the best of it. They'd only had the one child, and, of course, Charlie thought the sun rose and set on his little princess. Whatever she wanted—rocky road ice cream before dinner, the same Dr. Seuss five times over in one night, her best friend with them on a trip to Disneyworld—he couldn't tell her no. When she got to be a teenager, Selma set about to undo the damage. "Boys are tricky," she told her daughter. "Don't expect anyone to love you like your daddy." Lorraine had friends waiting for her at the mall. "I know all that stuff," she called back, already out the door.

Lorraine was thirty-one now, and Selma had no grandchildren. That was the shame of it.

Selma took her coffee mug to the sink, washed and dried it by hand, and put it away on a shelf in the cabinet. She sponged off the counter though it didn't need it and stared at her reflection in the window. She remembered the first time Lorraine brought Pieter home for supper on a Saturday. Selma had cooked a meal good enough for Sunday, even made her special dessert, crepes stuffed with cottage cheese and topped with orange-blossom syrup. "*Ahlan wa sahlan*, welcome!" She was all smiles as Lorraine steered him in the door. Oh, when Selma thought how good she'd been to Pieter, she could lay her head down on her arms and cry hot tears.

But that first visit, he'd made a good impression—white shirt and tie, clean shaven, and with a shy laugh almost like a girl's. And a trade, refinishing furniture, that meant he could be his own boss or hire himself out, anywhere, anytime. Charlie had taken to Pieter in a big way. In bed that night, he'd touched Selma's shoulder. "Our little girl's got a boy top of the line."

Just the same, Selma recalled that she, for one, had always had her doubts.

"Don't say I didn't warn you," she told Lorraine when the troubles started.

"You didn't. You said he was Mr. Wonderful."

Her daughter could be stubborn.

On her way upstairs to run her evening bath, Selma hesitated in the foyer. She glanced at her watch, then picked up the phone, dialed, and listened for the beep. "It's me." She fluffed her hair in the mirror while she waited, but no one answered. "The only mother you'll ever have," she added and hung up.

Eunice

The morning she looked in the bathroom mirror and saw her swollen eye and the bruise on her chin, she decided it was over. Elias had run around on her from day one, he couldn't or wouldn't keep a job, and she knew he pilfered money from her purse. He'd even roughed her up before when he'd been drinking. Twisting her arm behind her back, dragging her to bed by her hair, tripping her so she fell hard against a table. For a month, two purple blossoms on her thigh refused to fade.

But so far it had all been private, husband and wife. This was different, an announcement to the world. Livid markings, like ugly graffiti, on her face. She paid Elias off, twenty thousand from her savings, and he flew back to Lebanon.

Eunice was propped up in bed, playing with the sash of her silk negligee and thinking of her sister. Selma had landed the good cousin, the made-in-America cousin. Eunice remembered the banners in her college dorm—"When better men are made, Pine Grove girls will make them." The first time Selma came down to visit, she thought the banners were advertising motherhood.

Eunice wanted to blame the old country for Elias's temper. But that wouldn't wash—her bashful father who marveled at spider webs and made pets of ladybugs had come from overseas. She held up two posters in her mind—Elias on the left, Charlie on the right. And admitted that, even now and knowing what she knew, if she could pick, she'd choose the same. Elias had taught her that it took a bastard to make the blood pulse in her veins. Maybe for little Lorraine it was the same.

"I'll make her tell me." Eunice grabbed the portable phone from her nightstand and dared herself to do it. She was excited now, out of bed and pacing the corridor from bedroom to kitchen to living room. When the beep sounded, she announced herself, then waited. "Oh, pick up," she whispered. Her face felt warm. Her heart was beating fast.

Lorraine

It reached the point, Lorraine flushed with pleasure to hear the jangle of the telephone. She'd hurry into the bedroom and wait while her outgoing message played, then lean closer so she wouldn't miss a word of what came in. After a while, no matter whose voice it was, she didn't answer.

She found herself keeping a list in a notebook by her bedside. Names, dates, times of day, and messages enclosed in quotation marks. Before going to sleep, she'd read through the list like a diary of her day. At first, if the caller left only a name and maybe a number or sometimes neither, Lorraine was disappointed. But soon the intervals of silence began teasing her imagination, like taunts from someone playing hard to get. She erased commands to "call as soon as you get home." She invented messages to herself and wrote them down. The good news wouldn't stop—bequests from long forgotten cousins, a raise or a promotion, an old boyfriend getting back in touch, a lady telling her she'd won a raffle, an invitation to a party on a yacht.

Her few calls became fewer. Only her mother was persistent.

"Are you there, Lorraine?"

"Are you coming to supper, Lorraine?"

"Now, don't be silly, Lorraine. You pick up, I want you to pick up."

Lorraine would listen carefully to her mother's messages and sometimes she'd have to answer. Otherwise, Selma might show up in person, and she might bring Aunt Eunice or a policeman with her. "Hi, mom," she'd say, "I just walked in the door."

"Where have you been? What's keeping you so busy?"

Lorraine couldn't think how to answer.

"I saw the doctor, Lorraine. He says my sugar's up."

Lorraine gave a little "hmm" intended to show sympathy.

"A lot you care," her mother said.

Lorraine compromised. She allowed her mother one call a week and tried to drop by to see her for an hour on Saturday or Sunday. Eunice she cut off cold. If you asked her why, she couldn't tell you. "Aren't you lonely?" her mother asked her. "It's not healthy to sit in that apartment by yourself." She could kick herself she'd ever come up with that idea that started Lorraine not picking up the phone.

Eunice

Eunice changed her will. Lorraine out, Elias in.

Pieter

He felt strong. Like he could run uphill with a load of lumber in his arms. Like he could swim across a lake he knew in Pennsylvania. Like his heart would beat for days even if the rest of him were dead. And he was full of gratitude. For the trout in the lake in Pennsylvania and for wood fires at night. For farms with barns he'd slept in, for trails he'd hiked, for the girl with the red lips who laughed and tried to teach him Spanish, and for her brother who'd towed his car away when it died on the country road. Even for the waffles and bacon he'd had an hour ago in a diner this side of the state line. And now the breeze blowing through the window of the bus. He smiled at the passengers in the seats around him and noticed the girls. Not a one as pretty as his sweet Lorraine waiting for him at home. In the terminal, he hopped off the bus and headed for a phone.

Lorraine

When the phone rang, she had one foot out the door. She paused. No one had called in two days, and she was hungry for her fix. But then she changed her mind and turned the lock. This way she'd have something to look forward to all day. At the trolley stop, she was already imagining the wonderful surprise in store for her when she got home that evening. Composing in her mind the message that would make her the happiest girl in town.

Playing with an Invisible Deck

by Jessica Somers

Sam was holding a huge bunch of roses, mums, sunflowers and all else you could imagine. "For you," he said, pulling a bar stool up beside me. He chugged what was left of my beer and signaled the bartender for two more. Our usual. Sam worked in a flower shop so I got what was left at the end of the day. My bouquet was half dead, and beautiful. The summer was coming to an end, the bar was packed, and I was just about finished falling in love with Sam.

When we met it was raining, back in February. We were drunk and happy, and we've stayed that way. "Tell me about your day, Cheri," Sam said. And I told him. I told him about the patient with the horrible gingivitis. I told him about the little girl with four cavities and a cat named Candy Cane. And I told him about Dr. Mitvak, father of four, hitting on one of our teenage patients, again. I told Sam everything, because he listened. He really did. He listened intently to what I said, always. And he'd do the same for anybody. That was what got me about Sam. He cared what people had to say. A lot of guys I met, my ex-fiancé included, only acted like they were listening. But really they were just waiting for me to pause for a breath so they could interrupt. "Of course I am," said Sam once when I asked him if he was really listening to me at four a.m. in a bubble bath. "Every word you say goes in both my ears and stays there. You know why?" I asked him why. "Because, I believe I can learn all there is to know, really, all the important things in this world if I just listen. Don't laugh," he said, because I was laughing. "Everybody knows something. And I decided to collect all those little puzzle pieces from everybody and one day I'll be a very wise man." I thought Sam already was a wise man but I decided not to tell him. If he knew it, it would be gone.

"And how was your day?" I asked. I lived with Sam and so I loved to hear about this horticulture business. I had sworn I would never live with a man again until I was married. But after months of spending every night with Sam in his tiny apartment and wearing boxer shorts under my smock to work everyday, I gave up and moved my stuff in. I couldn't keep my hands off Sam and he was the same. Between us fights were rare and inconsequential. They were always more or less about tequila.

"Excuse me," a man at the bar stool next to me said. He startled me, I didn't even know anyone was there. When Sam and I went out together the world around us didn't exist. That must have been why we didn't mind spending so much time in a dive like the Seaforth. "I said: Excuse me, and I do mean to interrupt. How do you do?" The man was twenty-something or thirty-something, like us, and he was so emaciated I thought I was looking at a scarecrow. He wore black clothes and a top hat which he tipped to me. "I hate Owls. What about you?"

He smiled, I didn't. "Hi there. My name's Sam. This is Cheri." The man reached across me and shook Sam's hand and then tipped his hat to me again.

"I don't want to alarm anyone," said the man. "But I am a Magician." He pulled a five dollar bill out from behind my ear and offered to buy me a beer. I looked on the bar where my change from our last round wasn't.

"No, let me," said Sam. And that was how we met the Magician. Sam liked him right off, I could tell. For me it took a card trick.

"Here take this," said the Magician, thrusting an empty hand before me.

"Take what?"

"This deck of cards." I looked at his grubby hand again, but it was empty.

"What deck of cards?"

He put his hand closer to mine and said, "This one. It's an invisible deck." Sam was smiling at me, excited, so I mimed accepting the deck. "Take the cards out of their box." I did. "Good. Now fan the cards out for yourself and pick one. One you're attracted to. The Ace of Diamonds. Or the Nine of Spades. Pick your favorite card." My favorite card was a birthday card. I told the Magician this. He didn't think I was so funny, he just drained his beer. Sam ordered him another and I picked the Two of Hearts.

"Now what?"

"You picked a card?" I nodded. "Good. Now turn it over so that your card is facing the opposite way of all the other cards." I turned my invisible card over and the Magician had me shuffle the deck and put it back in its box. I handed it to him and he put it in his pocket, pulling a real deck out at the same time. He took a swig of his beer and said, "Tell me, what was your card?"

"Aren't you supposed to tell me?" The Magician just looked at me. I was being a jerk, trying to steal his stage.

"The Two of Hearts." The Magician took the real deck of cards out of its box and slowly fanned them out. All the red and black cards faced me except one that was turned around, only blue bicycles. He told me to pull this card out. There it was. I liked magic, I just pretended I didn't. I liked the Magician, too.

By last call we were old friends. The Magician and Sam and me. When we were leaving the Magician said, "Have a terrible evening!" We promised him we would and wished him the same. It was a funny thing, Sam and I had spent just about every night in the Seaforth since we met and had never seen the Magician before and then all of a sudden there he was the next night and the next and all the rest. We loved the Magician's company and spent all our time with him and when we finally went home, he was what we talked about. His tricks, his stories, they filled my imagination. If the Magician made any money at all it was from the magic, kid's parties, theater openings and stage shows he performed at, drunk. "Did I ever tell you guys about this show I did, it was a Corporate Christmas Party." He'd told us this one many times, but it was a good story so I didn't say. "I was hired to walk around, do a little magic, tell a few jokes, that sort of thing. Except, they had an open bar and everything. I was hammered by nine and this gig was supposed to go to midnight. Later on the CEO, who was going to give me my check at the end of the night, came round wanting to see some of my work. I launched into the Card in my Pocket trick, you know that one, don't you? Sure. Before it was over I passed out, cold. But apparently the CEO's card was lying next to me on the floor. He was very impressed and I did another show the next year, but I put my hand up his wife's skirt and had to leave early, no pay."

The Magician also had some small cons that got him by. There was a complicated scenario he worked out for his land lady where he couldn't pay rent for religious reasons.

He said it was working. His cell phone bill was charged to other accounts and every couple of months it would get cut off as the bill was being disputed. And he knew grocery check-out girls who stole food for him. The Magician didn't pay, that was his character.

We were so tight, the three of us, that the Magician had turkey with Sam and me in our little apartment that Christmas. We had mashed potatoes, cranberry sauce and everything. The Magician brought the bourbon. It was a wonderful night. But by New Years Sam and I were fighting. Our honeymoon was over and he wasn't listening anymore. "Where's all your money?" he asked me when I needed to borrow some of his. "Don't answer. I already know. You're buying the Magician beer every night and leaving me to pay the bills."

"I've never bought him anything," I said. It wasn't true. I did buy the Magician a few beers every night. But so did Sam, he must have. The Magician wouldn't buy his own. But, on we went. Fighting. About money and other stuff: the laundry, dinner, breakfast, sex. But there we were back at the Seaforth every night, drinking again. The Magician helped, his presence eased the bitterness. We could talk and laugh with him rather than fight with each other.

Sam was jealous and suspicious of me. He accused me of all sorts of things. And didn't hear my protests and denials. If I stayed late at work he said I was screwing Dr. Mitvak. Once he accused me of being infatuated with the Magician. I got too busy to finish falling in love with Sam and now I didn't want to.

But still, there we were staring at the Magician across a few pints as if everything was fine. In my head I pretended I was out with Sam having a great time like it used to be, but really it was the Magician's show. He controlled the conversation and we drifted along happy to have the pressure of each other's company lifted.

One night, coming up on Valentines Day Sam was kept at the flower shop, getting everything ready. I was left alone at the bar with the Magician. After a couple of tricks and a few beers he said, "I had a dream last night. About you, Cheri. I won't tell Sam. But I thought you'd want to hear it."

"Oh yeah? Tell me." I was laughing. But it wasn't funny. The Magician was so serious. I'd never seen him that way and I wanted to laugh it away. If this was an act it was a good one.

"The dream was about you and me together in a tiny old shack. Out in a field. We were screwing." I didn't hear it. But I knew he said it. "A heavy gust of wind blew the shack off its foundations and left us in the open field lying naked together."

I laughed him off, or tried to. But I couldn't tell Sam. Ever. This dream of the Magician's became a secret I kept from my suspicious boyfriend. Suddenly I was aware of the Magician. Had he been like this the whole time, making overtures and subtle comments to me. I ignored him. I hid it all from Sam.

I lived in fear of Sam's silence. He was no longer accusing me of things. He just looked at me with contempt. I didn't talk and he didn't listen. But we still shared a roof and a bed and beers till two with the Magician. I hated the Magician. I hated his anecdotes, his money stealing, and most of all I hated the magic. One night, at home, away from the Magician Sam broke his silence. "Just give it up," he said. "You don't need to keep lying to me. He told me. He didn't keep your little dream a secret."

"My . . ." My dream.

"Don't act dumb Cheri. You lie to me, but the Magician, he's my friend. He said he tried to keep you from telling him about it, but couldn't shut you up. He also said he's not interested in you and wishes you'd never said anything." Now it was Sam speaking and I listened. "He told me your dream Cheri. About you and him in that shack and what you were doing." There it was. How could he believe I wanted to be with that man, that Magician. I wept. We were tricked, and now the show was over. All that was left was to pay.

George Goes for A Walk

by Caitlin Hicks

On this slightly smoggy Southern California morning, dew on the cars and the short dry grass, George opens the scratched aluminum screen door of his wood frame stucco house, like he has for twenty years. A day like any other Long Beach day, and yet, for unsuspecting George, a surprise just around the corner. Something unexpected to disrupt the comfortable unease of his settled life. A thin cell phone in his palm chirps as he dials a ten-digit number. It's Saturday, and he steps down each wooden, paint-peeling step off the porch, wearing what he wore yesterday: slacks, a belt, wing tips, a crumpled white shirt, and something Weekend: his fuzzy blue sweater, the one the cats were sleeping on in the chair this morning. Today, no tie. He's on a Joe Job to pick up milk, bread, coffee and cigarettes at JP Liquor Store on South Street, the main drag in "the top of the town."

"Don't be askin' me to pick up anything exotic like endive or tofu," he barks back at Helen, who sits cross legged on the kitchen chair reading a thick paperback. Then inwardly, as the screen slowly inches shut behind him, "never, under any circumstances send me on a hunt for a 'feminine hygiene' product." He laughs at his own borrowed wit as he steps onto the bumpy concrete walk. He notices the cracks, the mini earthquakes, the heaved blocks, the crab grass in the raised dirt, and wonders when his share of taxes is going to filter down to improve his neighborhood. His foot crunches on a maple seed pod; spiked shells are littered everywhere. A busy signal buzzes in his ear. Ollie's low slung shiny yellow '74 Oldsmobile rolls past, rubber tires making a soft sound against the asphalt. George folds his cell phone into a flat deck of cards and slips it into his shirt pocket.

California Street is aptly named for this kind of crisp, sunny, winter day. It's not an upscale neighborhood, but its small yards are well trimmed, the palm trees are 70 feet tall and in the spring, maple trees, now without their leaves, fill in with a grace and elegance which George knows money can't buy. It's always been a working class area, and in the past ten years it has become more ethnic than George would prefer, a fact that irritates him when he thinks about it. The original residents were workers at the Naval Shipyard (which relocated out of Long Beach) and McDonnell-Douglas Aircraft, which is now Boeing. Today it's quite a mix. George knows by name the young Philippine family, several black families, a Chinese woman living with her parents, a Haitian family, a German widower, even a Cambodian, and a single white man whom George suspects is gay. They work at a variety of jobs: sales clerk at Robinsons-May Company, Supervisor for Parks and Recreation, construction worker, pipe fitter, insurance salesman, service station attendant, secretary, legal assistant, bartender, child care worker.

What bothers George is not the color of their skin, but the fact that they are all Democrats. George is a self-proclaimed "staunch Republican." The thought of Andrew, the suspected gay, participating in his gay practices (George doesn't like to think about it, but sometimes finds himself wandering off in that mental direction) does interfere with the serenity of George's Sundays, especially at Mass when Father Callahan reminds the congregation of what is, and what isn't, sin. Otherwise, George feels that by and large, these neighbors have the same values he has, except of course, George thinks that a person should not be given preferential treatment because of his or her skin color, and thank the Lord Affirmative Action was overturned when it was, enough damage was done during the thirty years of reverse discrimination. George rejects the notion that the playing field isn't level, and is firm in his belief that generations of people on Welfare is wrong. All the namby-pamby self-esteem bullshit, get them off their duff and out there, let them pull themselves up one minimum-wage hour at a time. He hates the thought of illegal aliens sneaking around and working at even low-paying jobs, and he's not sure who exactly, in his neighborhood, might be taking advantage. There is a black couple across the street, Bill and Doris, who rent a small house, and neither of them work. George knows that Bill limps, that he has MS, but that's just what bugs him about Bill: George blames Bill for being irresponsible and not buying health or disability insurance when he could. Now Bill is unable to work and is probably living off George's taxes. A sore spot. For all George knows, Bill never paid a cent into Social Security in the first place, and now he's depleting what might have been left for the rest of the hard working class. George never ventures into the despair that Bill's life might be filled with, he can't solve the problems of the world. "I stand by my family," he says in his most passionate moments. "I don't want the state to help them. I will take care of them."

With the Left Wing in power these last eight years, George was getting into more and more email rants with his college buddies about the wrongness of the American political situation, and finding himself increasingly frustrated about it all. How was he supposed to maneuver his way through the troubling landscape of Political Correctness, Affirmative Action, sexual harassment, this blind acceptance of people of every color and stripe like crack-addicted single mothers who get pregnant and then want abortions funded by public money?

Walking up to the boulevard, George's mind is still filled with this kind of talk. The ease his life has taken on with his recent money has been offset by the sense of injustice he now feels having to pay taxes. The target of his frustration today is funding of the arts, and although he's never been to an art exhibit, he's an expert on what kind of art he *doesn't* want to see. A traveling exhibit, *Sensation* invaded his morning calm by virtue of an article in the *Los Angeles Times*. The mayor of New York threatening to pull the plug on funding to the Brooklyn Museum if they insist on running that show! More power to the mayor! Flies infesting a piece of meat. Cross sections of a cow in Plexiglas. In 'political discussions' with his neighbors at the summer block party, George actually prefers trotting out the image of Christ on the cross immersed in urine, that usually shuts them up. In their arguments, his sister Margaret has told him that only $1.37 or some miniscule amount of every taxpayer's money goes to support the arts, but it still burns George that he can't choose the kind of art he would like for his $1.37. *Art? Let the marketplace decide. Give me an action flick with 'useless' nudity and sex any day—especially if it doesn't need my tax dollars!* He thinks of his younger sister, Jane, a smug liberal, a self-proclaimed artist who specializes in vanity productions and *I'm glad she lives in Canada*, as if that were a punishment. The way George sees it, 1% of the taxpayers pay 30% of the taxes in the U.S., and it's just so *unfair*. Lately, his rants have left him unsatisfied and cranky.

As he rounds the corner his inner pace quickens as if to keep up with the hum and roar of the traffic. He reaches into the soft pocket on his right buttocks where he keeps his wallet, squeezing the familiar shiny leather lump, *Yup, it's there*, stuffed with a month's worth of receipts. He puts his foot into the crosswalk.

A deafening clap assaults his ears, the screech of brakes and he finds himself staring at the body of a woman as it bounces like a rag doll off Ollie's shiny yellow Olds in the intersection and lands three feet in front of him. A heavy dread drops itself into George's heart, adrenalin washes in rushing streams through his veins. A red Camaro eats up the air with a low grumbling idle to George's right. His foot lands on the pavement as the limp pedestrian wiggles on the ground, trying to push herself up. *Oh, she's alive* and George notices blood splattered across her face like spray paint.

It takes a second, but George rallies. He can see he's the only one who has stepped into the intersection, so he must be the one. He puts his other foot forward, he's committed himself now to this woman lying on the cold asphalt who shouldn't be getting up. He sucks in his breath and remembers, yes, he took First Aid some years back! The thought of being a hero invigorates him. He deliberately listens to himself, waiting for the emergency questions to come rushing into his brain. Is this person breathing? Heart beating? George is now at her side. Obviously she's breathing, her heart's gotta be working. No CPR required, whew. Okay, calm down. He kneels at her head. He strips himself of his sweater, folds it into a flat pillow. *Don't get up*, he says, *Here put your head down on this, we'll call an ambulance.* The grumbling Camaro, George can't focus on what year, its windshield smashed in glass with the same splattered pattern as the blood, is backing up and turns right, moving around the woman on the ground. The engine revs, the car needles its way through the gathering crowd on the street and speeds away! George looks at Ollie, who's standing at the headlight, shaking his balding head. *Ollie, call an ambulance!*

George sees his neighbor, Mack, a stunned looking man in his Sixties or Seventies, George isn't really sure what his age is, holding tight the stretched leash of his black dog, George can't quite name the breed, and he says, *Mack! Your jacket! She needs a blanket.* Keep her warm, the voices say, Make sure she doesn't go into shock. George places the plaid wool jacket, the heat still in the silk lining, over her stomach and legs. He inches toward her, closing out the wind, his thigh in contact with her torso. Keep her calm. *How you doin?* he asks her almost cheerfully.

Now George really sees her, he's close enough to her face to notice the dark pores around her nose, her deep brown eyes, she's moaning a little, reaching for her leg, which George can't see because it's under navy blue slacks, and instinctively, he touches her hair, he pushes it over her ear in a gesture of comfort he learned from his mother. Just a simple touch, the hair between his thumb and fingers and he runs it down her temple and tucks it behind her ear. And again. She receives it, she sighs, she closes her eyes, and miraculously, George thinks, she relaxes the stiffness she's been holding, a stiffness he only feels with its release. Voices urgently surround him: does somebody have a cell phone? Call the police! Again he strokes her hair.

Did you get the license number? George hears the cries but he can't look up, he's been sucked into an orbit around this woman by a force stronger than curiosity and stranger than desire, something calm. George knows with a visceral certainty he's willing to succumb to, that his purpose is not to have the cell phone, or call the ambulance, but just to be there, just to comfort this woman, to stroke her hair. He can't believe how simple it is, how miraculous. *It's all right,* he says, *You're going to be all right,* in a tone he makes specially for her, a reassuring tone that would convince even himself. She tries to speak, her words come out in Spanish, now he notices her white blouse splattered with red, he can see the soft area just above her small breasts, *Yeah, she's wearing a bra,* he notices and looks away into her face again, *and she's young, her cheeks are round, just that downward wrinkle around *each side of her nose*, George can't quite place her age, thirty something? Her eyes bleed a little, it's quite bloodshot and a panic creeps in, George doesn't know what happened to her, exactly. Did the car hit her? *Internal injuries* he thinks, his heartbeat galloping, *She could be bleeding to death.* He calms himself, for her. *You're doing fine*, he says, cooing at her. *Bueno, bueno.* Is that a Spanish word? He's trying to remember the lessons he took years ago, when his company was doing some kind of trade deal with a Mexican company.

An eternity passes, and he's at the mercy of it, like he was a child, looking at the clock in the five hungry minutes before the noon bell. Someone has redirected traffic. The talkative crowd, a newly formed community of strangers, mills and stares, gawking and gossiping as if gathered around a barbecue for a family reunion. George notices blood on his hand where he's been tucking her hair. Oh, he hears, they've caught the hit-and-run driver. How fast was the car going? She bounced up onto the windshield? A policeman takes phone numbers. The belching panic rises and subsides in George's chest as the woman looks into his eyes. He can't look at her right eye, bloodshot as it is, so he looks at her left eye. He tucks her hair around her ear, he can't stop himself. Stroke, tuck, stroke, tuck. His eyes fall again on her long dark eyelashes, her brown skin, her thin nose. She sees him trying and she smiles stiffly, her eyes soaked in a suspended panic. Her lips are full and reddish brown and her teeth are so white, shaped so sweetly for her mouth. So many new synapses being created in his brain, he's swimming with a confused, euphoric feeling, he can't quite keep up with himself, and he hits on the idea of her beauty. A vague sense of recognition greets him at this moment, perhaps it's a reference to all the romantic movies he's seen where the moment of truth in the relationship, the epiphany is followed by the words, "You're so beautiful," words which somehow bestow legitimacy on the woman or the relationship, words which somehow wrap up all the loose ends in the story. What he does realize with surprise is that he hasn't been this close to a woman's beauty in . . . well, we can't remember when. He tucks her hair around that soft ear, and thinks pathetically, *I hope I brushed my teeth this morning.* Does he get this close to Helen's face when they make love? Does he look her in the eyes? He tucks the tendril around her brown lobe. She seems fine, but how could he know such a thing? *You're gonna be okay.* Tuck. *Bueno.*

Rushing paramedics in white slam ambulance doors behind them and suddenly George is obsolete. They've all got rubber gloves on their hands, they've had time to think, to protect themselves. It seems a cold, premeditated event but George remembers a burn on the knuckle of his hand which hasn't healed yet. The blood from the tucking seems to have found its way around the burn, avoiding it like water around an island. One of the men speaks to the woman in Spanish. As they immobilize her, put a brace around her neck, lift her onto the stretcher, George pulls his blue sweater from under her head. A souvenir. It drips in the middle, deep red, drop, drop, drop at his feet. A wave of dizziness envelops him, he feels himself swaying. His fingers reach in his pockets for that short pencil, it's not there, just his flat cell phone. He wants to slip his phone number in her pocket, but he thinks better of it. The sum total of the Spanish he remembers comes rushing out from under the hidden spot in his brain and he blurts out to her, *Como se yama?* He's not interested in her as woman per se, it would be tacky to be trying to pick her up, but he points to his chest desperately, raising his voice like a tourist. *Yo se George!* He's practically in tears. *Como se yama?* She whispers something he can't hear, they lift her into the ambulance. He catches Ollie's face, a squished frown, glances back at the soles of her shoes under the blanket. He thinks *Isabel, her name must be Isabel.* The siren begins its circular high pitched wail and George feels another rush of desperation. Is this it? This is the end? How is he going to find out what happened to her? Is she going to live? The twin back doors slam. *Excuse me, what hospital are you taking her to?* He hears himself, the sloppy emotional quality of his voice. The driver turns to him, *Are you related to her?* George lies, an instinct, do they give this information to non-family? *Yes, yes, I'm her brother,* and he realizes he can't speak Spanish, his eyes are blue, his face as Irish and freckled as it can be. *Her her brother-in-law!* he lisps.

St. Mary's Hospital. The driver clears his throat and hacks a wet bullet through his teeth into the gutter. George feels himself gathering back into his world warp-speed, sees himself back there on the crosswalk. *I forgot to pray,* he thinks, astonished.

The Trash Bag Kid

by Connie Noel

"We wear the mask that grins and lies."
Paul Lawrence Dunbar

He slumped on the neon orange plastic chair idly kicking the trash bag by his feet. He was an all-American, Fourth of July kid from his coarse, red hair, smattering of freckles down to his torn blue jeans and the tennis shoes with holes at the big toes. A secretary walked by and started to pat his shoulder, but he lifted up his bowed head with the frayed Jeff Gordon cap, and she smiled hesitantly and moved on. The name on his file was William Jack Daniels Henson, but the caseworkers called him Bill, or Billy, and when he couldn't hear them, the Trash Bag Kid. His mother had called him Jack Daniels because without a bottle of it, he never would have been conceived. The agency called him the Trash Bag kid because he moved so frequently that his few shabby possessions resided more in a trash bag than they ever did in a home. Unfortunately, while Billy had overheard what the welfare department called him, he did not know how much it bothered Mrs. Romeros, his caseworker, who hated the epitaph with its connotation that he was trash, a throw-away child. He had heard Mrs. Romeros ask that a suitcase be bought for him to give him dignity. He didn't know what dignity meant so he asked Mrs. Phillips, his teacher at school. She told him dignity meant having pride and a sense of worth. He didn't understand how a suitcase could do all that, but it didn't matter because Social Services never got him one anyway. Suitcases weren't in the budget.

Through the closed door, Billy could at times hear Mrs. Romeros and her supervisor Mr. Roshelm discussing his new placement. He had heard Mr. Roshelm's loud, "There have already been twenty-two placements, and the kid is only seven!" He could hear the faint murmur of Mrs. Romeros' voice but none of the words. Billy tried to think of all the twenty-two placements, but neither his memory nor his math was good enough to make the effort worthwhile. Besides, he usually tried to forget the past.

Billy did remember the first placement with Tim and Sally Feldon, although he had only been three at the time. Billy had lasted a whole year with them until Tim and Sally moved out of state. Since he wasn't really their kid, they left him behind. In the black trash bag, he had a dirty, tattered, brown teddy bear named Fred that they had given him for Christmas. The fur was rubbed from Fred's ears and one of his eyes was missing. Yet, Fred had faithfully moved with Billy to each new home, Fred and a broken earring that had belonged to Billy's real mother. Usually, Fred lived in the trash bag, but late at night when no one could see him, Billy would hold and talk to his only friend. One old biddy at a placement had tried to throw Fred in the garbage, calling him dirty and disgusting. Billy had stabbed her with a fork and rescued his friend. Billy was moved again that night and was, thereafter, labeled "incorrigible and special needs."

Roshelm's loud query, "What are we going to do with the boy?" made Billy jump.

Probably send me to another stupid foster home where they'll blame me for everything, thought Billy, *but I don't care! They're all a bunch of idiots, the whole stupid lot.* "They don't know nothing about nothing," Billy mumbled as he picked a scab through the torn knee of his jeans while he began to play "The Game". Listening to the murmur of voices, Billy watched the warm red blood trickle down his leg.

The voices finally stopped and the office door swung open, but Billy sat transfixed by the blood on his raised leg. The Game had begun!

The Game was simple and the rules were few. The most basic rule and the object of the game was to never let anyone know what you were thinking or feeling, for that knowledge made you vulnerable. If people knew your weakness, then they had power over you. Inevitably, they would then use that knowledge to hurt you more and hurt would feed the Blackness. Survival was the purpose of the game.

Other people never knew that they were playing the game with Billy, but he never thought of that as an unfair advantage for him. After all, they usually had all the power.

Indifference, cockiness, anger, and passiveness were the only weapons in Billy's arsenal, but he had learned to use them well. If Billy could cause the others to get angry then that meant that they had lost control, and Billy could declare himself the winner.

There was, however, the danger that Billy too would lose control and that was scary because then the Blackness would come. Billy feared the Blackness more than anything, more than ghosts, more than pain, more than unfairness, more than even going into a new place. The Blackness was terrifying and was always watching and waiting to devour him. Still, the compulsion to play the game was overwhelming since it too meant survival.

"Billy, we have decided on the placement for you," declared Mr. Roshelm.

Billy continued to silently contemplate his knee. *I'm not listening; I don't want to hear this!* thought Billy, terrified, as the Blackness settled in the pit of his stomach. *Think of something else!* Billy's mind cautioned. *Think about what an ugly tie Roshelm is wearing with that big old horrible stain. Looks like coffee, but I bet it's blood. Old Roshelm probably turns into a vampire after dark. Nah, if he was a vampire, he couldn't come out in the daytime. I bet he's a werewolf. Yah! Look at his hairy hands, he's a werewolf alright!*

"Billy, are you paying attention to me?" queried Mr. Roshelm as he jerked Billy's chin, forcing Billy to look up. Billy heard the impatience in Mr. Roshelm's voice but failed to see the weary concern. Billy never knew the sleepless nights that Mr. Roshelm had or the ulcers caused by worrying about a hundred different Billys. The names might change, but unfortunately, the tragedies were dismally similar.

"Billy, Mrs. Romeros and I have decided to send you to the Walkers, Edward and Cathleen Walker. I don't know why we didn't think of then before. They are much older than the former foster parents that you have had, and usually, they work with teenagers, but we think this will really be a good placement for you. Billy! What do you think?"

"What I think don't matter none," answered Billy, "I'll go stay awhile and then leave, just like always."

"No, Billy," said Mrs. Romeros softly, "the Walkers don't send children away."

"Never?" demanded Billy.

"Once, but only once," replied Mrs. Romeros truthfully.

It will soon be twice, thought Billy, as the Blackness grew within him.

Mrs. Romeros stooped to pick up his bag. "The Walkers aren't expecting us until half past noon so we have time for a sandwich. Where do you want to eat?" she asked Billy.

I'd like to eat at McDonalds, thought Billy; *they are giving away Jeff Gordon Match Box cars; if Mrs. Romeros really cares about me, she'll know that.*

"I don't care," replied Billy, playing the game.

Mrs. Romeros, whose children were teenagers and beyond fun meals at McDonalds, knew nothing about the Jeff Gordon promotion.

"Wendy's okay then?" she asked. "I'm hungry for a salad."

"Yah," Billy replied as he thought, *I knew she didn't care.* Mrs. Romeros had lost points in a game that she did not even know that she was playing.

As Mrs. Romeros munched on a salad, Billy tried to eat his hamburger. Still, when the Blackness settled in your stomach, it was hard to choke down food.

"Not hungry?" Mrs. Romeros asked as she pointed to his french fries and half-eaten hamburger with her fork full of salad.

"We had a big breakfast at the shelter," replied Billy untruthfully.

"The Walkers are different, Billy; I really think you have a good chance of a permanent home there, but you are going to have to try," cautioned Mrs. Romeros.

Score one for Romeros, thought Billy; *she knew what I was thinking.* Billy quickly dipped a fry into his Frosty. "I like moving," he lied.

Mrs. Romeros sighed and picked up the trash from their table. *Seven years old and already such a tough, uncaring child,* she thought.

The Walker house was large and faintly shabby with huge maple trees shading the front porch. On the porch beside a wicker rocker covered in fat fluffy pillows was a half empty glass of ice tea. Billy immediately liked the porch. On the side with the swing, the porch was shaded by a trellis full of summer roses, their fragrance warm and lush in the hot sun. Billy even liked the shadowy pattern of leaves from the hanging plants which danced upon the cool gray floor. The porch was a breezy hidden place. He could sit here and silently watch everything, and if he was very still, no one would even notice him. From the back, Billy could hear splashing water, laughter, and the shouts of children. Mrs. Romeros had already told him that the Walkers had a pool. *This looks like a house that would be lived in by Davy Johnson*, thought Billy, which was the highest accolade that Billy could pay.

Last year in first grade Davy's mom had sent balloons to Davy on Valentine Day. There had been a knock on the classroom door, and when Mrs. Phillips opened it, there was this guy wearing pink tights with small pink wings. Everyone laughed. This guy whom Mrs. Phillips said was supposed to be Cupid was carrying five big balloons with a big box of candy. "Davy Johnson?" Cupid had asked. Davy turned pink with embarrassment, but everyone in the class wanted to be Davy Johnson at that moment. The next day at recess for no apparent reason, Billy bloodied Davy Johnson's nose.

Mrs. Romeros knocked on the open screen door and called out, "Cathleen." From inside Billy could hear a voice shout, "Mom, they're here!"

Cathleen Walker came smiling to the door. "Sorry," she said, "I was canning peaches and I didn't hear you. Come in. Come in." Billy could now smell the cooking fruit. Cathleen Walker, plump and merry, wiped her hands on her apron before shaking Billy's hand. She motioned for them to be seated.

Billy sat with his head bowed but took quick glances around. *Not too fancy,* he thought, *that's good! Maybe I won't break nothing.*

Billy also noticed that the room was tidy but not unbearably so. It would have surprised him to learn this, but deep down Billy was fastidious and hated mess and filth.

The room seemed just right.

From studying the room, Billy went to surreptitiously watching Cathleen Walker. *She is old, but she don't look too mean. I like her eyes and her hair,* thought Billy. Her hair, brown with lots of gray, was pulled back into a bun, but stray wisps had pulled loose and haloed her plump face. Billy was a little startled to see her brown eyes keenly watching him. Billy quickly lowered his head, his cheeks flaming scarlet. From then on, Billy kept his eyes on his tennis shoes so he could not see the boys who took quick glances at him from the doorways, but he did hear their whispered laughter.

"Boys, come in here and meet Billy properly," demanded Mrs. Walker.

Billy was dismayed to see so many boys, five of them and all older and much bigger than himself. The Blackness that had begun to recede came back to fill his stomach and started to creep up his throat so it could choke him. Billy had learned that the smallest foster child always got the brunt of the bigger child's anger. Your things were taken, and you were knocked around with no recourse because usually the foster parents never knew. You didn't snitch, not if you knew what was good for you.

"Billy, this is Tom," said Mrs. Walker. "Tom, show Billy his room and help him get settled in and then come back down. Mrs. Romeros and I need to talk in private. The rest of you go back to the pool. You can meet Billy later when he is not so overwhelmed."

Billy looked up and saw the oldest boy smiling at him. Warily, Billy started to pick up his trash bag full of stuff. Tom grabbed it and hefted it over his shoulder. "Come on, Billy," the boy Tom said as he left the room.

Billy looked hesitantly at Mrs. Romeros. She smiled encouragement. *Oh no!* Billy thought dismally, *they are going to talk about me. Once that old woman knows how bad I am, she won't want me here.*

"Hurry up, kid!" demanded Tom impatiently from the other room. "It ain't too bad here," Tom stated as he took Billy up a flight of stairs into a large room with gold and brown plaid wallpaper. The shiny floor was painted dark chocolate brown and gold curtains hung at the large windows. Two sets of bunk beds, covered with dark brown bedspreads, were flush with the walls. Yet, what Billy noticed most was three thirteen inch color TVs, each with its own game system. There was a black X Box, a black Play Station 2, and a purple Game Cube.

"One of the video games yours?" asked Billy, pointing to the TVs.

"No, this ain't my room. I have my own room. Its small but all mine. I have far more electronics than the others since I have been here longer," bragged Tom, throwing the trash bag onto the bottom of the closest bed.

"What about them?" asked Billy, jerking his head towards the floor.

"Mom can holler if you make her mad, and she has lots of rules." Tom laughed, "Even Dad stays clear when she's on a rampage. But she doesn't usually get mad unless we deserve it. She's got this thing about making us into 'men of honor.' When she says something she usually means it, but sometimes if she thinks that she has been unfair, she'll change her mind. When is your birthday, kid?" asked Tom.

"February seventeenth," answered Billy.

"We get fifty dollars for birthdays and presents on the other holidays. Besides candy, we usually get summer clothes on Easter, new clothes at the beginning of school and more clothes at Christmas."

"We just get clothes at Christmas?" asked Billy.

"No way!" replied Tom. "That big room down stairs is just full of presents. Mom has five grandchildren and three grown kids so the house is full. But her kids don't buy you nothing unless you haven't got any other folks. That's to make it fairer for the foster kids who don't get presents from their other home. Mom lets each of us get one big present worth $150 dollars. Usually, we get video games, but Ma always breaks down, and the first year she also gets a TV to play it on. It will be the best Christmas you ever had!"

"This my bed?" asked Billy as he bounced on the bottom bunk.

"Yes, but Mom will get you new sheets, a new bedspread, and a pillow. Mom always buys extra bedding so each new kid gets their own," answered Tom.

"Do we have to call her Mom?"

"No, I call her Mom cause I've been here five years. You can call her Cathleen or Mom."

"Do they ever send kids away?" asked Billy nonchalantly.

"No, Mom will tell you she's going to call the agency when you're really bad, but it's only for weekend detention."

"What about him?" asked Billy.

"Dad talks a lot and hollers more than Mom, but he doesn't ever punish much. We just let him get mad. We even have his lectures numbered. Sometimes, Mom and Dad will make you really mad, but it's the best home I've ever been in, although I'd never admit it to them. They really do care. Besides, the food here is good. Mom cooks all the time, but you will have to do dishes. You'll also have to learn to clean, cook, and do laundry. The best thing is Mom and Dad really understand what we're feeling. You don't have to tell them much."

"Boys!" shouted Mrs. Romeros. "I'm leaving so come and say good-bye."

Tom ran down the stairs. Billy slowly followed.

"Good-by Cathleen, Tom," said Mrs. Romeros. "Billy, walk me out to the car," she added as she turned to pick up her briefcase. Billy slowly followed her to her car.

"Billy, I want you to really try to get along here," said Mrs. Romeros. "Don't you think you'll like it a lot?"

Billy did think that he would like this home. Tom hadn't threatened him and the Walkers seemed bearable, but the problem wasn't whether he'd like them but rather if they'd like him. Billy was very afraid they wouldn't like him or even if they did at first he'd do something to screw it up. The Blackness shouted inside Billy's head, *You'll screw it up! You'll screw it up! You always do!*

"Billy, promise to try!" pleaded Mrs. Romeros.

"Do they know I wet the bed?" asked Billy.

"Yes, but Cathleen said that it did not matter to them."

They all say that in the beginning, thought Billy. *No matter how hard I try to stay awake, I fall asleep and wet the bed. After awhile, they all get mad, no matter what they say at first.*

"If I stay, I stay; if I leave, I leave! It don't matter to me none which I do," lied Billy emphatically.

Mrs. Romeros sadly got into her car. *I wasn't able to reach him. This is probably his last chance, and he doesn't even care.* Billy watched her, and knew that he had fooled her. She never guessed how badly he wanted to stay. He had won the game. Yet, he could not claim victory until he admitted to himself the biggest truth. *Just once, I'd like to lose,* Billy thought. *Just once, I wished someone besides me would win the game, and then maybe, just maybe, they might be able to make the Blackness go away.*

Billy, the Trash Bag kid, watched Mrs. Romeros' car drive slowly away and then he hunched his shoulders as if for combat. It was again time to begin a new phase of the same old game.

Fisherman's Daughter

by DeAnna Jarrell

In my dreams I breathe in the pungent odor of creosote. I trail my bare toes in the thick green water of the bayou, tracing rainbows in the iridescent ribbons of fuel that spill out behind our boat. In my dreams I am home again, sifting through piles of shrimp and seaweed muck, pulling out the baby crabs and setting them free. *You can't save 'em all, baby.* To me the freshest air is that heavy breeze that sweeps over Lake Ponchatrain, saturating my skin with the smell of salt, diesel, and fish. Comfort is the sputter and gurgle of a boat motor at three a.m., the sound of a ripe watermelon cracking wide to show us its bright insides in the picking box. *Ya'll don't pick out all the heart now. Leave some of the sweet part for someone else.* It's smashed peanut butter and jelly sandwiches and waking with my face pressed against sticky nylon life jackets.

I know what it is to stalk an underwater prey you cannot see, dodge dangers just as invisible. I know how to circle wide the nets, sweep along the deepest places, and scoop up the tiny life forms that give their lives for ours. I have held a mother catfish, slick and heavy in my hands, and watched eggs drop from her whiskered lips into the waves. *Were they her eggs, Daddy?* I have pried open oysters and never found a pearl. I can catch a blue claw crab with my foot and pinch him by the hind legs for all to see just how big he is. *He's a fat one, him. Lots of flavor in those big ones like that.* I know which fish have poison "stickers" and which ones make good bait.

Hurricanes still loom in my nightmares. White crested waves trigger panic for the children of fisherman. My body still remembers the way a boat sways between waves, how the wind pushes and pulls. How wet fiberglass feels sliding under my bare legs as the boat is forced vertical. *Tie those lifejackets tight! Shut the windows in the cabin!* Today, when storms rise around me, I struggle with the need in me to tie things down.

Sometimes, rough water sets you drifting, and the greedy wind steals the things you love. *We have to cut the trawl. I don't want to lose it, but we can't ride this one out.* What is it that causes my heart to ache when I remember watching the end of a ragged green shrimp net, severed from our lines, slip over the edge and be forever lost? Is it only the net that's slipping away?

In my dreams my father speaks to me from his captain's chair. He gives me half of his root beer and lets me steer for a while. *Slow, slow. Steady. There ya' go. That's it now.* When I can't breathe, when the noise and confusion of life swells around me, I almost expect him to be there next to me. He puts his big rough fisherman hands over my little ones and talks me through. He smells like sweat and Louisiana summer. I haven't stepped foot on a shrimp boat in years, but I still rock myself to sleep every night, and I swear I hear seagulls.

Reunion Underground

by Jewel Seehaus-Fisher

The rain fell steadily in Cozumel, where I'd come to bring Pamela a sweater Mama made when she was well enough to knit.

I was to meet her at: "The Pyramid Hotel, August 23rd."

The airport was empty. No FBI.

I walked outside into the rain.

The Feds used to drop in on Mama so often, she'd put on the coffee pot when she saw their car pull into the driveway. Now, of course, they didn't bother her any more, because her cancer was terminal. "Federal Law," they said, if you could believe them, if it wasn't a ploy to make her careless on the phone. I blamed Pamela for that, too. The cancer.

But me they still questioned, and I still answered that I didn't know where she was and didn't want to know. The first part was a lie.

"Taxi, Senora?" I gave the address of the hotel, and a half hour later, I stepped out, expecting to be arrested any moment.

Though it had stopped raining, the rain water still swelled and overflowed in the streets, and Pamela was standing in ankle-deep water outside the hotel when I pulled up in the cab, her hair stuck to her head, her dress plastered to her body, reminding me of one of those turkeys who drown because they're too dumb not to look up at a storm with their mouths open.

I stared at her. She was just the same, careless of her own well-being.

"It's me, all right," she said, when she was close enough to talk.

"The FBI got the computer age enhancement all wrong. You haven't changed a bit."

"What computer enhancement?" She hurried me to the entrance to the lobby.

"On a 'Wanted' poster in the post office."

"Did you bring it?"

"Of course not. Suppose my suitcase was examined at the airport!"

"You'd invent something—" And suddenly her arms closed about me, and she was crying, and even though I hated what she'd done to all of us, I patted her back and cooed.

She disengaged. "You should have warned me about the poster. This changes everything. This means that they're still after me."

"How could I warn you? Did you send me a phone number I've forgotten about?"

"Obviously if you didn't come, that would have told me there was danger." She looked at me appraisingly, the same look from her arraignment all those years ago.

"I wasn't followed."

"The bad guys don't announce their presence."

"The bad guys? And do you still call the cops 'pigs'? The world has changed, in case you haven't noticed."

One entire glass wall of the lobby overlooked the beach. In front of the window, a swarthy man sat on a modern couch. He stood up. The child next to him stood, too.

"My husband," Pam whispered.

"Oh, you got married? Does Mom know?"

"We don't have papers, but we live as a family." Loudly, she added, as the two walked towards us, "His name's Miguel. He's very sweet."

Miguel reached us. "A pleasure," he said in a clipped Hispanic accent. "This is our daughter, Melody."

"Mi Tia," said Melody.

"It is good she meets her aunt," said Miguel. "Very good for her language. Baby, you hear me? Speak in English to your aunt."

"How old are you, Melody?"

"I have nine years."

Pamela touched Miguel's arm. "There's a problem. My sister can't stay here. Put her suitcase in our car," she said. They exchanged long looks. "This hotel will not do for all of us, Baby," she said to Melody, who was beginning to object. "Your aunt will need a room of her own."

"This hotel is too far from the reef," said Miguel to Melody. "Very bad snorkeling."

Miguel pulled Pamela aside so they could whisper together. He nodded decisively. He and Melody left with my suitcase, while Pamela and I sat down.

"Miguel thinks you might have been followed. What did I look like on the poster?"

"Thin, hard-bitten, old."

"I wouldn't mind being thin. What did it say? Armed and Dangerous?"

"Actually, yes. And that you'd been wanted for years. But the FBI told me that they're ready to deal."

"Told you! You talked to them? When was this? Miguel will have a fit!"

"Two weeks ago. They called on me."

"They still call on you! On Mama, too? She must be so frightened!"

"No, not Mama," I said. I reached into my tote bag for the sweater. "She sent this along for you."

"A sweater to Mexico in the summer!" In one of her typical excesses, she held it to her face, kissing and crooning. "Mama never did know which end is up."

"And you did?"

"Tell her I treasure it." And now I realized that the plastic bag near the couch was for me, as she handed it over. "I made this quilt for Mama."

"A quilt," I said flatly. "How will I explain a quilt to a customs clerk?"

"You'll think of something."

"Nobody has ever opened one of my suitcases before. Never. But now they have random searches. It could happen. They'll think it's folk art, something expensive. They'll want a receipt! This'll be the one time—"

"Is Mama in a hospital?" asked Pamela.

"She's at home." Before her face brightened too much, I added, "In Hospice care. That's when they get you ready to die."

Pamela shook her head, unable to speak.

"She wanted to come with me, but she was too sick."

"Then she's forgiven me."

"For jumping bail and leaving her with that huge mortgage? Of course. You were always her favorite." There! I thought. I've said it!

But Pamela hugged her again. "How I've missed you. My acerbic sib!"

Miguel returned with Melody. "Come," he said, directing us to the elevator. "My father want to meet you."

"Don Pedro doesn't know English," explained Pamela as we rode up to the fifth floor. "He speaks Zapotec and Spanish. He knows me as Dolores."

Inside the suite stood a tiny old man with leathery skin and keen dark eyes.

"Buenos Dias, Senora," said Don Pedro, rushing into a long speech in Spanish. Melody snuggled beside him.

"He says you are very beautiful," said Miguel.

"Tell him 'thank you,'" I said.

As Miguel spoke with his father, Pamela whispered, "What he really said is you are dressed immodestly. He hopes you will change before we go to dinner."

"What does he think of your politics?" I asked.

"I have no politics. How can I? I go to church. I live quietly."

Melody came over to us. She said, "Don Pedro want to visit you in New York. He want to bring me."

"We can discuss this later, Baby," said Pamela.

"He want an address. For to write."

"Your aunt is moving to a new apartment. She'll send us the new address."

Melody returned to her grandfather's side to explain.

"Miguel insisted on bringing his father along," whispered Pamela, "even though the old man asks many questions. But Miguel says it's important that his father sees you. To a Mexican, if your family doesn't value you, you're a thing of no worth. Don Pedro has wondered why no one of my own family has traveled to see me in all these years. They'll respect me after this."

Miguel opened bottles of beer, which he handed around. He announced "Don Pedro want to ride the ferry to the Yucatan tomorrow and to swim at the base of the pyramid in Tulum."

Melody clapped her hands in excitement.

"Sounds lovely," I said.

"I wish you were coming with us," said Miguel. "I've explained to my father that there was a message at the desk, telling you that your husband had a heart attack."

Pamela gasped.

Miguel continued, "I tell him that your husband is to have an emergency operation, and of course you must go to him."

"I can't bear it," said Pamela.

I felt sick. After all this! The hesitation, the determination, the fear! I gagged on the beer. I couldn't swallow. I put the bottle down.

"Your sister must go this evening," said Miguel. "She bring danger to us."

Don Pedro patted his own chest in sympathy and everyone began talking at once: Don Pedro in Spanish, Miguel translating, Melody translating, as Don Pedro said how pleased he was to meet me, and that when I next come we will travel together.

"We've always used your husband as an excuse to explain why you don't come," said Pamela.

I began to feel spooked, as if I should call David to see if he was all right. Not that I believed in jinxes, but this was just asking for trouble.

The old man began to question me through Melody: Did I have children? Did I bring pictures? Did I have cousins? What was Pamela like as a child?

"She was adventurous," I said. "Always disappearing. We wouldn't know where she was."

Melody translated. Pamela gave me a look that said: Don't! No more!

But I continued. "She liked to explore caves. To be underground. Her family worried about her."

"You're upsetting me," whispered Pamela.

"I won't tell them," I said quietly, so that Melody couldn't hear, "that I always knew you'd end up in big trouble, what with all those changing phone numbers, where you could never be reached! What if something had happened to Mama—!" I was crying. Anger always made me cry.

"It was so long ago," said Pamela.

"And now something has happened to Mama, and you didn't know about it for almost a year."

"I wish I could see her. I wish I could explain—"

"That you helped set off a bomb? There's an explanation for that?"

"No one was supposed to be hurt—"

"Well, someone was hurt."

"I was very young and idealistic—"

"Oh, please!" I said, choking out the words. I wanted to say something like: Oh? Tell me I just had to have been there, as one says when a joke fails. Or the flat truth: You were over eighteen and highly intelligent, so tell me you didn't know bombs were dangerous! But I felt sick at the sight of her. I should have said no to Mama. I should never have come!

"You don't know what it was like to have been—"

"—You ran," I said.

She looked as if I had slapped her in the face. "I ran," she said at last. "They were going to throw the book at me. Possession of explosives. Conspiracy to commit arson, malicious destruction of federal property, depraved indifference to human life, leaving the scene of a crime—!"

"—Flight to escape prosecution," I cut her off.

"It's still in my head. When I talk about it—"

"You talk about it?"

"No, of course not. I mean now, with you. Not in Mexico. Do you know what it's like to never let anyone get close, never to have real friendship—"

"Talk about sad!" I snapped sarcastically.

"When I talk about it with you, it's as if it just happened! And yet—almost—nothing happened."

"It happened all right. And no one in the family's been the same since. For us it goes on and on and on."

"The bomb didn't go off at first, and Joe looked through his binoculars and said the fuse must've fizzled out—"

"—I wonder what translation your husband is giving to Don Pedro—," I interrupted.

"Never mind that. I want to tell you—"

Some day I might want to hear her story, but not now,

not with the obviously false translation given to the old man, who smiled and smiled genially. Not with this upsurge of anger that I thought I had finished long ago. Not to hear her same old excuses.

"No, really, what is he saying?"

"Miguel is telling Don Pedro that I was a lively little girl once and that I wanted to be an actress," said Pam, looking lost, as if she had just come back to the reality of the day, after being dragged into the memory of the bombing and her arrest.

"Well, you are an actress," I said. "You act a role every day." Suddenly, I couldn't go on. It was kicking a sick horse.

"Afterwards, I didn't care if I lived or died."

"You cared," I said. "You jumped bail."

"We had just wanted noise and publicity. And we wanted to get rid of the war and the bomb."

"Oh?" I said. "What bomb did you want to get rid of?"

"THE bomb. I grew up with it. Maybe you were just young enough not to know what it was like. Unbelievable. Little kids hiding during air raid drills in school. We used to say, in the event of a nuclear attack—step one, get under your desks; step two, pull down your pants; step three, kiss your ass goodbye."

"You crossed a line."

"We crossed a line. The government had its war, whether we wanted it or not. We got desperate."

"And what did you accomplish? A life in hiding."

Miguel announced that it was time I left for the airport and that he and Pamela would take me. Melody would stay with her grandfather.

"Come home," I said to Pam, as we rode down in the elevator.

"Home? My home is here!" she said, but her eyes were filling. "Home, how could I go home?"

"The FBI will deal."

"I can't take that chance. I have a daughter."

"You're still running," I said.

Miguel said he would try to set up an address in Mexico where I could write to Pam, but I didn't believe him. He wanted me out of there.

"It is better every one of us leave Cozumel," said Miguel. "You bought tickets and made a reservation through a travel agent?"

"Yes."

Miguel shrugged, as if that explained all of his concern. Pamela was crying. I was crying too.

Something had happened. Some wall in my heart had cracked. All the way to the airport, Pamela and I held hands and talked: Remember when you climbed the railroad trestle? Remember when you caught your first flounder and wanted it mounted on the wall? Remember when you wanted to join the circus and I told Mama because I was afraid you'd really go?

Miguel dropped me off at the entrance. I wheeled my suitcase up to the desk, feeling painfully alone in a foreign country.

The clerk changed my ticket and handed me a boarding pass.

I knew what was happening, all right. I'd forgiven her, even though I'd sworn I never would, and, in that moment, I began to mourn the loss of my sister.

The Ballad of Geezer Malone

by Evelyn M. Perry

Emer Killian sang softly to herself behind the bar. Across the pub, in a mirror flecked with age and offset by a bright, brass chair rail, she could see the reflection of her face and torso, and framed behind that still, the back of her head in the mirror behind her, and her shoulder blades cut across by a skyline of bottles and stoppers. First the skyscraper whiskeys, fluid ginger: Jameson, Tullamore, Bushmills; then the squat, noble flathouses of the liquers half full with thick nectar: sweet, plum-like Blackcurrant to swirl into Snakebite, the oranges like stagnant factory water. Peppering the skyline were the smokestacks and the Georgian outlines of ale and cider, and the deep crimson and pale peach sunset of the ports and brandies.

She watched her mouth move slowly as she drew out the chorus of her song, smoothed her green silk shirt and combed through her cropped brown hair with fingers sticky from cocktail cherries and clove dust. Emer pulled a snifter from the rack and laid it against her cheek, hoping to cool down the flushed, red color, but she knew it was no use. Her cheeks bloomed tirelessly, whether she was out in the soft, misty morning, watching telly in front of the fire with her family, or asleep in cool, damp-smelling sheets.

It wasn't a bad chorus after all. The tune was simple and strong, the lyrics just this side of saccharine, just enough to be romantic and nostalgic. But, Emer sighed to herself as she washed down the bar, that was just her opinion. She knew that the lads in the band would be watching her, testing her, judging her. She supposed that it was her own fault.

Emer had been delighted when she saw the ad in the *Donegal Examiner*. "Vocalist/Writer Wanted for a New Band. Talent and Experience Preferred. Phone 043368," it had read. She had pulled Mammy's sewing scissors from the basket on the hearth and carefully clipped out the advertisement, making sure not to cut into the phone number. She folded the thin piece of newspaper into her Irish *Pegeen* textbook on page 26 (for Boxing Day), where Bride and Maura, the younger sisters with whom she roomed, would probably not care to look. She had been ebullient. For days after she phoned for an audition, she would sneak into the textbook and stroke the piece of paper. This would be her chance, her chance for so many things: to get from under the eight pairs of feet in her house, to speak her mind, to caress the words of the old stories and make them proud again. She ironed a white blouse in the kitchen, explaining that she would help Mammy by doing all the ironing, and in her absent-mindedness ruined the pleat on Brendan's school trousers. "Emer, you idgit," Brendan had declared upon finding her ironing the crease flat. Emer looked at the thin gray pants in her hands. "Right, sorry," she said lamely, laying the pants out again and covering the scorch mark she had made in Colm's maroon school tie.

VOLUME II

The Sunday after, Emer knicked Colm's smooth new jumper, slipped out of Mass and went to her audition. "Right then," said the pink-faced drummer in a most professional manner, "Your qualifications?" Emer stammered her response, thinking that a strong and gentle voice would make her sound like an experienced singer, but failing miserably. Her voice came out squeaky and nervous, constricted in her neck. "I had O-Levels in Irish and Reading. I took my degree at UCG. I . . . I was in the chorus there . . . and I can write." 'You dumb cow,' thought Emer to herself, 'not very impressive.' Apparently the lads didn't think so either. "We weren't really in the market for a *colleen*," said a guitarist with a Horslips sticker on his case, growling out colleen like an insult and twisting his mouth into a sneer. "Now, Lorcan," said a fiddler, presumably the appointed leader for the band, "give the girl a chance."

First Emer had written a song called "The Vindication of Queen Maeve," which she howled and shrieked like Sinead O'Connor. She tested it by singing it out loud in the kitchen. "Would you ever shut up, for feck's sake? I'm watching the hurling," said Colm. "What kind of a stupid song is that?" asked Bride. It's . . . I wrote it myself. It's about Queen Maeve. Maura and Bride snorted while the boys rolled their eyes. "Na, 'tis a fine song," her Da said, bouncing Shane on his knee. Shane gurgled and burped. Bride laughed and said, "Even Shane's song is better than Emer's!" Mentally, Emer scrapped "The Vindication of Queen Maeve," who was a dubious hero anyway. "You're as cracked as Auntie Jane," Brendan said then. Brendan was unkind. Mammy said as much, for Jane was her sister for good or ill. Brendan mimicked Auntie Jane in a high-pitched voice, "I was walking on the path and I saw a ghost come, right in front of me, and I walked into a tree." Maura joined in, "I had Father McGuire down to dispel the fairies in the house, they were bothering the cats so." Mammy had frowned while she set out the smoked trout, but said nothing. It was hard to argue with the truth. Emer had frowned also. However cracked Auntie Jane might be, Emer had grown up with her stories, they sang in her veins with her blood. Emer alone would listen for hours on end while Auntie Jane talked, discarding the unrelated bits ("the Irish youth are red rotten, I tell you" or "Your Da's a bad one, black as a jackanapes to be sure"). She savored the stories themselves, stories of how CuChulainn—whose wife shared Emer's name—had killed his own son, or how Finn MacCool had burned his hand in the Druid's fire and, sucking on the burn, learned the truth of all things. It was Auntie Jane who had told the story of Geezer Malone, the local who still lived in a cottage by the Moy and strolled the banks talking to a swan.

It was Geezer Malone's story that she now sung to herself behind the bar, a sad and romantic song about how the Geezer had loved a girl whose father was a broke gambler, how the girl's father had arranged for her to marry an old man just for money, and how the girl had thrown herself into the Moy rather than marry the crude old man—and for love of the young Geezer Malone. Emer had pieced it together from Auntie's story and from Geezer Malone himself, who came into the pub every day at five o'clock, when he was done digging graves in the churchyard or cutting turf for Mrs. O'Leary on her land. Geezer Malone was so old that no one remembered his Christian name anymore. No one cared much anyway. He spoke to no one except the swan on the Moy and his glass of stout, sometimes in Irish, sometimes in English. Emer would stand at the end of the bar, looking at the crowd or drying glasses but listening to the whispers he made into his glass. One pint of Guinness would last an hour or two (Emer suspected he was as poor as a Galway farmyard). He would lay his coins on the bar, nod to Emer, and leave again. He almost always missed the thickest crowds.

Some said that Geezer Malone had killed that girl, had thrown her into the Moy and watched her skirts fill up with dark water, pulling her down and swallowing her. Geezer Malone spoke to no one and no one spoke to Geezer Malone either. Sometimes they told the story of the swan who spoke, especially on All Hallow's, but the words of the story always tangled themselves up with "The Children of Lir" so that both stories were caught and swayed in the grasses at the bottom of the Moy like the young girl herself. And once when Mrs. Dunn, who ran the bakery, had had too much scotch, Emer heard her say in a loud voice that Geezer Malone bought two sliced pans every Monday—one a day old and one fresh that morning. Mrs. Dunn wrapped the old pan in brown paper and put the new in a waxed white pan. That's how she knew that Geezer Malone fed the fresh bread to his swan and ate the old bread himself. "Cracked as a brush," Mrs. Dunn had concluded.

Emer checked her digital watch. 15:23. At any minute, old Betsy Fitzpatrick would come to cash her pension check and knock back two stiff whiskeys as fast as she could before her sister Eileen came into the pub to catch her in the act. Eileen was slow, arthritic, and Betsy could drink with the best of them. Emer poured the two whiskeys and set them on the bar. She sliced an orange and pulled some cloves out the jar and set them on a little plate. Old Betsy would want to kill the smell before Eileen came and sniffed her breath. Emer knew that when Eileen caught up to Betsy, Betsy would already be pulling the old pink lipstick from her purse—the brand so old that it smelled faintly of pills and hospital waiting rooms—and do herself up in the mirror, her long, graying hair covered in a plastic rain hat, her withered and kindly face collared by the pub bottle skyline.

Emer smiled at Betsy Fitzpatrick as she came in and busied herself by pouring three pints of Guinness. The foam stood tall on top of the rich brown stout. Emer watched it settle slowly and topped off the pints. Tomorrow was the last Bank Holiday before Christmas. The pub would be busy all night. Crowds of young people would gather, some of them home from Londontown for the holidays and the craic. Men with their wives and children would come for a sing-song. Those who hadn't made it to the bank would add their tabs to their accounts, stretching it for years and histories across the ledger. Others would come, paycheck in hand, and spend all they could cash that night.

Emer heard the pub manager, Frankie Butler, cough and clear his throat in the back room. She rummaged about in the ice bin and swept the tile floor loudly to make him think that she was busy enough. Frankie Butler was worried about the tinker wagons that had stood parked outside the pub for the last week. He had complained to the Garda that the tinkers were bad news waiting to happen, and he didn't want it to happen outside his establishment. The Garda had just shrugged their shoulders. There was nothing that they could do short of getting knifed by the tinkers and pulling bloody victims of their fist fights from the ditches to load them into an ambulance and take their twisted bicycles back to the station for the broken-nosed and fence-post battered to claim later.

Eileen Fitzpatrick was very slow today, almost half an hour slow. Betsy had her whiskeys and was half way through a Coke when her sister came in. "Well now," said Eileen to Betsy, "Coke would be nice." She winked at Emer and said, "I'll have everything the same as Betsy but not *before* the Coke." Emer smiled. "I don't know what you mean," said Betsy huffily.

At the end of the bar, Father McGuire ordered a coffee. Emer poured the Jameson's more than half way into the glass, and filled the rest with coffee. She had learned the hard way that when Father McGuire said coffee he meant Irish coffee—just like when he said sin he really meant sex.

They kept on coming. Bully Morgan sauntered in with his crowd. Emer could tell they were already well locked. She set out the beer, avoiding Bully's groping hands and leering comments. It was Brendan who had started calling

Billy Morgan Bully. The name had fit so well that it stuck. Even Bully called himself so.

Emer poured the drinks quickly, then over again, hovering as long as she could near Geezer Malone, straining to hear his voice above the din in the pub. Just as she caught the words "la breagh tsamhraigh," one fine summer's day, a group of five tinker children came in, their clothes dirty and ripped and their faces smeared. They clung together in a group in front of the hearth, by the turf bin, and started in on an out-of-tune rendition of "Good King Wenseslaus" with their dirt-streaked palms outstretched, waiting for change.

Emer's Da had told her many times that the tinkers had more money than the President herself, and that they made themselves dirty so that they could do a better begging. The government gave them money and pre-fabricated houses, but the tinkers broke down the walls and parked their caravans in the houses instead. They beat their wives and tied up their sad and filthy horses in the public yards. "Money won't make dirty people clean," Da had said disgustedly, "We should fuck out the lot of 'em." But Auntie Jane had told Emer that the tinkers were once the noble kings and queens of Old Eire. She said that they know who their people are and what their history is, that they know where they belong. "Proud people, the tinkers. Money won't buy their freedom," Auntie Jane had said.

The crowd was snorting and ridiculing the tinker children now. They had moved through "God Rest Ye Merry Gentleman" and started on a strange version of "Arthur MacBride." Though it was getting mauled by their tuneless voices and vacant eyes, and by the comments of Bully Morgan and his company, it was one of Emer's favorite tunes. She pulled a pound from the pocket of her jeans and placed it in the hand of the eldest (or at least tallest) tinker boy. Frankie Butler flashed her a smile from where he stood hanging over the bar and laughing with Betsy and Eileen. It was clear that Frankie Butler thought that Emer was buying him some peace from the tinker parents outside.

"Jesus, Mary and Joseph, Emer," said Bully with hot breath in her face, "What the fuck did you do that for? Those little shits will bother us all night now, stupid cow." Emer moved past him, into her refuge behind the bar, and stood near Geezer Malone. Bully would forget this night, there was no point speaking in her defense even if she could think of something to say. While he mouthed into his glass, his head bent down and his shoulders stooped, two men next to Geezer Malone feuded passionately over the new dual carriageway that was getting built. "End of Ireland as we know it," said one of them mournfully. "Get to fuck," said the other thickly. "There's plenty of jobs to be had on the new road, and houses to be built as well." "New houses for who? Those Dublin fucks? Or worse, the Northeners coming in? Donegal will become a suburb. It'll kill the fishing here just like it did the farming in Mullingartown." A third man entered the debate, "'Twas the EEC that killed the farming—asking 'em to plant trees and go into tourism, for fuck's sake." They argued until a fourth man came in, "Now I'll tell you what the new dual carriageway will do, bring all them flat-dwelling tinker fuckers even closer, those bastard lads from Dublin would never have killed that poor old lady in Clare but that they got there on a new road. We should build high walls and charge for use of the road, just like the Americans do." To which the first man responded, "Well I care now what you say. My Johnny lives at home and works in the town. He's home for tea with the new road." Emer listened to the men arguing, still watching Geezer Malone's mouth work words like spells into his nearly-empty pint of Guinness. Geezer Malone didn't even know they were there. He mouthed out 'swan' over and over again.

The tinker children finished the last long verse of "Frosty the Snowman." The tall lad that Emer had paid pulled a penny whistle out of his sleeve and started a reel, "The

Connacht Heifers," maybe, or was it "Miko Russell's Reel"? Emer kept filling the glasses, humming her first verse. She hummed quietly, the words in her head set against the reel and the loud voices that spilled from every corner. She had pieced the verse, putting Geezer Malone's Irish and English whispers together, the taste of stout giving them a backbone, and weaved like his ravelly fisherman's knit. Frankie Butler worked next to her taking orders, his "Now, lads," and "What can I do for ye, dearies?" punctuating Emer's thoughts. The tinker children stood idle while the whistle called out and bursted suddenly into "Rudolph the Red-Nosed Reindeer."

"Ah, for feck's sake, Butler," called Bully. "Would you ever shut 'em up?" Bully's words were a question, but his tone a half-hearted demand. Bully knew, as well as Frankie Butler, as well as Emer, as well as everyone in the pub, that no one would throw the tinkers out. It was too risky. But Bully was well on. Emer counted eleven pints poured from her own hands, maybe more. Emer looked at her watch, it was getting late. Betsy and Eileen Fitzpatrick were long gone, so was Father McGuire. The families had gone home to have a sleep. Although he stayed much longer than usual, his eyes dark and brooding under thick eyebrows, there were only the last few swallows of his pint between Geezer Malone and the door.

Bully Morgan stood up from his stool, weaving with his drink in his hand. "You fucking, cock-and-blood sucking, mother fucking tinker, shut the fuck up," he yelled. He hurled the full glass of Guinness at the tinkers, his aim skewed by drink, and roared out a laugh while the glass smashed against the chimney. Beer and glass fell on the children like rain. The tall boy rushed through the crowd, stabbed Bully Morgan in the belly with his whistle, grabbed the other children, and ran out the door. Emer heard Frankie Butler hiss out "Shit," grab the phone and call for the Garda. Bully Morgan was hunched over, holding his belly, but his fire was not put out. "Cocksucker tinker shit," he yelled. "Fuck the lot of 'em." Still holding his belly, he stood up, almost majestically. "This town is a fucking hole," he said. Silence fell around him just as the pub rain had fallen onto the tinkers. The four men arguing over the dual carriageway glared at Bully, their mouths hanging open. The man against the EEC turned to the man in favor of the dual carriageway and punched him in the nose. He fell to the ground. "What the fuck did you do that for?" asked another one. "Save the tinkers the trouble," he growled, pulling on his mac and leaving by the back door.

Everywhere people were moving, their feet dancing and slipping over the broken shards of glass like a bunch of heifers at a ceili dance. Fingers were pointing and accusations were flying. The turf fire spluttered and sang with beads of stout. Factory workers screamed at fishermen. Women screamed at their lovers. Townspeople and farmers cried out their pain and frustration. Above it all, Bully Morgan reigned supreme, his voice the loudest and his finger the longest. Emer stood motionless behind the bar, staring into the chaos, thinking of the druids and warriors who had had their right hands cut off by Roman soldiers. This was just another argument over a new road system and a change in the way of life. Stories had a way of staying the same.

Frankie Butler grabbed Emer and pushed her behind him. "Now folks, you'll all be leaving," he yelled out. "Get the fuck out," said Bully, though he was buttoning up his coat unevenly. Just as Bully started to leave, flanked by the lads he lorded over and protected like a chieftain, he turned towards Geezer Malone. For the first time that night, Geezer looked up from his glass. There was a long silence. Bully hissed out his final accusation of the evening, perversely blending together the Catholicism and ancient lore that hung in the clouds of cigarette smoke in the pub. "Geezer Malone," he said with strain, "You have cursed this fucking town with your sin. You killed that woman; her bones carpet the Moy. Your shame is our Hell." Emer marveled at Bully's drunken poetics. She held her breath waiting for the old Geezer to set them all straight, to tell his story. But Geezer Malone just watched Bully leave through the door, turned his back on his stout, finished it, pulled some coins out of his pocket, and laid them on the bar. As he did so, Emer reached out touching his hand with hers. Their eyes met; hers hopeful and pitying, his sad and resolute. "Nah, Emer, don't fret," he said. "What they say, it may be true. I don't rightly know anymore." Then he pulled his hand away, settled his cap on his old and sorry pate, and left through the back door. Emer watched him go, the knots in her stomach loosening and recoiling with each thought of what had happened, her eyes focusing and her mind dizzying on the diamonds and cables of his old fisherman's knit. Turning back to the bar, Emer had found that, for once, Geezer Malone had been the last to leave.

Now, where the crowd had been, cigarette stubs flowered the tile floor, glass and alcohol shined like dew, pints in varying stages of undress sunned themselves against the dying fire. Frankie Butler's voice drifted in from the back room. "'Twas nothing, James. There was a bit of a row earlier on, but it's okay now." Then James's voice, the Head Garda and Frankie's brother, "The tinkers are quiet enough now. I'll help you out here then see you at home." James Butler came out of the back room with Frankie and smiled wanly at Emer. The three of them stood, surveying the damage. Frankie started to sweep up the glass, while James turned the chairs and stools over on top of the tables and the bar and Emer ran hot water for the mop. She sang while she squeezed the Fairy liquid detergent into the pail ("hands that do dishes can feel soft as your face with mild, green Fairy liquid"). For good measure, she added a dash of Mr. Tidy and Detol in to the pail, and sang out the second verse of her new song.

"That's your new song, is it?" asked Frankie. "Well, that's the second verse, anyway," said Emer. "Well, I like it. I'll see you in *Spin* magazine yet," said Frankie. Emer was grateful for Frankie's kindness, also somewhat puzzled by the fact that she had shared this dream with him, this dream that she was keeping from her own family. "How about finishing it off?" asked James. Emer blushed, but she obliged, happy to have a receptive audience. She ended with the chorus, mopping while she sang.

When she was done, there was a pause. "Well, now," said Frankie leaning against the bar, "that's lovely. But you said it was finished." "Well, it is," said Emer uncertainly, "isn't it?" "Don't listen to him, Emer," said James, "it's finished enough. Well, maybe one more verse will do it, like how the love-sick fella found himself a new life, a new wife." "And there's a rhyme for you, too," Frankie added, laughing. "Right," said Emer, "thank you." Terrible rhyme aside, she new Frankie and James meant well. The only problem was that that was story as best she knew it. There was nothing more to say— and making up an ending just didn't feel right.

James Butler was kind enough to walk Emer home, holding open the door and looking left and right for any members of the pub crowd who might be getting into trouble in the dark, wet street. Most of the crowd could be seen through the window of the chip shop. The four men who had argued and fought stood by the off-license singing "O Come All Ye Faithful" with their arms around each other. Emer smiled to think of it.

"Your song is real nice, Emer," James said again, "You'll finish it soon enough." Emer said nothing while James hummed her own tune. "'Tis a bit like old Mr. Malone, isn't it?" asked James. Emer looked at James quickly, taking in the dark hair streaked with gray, the smooth ivory skin and blue eyes. Mammy had once said that James Butler had been mad to marry Auntie Jane, but Auntie Jane would have none of it. She lived alone, never married, in Grandfather and Granny's old house next door to her own. Emer had laughed at the time, but now she wondered why Auntie Jane didn't marry such a good man. "What do *you* think happened to that woman, Officer Butler?" she asked.

James breathed in through his teeth before answering, and when he finally did, he answered with a question. "Is that what the row was about tonight?" "Well, not really. A little, maybe," said Emer. "Bully Morgan was there. He said that the auld fella shamed the town with his sin." "Well now," said Officer Butler, "most of us weren't even born yet, and stories change. But it has been said that that woman was promised to Bully's great, great grandfather. The Morgans were always ones to hold a grudge . . . runs in the family." Emer nodded, though she didn't know whether that was true or not, and they walked in the rainy silence until reaching her hedge. "All the best to the family, and to your Auntie Jane," James said, then spun on his heel and disappeared into the dark like a ghost.

Emer was up late the next morning; so late that the house was empty. The kids were all at school, Da was at work in the factory and Mammy must have gone to the shops with the baby. Emer made herself a fry, pressing down the black and white pudding with a spatula and grilling a tomato in the fat of the rashers that she never bothered to soak. Relishing the empty silence of the small, three-bedroom cottage, she wrote out the words of her song on a serviette, even though she had memorized them, and tried to understand why the song wasn't finished.

After Mammy and the kids had returned in a good mood, Emer sang her song to them. Mammy was sidetracked by Shane's squealing, and the kids were arguing over who ate the last sliver of Sunday pudding, but they all agreed that it was a nice song. "All you have to do now is finish it," Maura said. "Make it a happy ending," added Colm, handing a fishing pole to Brendan and walking out the door with him.

It wasn't season yet, they would have to throw the fish back into the loch, and it was cold and wet, but they went fishing almost every day anyway.

Emer sighed and pulled on her coat. She decided to walk by the Moy for inspiration. Maybe she would see Geezer Malone there, talking to his swan. That could help her finish her song. She went alone as she often did since her three best friends had taken their degrees and left Ireland to work, two in Australia (together) and one in Londontown.

Emer hummed the chorus over and over again, trying to find a way into the last verse while she crossed the soft green grass of the fields, passed the old fairy fort that the farmers knew better than to mow flat (the fairies would burn down the barn or kill the crops if they did), and followed the canal to the Moy. But Geezer Malone was nowhere to be found. The swan, alone like her, looking for the old Geezer like her, circled slowly in the water. "Do you know the last verse?" Emer asked the swan, but the swan just turned away, glaring at Emer sideways. Emer headed for home again. Stooping to tie the laces of her runners behind the old Ogham stones and deciding to take off in a run, Emer did not see Geezer Malone stroll up the banks of the Moy.

Geezer Malone reached into the pocket of his trousers, pulling out Mrs. Dunn's bread and picking the threads of his fisherman's knit out of the crumbs in his hand. He whistled softly to the swan and called out, "Mary, Mary. Here's bread, Mary." The swan floated gracefully over to Geezer. "Michael has brought you bread, Mary," Geezer Malone said softly. The swan, Mary, looked sideways at the Geezer, Michael, and trumpeted. "Is what they say true, Mary?" Michael asked the swan as he had so many times. Mary bent her head down to his palm, pushing at the crumbs with her bill, and floated backwards a bit. Anyone looking would have said that the swan bucked her thin, white head and fluttered her clipped wings a bit, but Michael knew better. Mary tossed her thick black curls and laughed so hard and quietly that her hands shook. Michael threw some bread into the water and watched Mary pick it up, turn her head demurely and swallow. "Emer Killian has your job at the pub now, Mary," said Michael, though he had told Mary as much before. "She's a fine lass, kindly-like," he added. He threw some more bread into the water, politely watching the waves of the Moy lap at his Wellies instead of watching Mary eat. She had always been shy like that. Mary had always been a real lady.

"There was another row with one of the Morgan's last night," Michael said carefully. "It seems I've killed you. Is that true, Mary?" he asked. Michael threw the last of his bread into the deep, still waters of the Moy. "Oh, I would that you had not left me, Mary. We could have run away. Old Morgan didn't have to take you from me. But why, Mary, why?" Michael asked again, his voice cracking. And again Michael asked, "Did I kill you, Mary?" Mary beat her wings softly against the water, trying to fly, trumpeted angrily and fled to the far bank. Michael stood alone at the edge of the water, his head in his hands, and tasted the first tears he had cried in a long time. From the far side of the water, he heard Mary call out, "It's time, Michael."

Michael Malone wiped his face with his ravelly sleeves and walked slowly back to his one-room cottage. Carefully, he banked the fire and cleaned the old crumbs of brown bread and sausage from the cooking pot, took his last tin of sardines down from the shelf, and put it in his pocket. He piled up the turf that Mrs. O'Leary had given him and laid the few coins he had on top of the turf. Shutting the door softly, Michael walked back to the Moy, picking up small, heavy stones along the way.

Michael Malone stopped at the bank, putting his Wellie-clad feet back into the prints he had left in the mud. He opened the sardines stiffly, holding the key between his finger and thumb and breathing in the thick, sweet-smelling sardine juice. "Mary," he called to the swan still on the far side of the water, "I've brought sardines this time, Mary, a

Christmas treat." But Mary wouldn't look at Michael Malone. "It's time, Michael," he heard her say again. Michael sat down in the mud, thinking that he might as well get used to it. He dumped the collection of stones from where they were bundled in his fisherman's knit and, one by one, tossed them into his Wellington boots until they could hold no more. He lifted out a single sardine and swallowed it whole. Then he put the full tin into his pocket, letting the oily fish juices run down his leg and seep through his trousers. To the other pocket he added the sardine key and a few more stones. Michael stood up. He felt younger than he had in years. Breathing in the salt air of Ireland, and licking the sardine taste from his lips, Michael waded into the Moy. He swallowed the water as fast as it swallowed him, and noticed, just as his head dipped under the water, that Mary was floating back to him.

Michael's head swam from the lack of air and the intake of water. He felt sleepy. Dream-like. Visions of Mary and Emer behind the bar, and old Mr. Morgan and young Bully, flickered back and forth in his mind. Michael fell asleep into death just as the swan bent her graceful head down and pulled the sardines from his pocket.

Whether it was because of the holidays or because of the row, Emer did not see Geezer Malone on his stool at the pub for several days. She didn't have much time to notice how many days, since all three of her friends had come home for the Christmas, the one in Londontown begging Emer to go to Germany or America with her. Emer told the girls about the lads and the band, about the row and the unfinished song, and about how Colm had said to make it a happy ending. On the fact that it was unfinished, the girls agreed. As to the ending, opinion varied. Sheilagh wanted Emer to end it tragically. Susan wanted her to change the story altogether so that the couple run away to America and strike it rich. Aisling wanted the young woman to turn from a swan back into a girl, like "The Children of Lir." They laughed over their pints and traded stories—both old and new—of their adventures. Together, they went to the Christmas dance where the fiddler from the band introduced himself as Kevin and kissed Emer under the mistletoe. Emer laughed and sang with her friends and danced with Kevin, and made Christmas cake with Auntie Jane, but she still couldn't finish her song.

On Christmas Eve, while Emer was helping Mammy with the pudding, Colm and Brendan came in with their fishing poles and a story. Two swans had trumpeted while Mr. Dunn pulled a dead body from the waters of the Moy. His skin was bloated and his eyes eaten out by fish, he had floated right out of his Wellies and gotten tangled in the grasses, but it was Geezer Malone. Officer Butler could tell from the weave on his fisherman's knit. "I'll bet it was Bully Morgan who pushed him in," said Brendan. "I'm gonna be a garda officer," said Colm definitely, "it was very cool." "The poor, old soul must have killed himself," remarked Auntie Jane. "No," said Emer softly, "no. It was the swan."

At midnight Mass, Father McGuire spoke about the baby Jesus, how he was a fisherman for God and saved the drowning souls of people. Everyone else talked about Geezer Malone, some of them saying his name out loud for the first time in their lives.

On Boxing Day, the day after Christmas, when the whole town awoke with sore heads and stumbled into the pub for a bit of the hair of the dog that had bit them, Emer, still without a final verse, washed and dressed and pulled her old Raleigh out of the garage. It was a soft day. The wind was whipping the rainy mist into her face as she rode her bike past the churchyard to her audition in the town. On impulse, Emer stopped, leaned her bike against the concrete Virgin, and walked into the yard. Father McGuire stood over a grave, talking with a gravedigger. He looked up with surprise at

Emer. "Now, Miss Killian," Father McGuire asked, "What can I do for you?" Emer looked at the plain, pine box in the earth. At least the congregation had chipped in for that. Father McGuire would have to take the money out of the church funds himself for a gravestone. "I knew Geezer Malone a bit," Emer said, "He came in to the pub every day at five o'clock." Father McGuire nodded. He held the umbrella over them both while they said a prayer. Then Emer and Father McGuire and the gravedigger threw the fresh, soft dirt into the grave. Before leaving the churchyard, Father McGuire squeezed Emer's shoulders and said, "Don't worry, child. Mr. Malone is with Mary now." Emer nodded, her head bent against the tears at the backs of her eyes.

Emer rode her bike the long miles into town, humming her song to herself. She was hoping that a kiss from Kevin would make up for the missing verse—or that the lads wouldn't notice it missing. But she didn't have to hope, after all. In a strong, delicate voice she sang out her song to the lads in the band seated in front of her like a jury with their tea in their laps. She started with the chorus. Then, finding her rhythm, Emer went through the verses, running through the chorus after each one. And just as she drew out the last lines of the chorus, thinking to end her song, the final verse came to her as if it had always been there. She sang about how Michael Malone had joined his love on the Moy, and how two silver swans now glide together over their cold graves; she sang about how they had lived for each other, died for each other, and how the lovers were united at last. And then Emer sang out her chorus again, sure that her song was finished now, sure that Geezer Malone would rest in peace.

The lads, who had been quiet and still while Emer closed her eyes and sang her prayer, now stood up, clapping and knocking their teacups to the floor. The drummer, Lorcan, extended his hand to Emer while Kevin kissed her cheek. "It's a great song, Emer. We would be honored to have you sing for us," Lorcan said. Kevin kissed her again, stating, "Now lads, I told you that she was alright. What d'ye call the song, Emer?"

    Emer paused at the question. She wasn't sure. She had called it 'her song' for such a time, but that was wrong. It wasn't her song at all. It was the town's song, even Bully Morgan's. It was Father McGuire's. Auntie Jane's, Mr. and Mrs. Dunn's. But most of all, it was Geezer Malone's song. Emer smiled then and, without hesitating, said, "I call it 'The Ballad of Geezer Malone.'"

Franny & Mary

by Heidi Wohlwend

Franny gave it a month. Go to Ricks college, obey all the rules, perhaps she'd find God, make her parents happy. But after thirty days all she felt was grizzled, haggard and alone. She made the preliminary decision that this religion was not what she wanted to do for the rest of her life. But getting out of it was another problem. The three women she roomed with at Pinecrest Apartments (the only Church-sanctioned housing off-campus) did not want to talk about anything but temple weddings, hair spray, and clothes that looked alluring even if they were modest. They liked the dress code: no hair cuts with unusual shapes, no hair dye, bras worn at all times, no jeans or clothes with rips, no androgynous clothing.

The home teachers came over, two young men from the same college ward, to make sure their apartment was blessed. And to flirt, of course. Krissy, the one from Oregon, was the prettiest, bouncy long hot-rollered curls, hot pink lips. Franny saw the looks between the return missionaries. She knew her own short cropped hair and big shoes were not acceptable. Franny smiled and listened to a gaunt boy from Montana read a verse from the Book of Mormon.

Rexberg, Idaho, was subarctic, and Franny missed the sun and fog of California. She looked out into the parking lot and saw the tall girl from next door puttering around on skis. Franny went outside in the cold to watch her breath turn to fog and to wander in the snow. She made trails where the snow was fresh, made a peace symbol with her feet. The girl on the skis came over to look, then pointed to her car in the parking lot, a yellow VW bug with Utah plates. It was covered with bumper stickers and spray paint. *Visualize world peace, Cocaine Import Agency. Care you spare a paradigm? Question Authority.* Franny laughed and said, You must be as watched as I am here. I've been sent to the Dean's office twice for wearing too much black clothing. You too? the girl said. She held out her hand. I'm Mary Catherine and I'm a Mormon, she said, as though she were announcing that she had an inoperable liver tumor.

Franny traded places with Mary Catherine's roommate from Arizona because she felt her own roommates were giving her neurological damage from all the hair spray. Mary was better to talk to, she was smart and wanted to be a botanist. She knew the names of tons of plants. Franny helped Mary Catherine memorize: *Alnus rhombifolia* was white alder, *Sequoia sempervirens* was the giant redwood. Oh, I want to see that tree, Mary squealed. Have you seen the redwoods in person? Franny laughed. Yes, I've been to "The Trees of Mystery," they have a gift shop and a tree you can drive through, but it's sad. They walked to the grocery store and hookey-bobbed behind cars on the way home, nearly losing their groceries as they clung to bumpers and slid on the ice; water skiing of sorts behind moving cars. Their laughter rose in the cold air, notes fading away in the black sky.

They told each other their stories. Mary Catherine's dad was an engineer and worked for a defense contractor. She deemed this far more immoral than drinking or having premarital sex, but of course she couldn't say anything. What do they think of your car? Franny wanted to know. I did that the week I came up here, Mary said. Franny told how she had stopped eating meat in high school and her parents thought it was cute. Her mother kept cooking beef for dinner anyway and still offered it to her even though Franny had tried explaining about how much water and grain it took to make one pound of beef. Her dad said, God has a plan for everything, he said, God put cows on the earth for us to eat.

Franny asked Mary Catherine if she wore tampons and Mary sheepishly said, Yes, but my mom doesn't like it. My mom doesn't either, Franny said. I put one in upside down once, you know, so the string wasn't hanging down. Mary hooted and snickered. Well, what did you do? Franny's face turned red. I was afraid to say anything to my mom, so I waited for a day. But then I thought I would die of Toxic Shock Syndrome, so I went into the bathroom with some kitchen tongs to see if I could grab it, but I ended up using my fingers. It seemed so bad. Mary put her hand on Franny's cheek. Oh honey, she said.

Mary Catherine was a tomboy, she told Franny, and her friends back home in Logan called her Granola because she was so into nature. She climbed things. She climbed onto the roof of the boys' dorm to see if she could see in. Instead she found a jug of vodka and lugged it back to the apartment. Look, she said, I'm Indiana Jones! They made grape Kool-aid for mixer and drank. They ran giggling into their bedroom when the other roommates came home. Later they had to clean purple puke from every nook and cranny of the bathroom. It took hours. Their eyes met in the bathroom mirror and they smiled.

They talked about God while they drifted off to sleep at night. Franny said that the closest she'd ever felt to God was when she was hiking at Eagle Cap Wilderness for her final badge to be a Summiteer at church camp. She followed a different trail from the others because she thought she saw some deer, and when the trail broke open, out of the trees, she landed in a meadow full of mountain blue bells and Indian Paintbrush as far as she could see. Mary Catherine agreed, shaking her sandy hair; she had only seen the ocean once, she said, and that was where she'd felt it. Her grandmother lived in California. Really? Franny said and sat up in her bed. I don't think I'm coming back next year, she said. Mary Catherine was silent, her face to the wall. What will I do? she asked.

Franny fired up her station wagon, the tuna boat, and they piled in for a trip to Jackson Hole, Wyoming, to buy alcohol. It was only an hour drive. The drinking age was nineteen in Wyoming, and they had drive-through liquor stores. The Grand Tetons were jagged and capped with snow. Fraxinus oxycarpa, Franny said, pointing at a grove of Mountain Ash. Franny, stop, Mary Catherine said. Let's get out and take a breath of this air.

They pushed their twin beds together at the center of the room to make more room for cleaning, and then they left them that way. It would be easier to talk late at night in low whispers if they were closer, Mary Catherine said. Franny agreed, turned out the lights and lit a candle. Do you ever think that they're wrong? Franny asked. All the time, Mary replied, sighing. They laid flat on their backs looking up at the glow-in-the-dark stars Mary had put on the ceiling. Mary said, You know what I'm really worried about? That I'll end up marrying someone and then on our wedding night I'll discover that he has a tiny penis. They both laughed out loud. Right, Franny said, if only you could try before you buy.

Mary held up a large ball of twine. Let's string all the doorknobs together, she said. Franny looked up from the script she was trying to memorize for acting class. She was playing Emily from *Our Town*. Franny looked at the way Mary's mouth curved when she was up to something; there was nothing quite like her lips, the perfect cupid's bow at the top and the pouty little-girl lower lip.

Mary Catherine held Franny as they slept some nights because of her nightmares. Franny dreamt about a large man who looked like David Bowie, but meaner. He held a curved knife and when he smiled his teeth were black. He cut off Franny's hands while she watched. This was where she woke up, shivering, waving her hands to see if they were still there. Mary rubbed Franny's back and held her tighter. I'm here, it's okay, she said. Mary kissed the back of Franny's neck lightly and Franny felt the down on her neck stand up, erect. Mary's hand lightly brushed Franny's chest and slid down her hip. Franny turned her head and let her lips touch Mary's, then took Mary's soft lower lip between her teeth. Mary tasted like milk.

Franny brought up cans of Diet Pepsi from the machine downstairs. She told Mary about the mistake—instead of Country Time Lemonade the delivery guy had put in Diet Pepsi. Mary dug through her top drawer of junk for more quarters. Let's see how much we can drink, she said. They stayed up all night making a pyramid of cans while Franny helped Mary study for her plant ID final. *Cedrus Deodara?* Franny asked. I think I want to take flying lessons, Mary said. Franny fanned the ID cards in front of her, Latin names of

VOLUME II

trees. *Cedrus Deodara,* Franny said, is Incense Cedar. Do you ever feel that you should just break out and have an adventure? Mary asked. What, sitting in Rexberg drinking Diet Pepsi isn't enough for you? Franny said and smiled. She looked back down at the cards. Mary swept her arm across the table, knocking the cards off, grabbing Franny's chin, pressing hard. Franny's blue eyes locked with Mary's green. Save me, Mary whispered.

After Christmas break they flew at each other. I missed you so much, Mary said breathlessly. Franny felt how Mary's hot hands left impressions on her back as they held each other in the doorway. Let me show you what I brought, Mary said. I made you a present when I was at home. Franny looked at the stooped line of Mary's back. Mary pulled a purple tie-dyed sun dress out of a paper bag. You made this? Franny asked. I didn't know you could sew. Well, I am a Mormon, Mary laughed. You can wear it in the sun in California, where it's warm. You can look at the ocean and feel God. Franny looked at Mary's sandy hair slicked back from her face. She seemed scraped out, something missing in her eyes. Franny held the dress in front of her, feeling the soft cotton, picturing Mary over the sewing machine as if she were in occupational therapy. A vegetable making lanyard key fobs. What did they do to you? Franny asked, biting her lip. Mary said, They made me confess to the Bishop. They want me to come back to Utah. Mary looked at the floor, but then brightened. *Salix babylonica?* Mary asked, smiling with her beautiful mouth. Weeping willow, Franny thought, but couldn't speak.

On a day of spring renewal Franny drove them to the sand dunes ten miles out of town. Like a mini Sahara, huge dunes of golden sand appeared from out of nowhere and students came to suntan or slide down the dunes on scraps of cardboard. Franny and Mary were dressed like Bedouins, sheets swathed about them, hiding their faces. Franny's idea was to make a fort in the sand where they could enjoy the sun without being discovered—they wanted to try nude sunbathing and Franny was afraid everyone would see. They trundled up the dunes getting sand in their shoes, toting a cooler full of food and sodas and beer from Jackson Hole. Mary had an armload of PVC pipe for the walls of the fort. Here, rub this on my back, Mary said, and took off her shirt. Franny took off her shirt too, and then watched Mary lie on her stomach, and looked at the curve of her muscular freckled back. I don't believe in this anymore, Franny said, watching the play of shadows on the sand. Why don't you come to California with me? Your grandmother lives there. We can go to a real college together. Mary took a deep breath and let it slowly out. Because I can't, she said.

Franny looked out into the audience after the house lights came up and saw Mary Catherine standing alone with her hand over her mouth. Did you like my good-bye speech? Franny gushed. Mary said, My mother is here. She is packing my things.

When Franny told her parents on the phone that she no longer believed in the same God that they did, they told her she probably should find her own place to live in California. When the semester ended Franny packed up the tuna boat with all her belongings and headed towards Utah. She called Mary Catherine, tearful, from a pay phone at a gas station in Logan. Mary wasn't allowed to speak to her. Mary's father said she should continue to California, they didn't have space for her to stay the night. Why are you doing this to me? Franny asked. The silence at the other end of the line crackled and snapped with indifference.

Mary finally wrote a letter to Franny: Dear Franny, things are going well here with my family. My two brothers passed the sacrament today at church. My mom was really proud. I've started classes at U of Utah. You'd be so much of a help to me if you were here—I've got this really complicated set of plants to learn for my botany class. Oh, and I actually found out about flying lessons—I can take them at the university. At last, an adventure! I may be able to come out for a visit later. I'll try to call soon. Love, Mary Franny wrote: *Populus temuloides. Quercus agrifolia.* The quaking aspens are beautiful this time of year. Send me some leaves. Here is the leaf from *Quercus*, the Coast Live Oak. I touched an oak today, wrapped my arms around it, as far as I could. It must've been at least 300 years old, and I could feel the knowledge in this tree, the wisdom coursing through it. What things that tree has seen! I thought of you as I hugged the bark. I wish you would call. I need to hear your voice. All my love, Franny Mary never called, but did write letters that seemed more and more like someone else was writing them. They said cryptic things like, My mother is happy to have me help in the kitchen. Then the letters stopped. Franny looked up the grandmother, and went to her house out in Hayward. No one was home but she left a long note with her phone number.

Three years passed and Franny came home from work, her first job after graduating, a beige job. Franny missed trees. She was sweating from struggling with the traffic on 680 and as she started to unlock the door of her Fremont apartment, her roommate Jill threw it open, said, I have to talk to you. Franny paused in horror and thought for a moment that she'd left a turd in the toilet on accident. Their roommate relationship had been strained lately. Jill said, Your friend Mary Catherine has died, Franny just stared at her. Oh, she said, not knowing what to do with her body suddenly. Oh. An hour later while watching *Married With Children* tears began rolling down her cheeks.

Franny went to Mary Catherine's grandmother's house to watch a videotape of the funeral. A woman said that Mary had made a change in her life recently, was preparing for a mission, and wasn't she the most spiritual young lady in our ward, the most prepared to rear a family and serve the Lord? They had an awful high school picture of her sitting on the pink casket. Mary detested pink. Mary hated that picture too, Franny had heard her say that she'd be embarrassed if anyone saw it. It was closed casket because Mary had died while practicing touch-and-go landings in a Cessna at the University. She had been flattened on impact. Franny could not imagine the perfect curve of Mary's lips being marred in any way.

Franny fumbles through her closet one morning, getting ready for work. Since her pregnancy, getting dressed has become a battle. She comes across the old purple sundress. It is like stepping on a tack, breaking the skin, but then the tack must be pulled out.

Touch and Go.

Franny wonders again about the touch-and-go part. They never said the plane had failed. Pilot error, they said. But if Mary was in control, she was in control. That was how she did things. Franny decides she will iron the dress flawless and place it in a special box with bunches of lavender and rosemary for remembrance. She rubs the cotton across her cheek, smells Mary Catherine as clearly as if it were yesterday. Flimsy cotton fabric, barest fibers, how could it outlast you?

After work, Franny trudges slowly up Dolores in a heavy mist. It falls over her hair and she feels it on her face. The air is pregnant with water, as Franny is pregnant with a baby she wants to love as much as she loved Mary Catherine. Franny stands at the pinnacle of Dolores looking east, down over the city. She turns slowly north, to see behind her, south to see the future, and then turns west to see the faint glimmer of last sun. And she feels Mary for a moment. Is that you inside me? she asks the mist. Is that you longing to fly? She wants to protect the baby from so much, the way, she decides, that she wanted to protect Mary, but couldn't.

Franny will tell all of this to her daughter when she is old enough: this is how love was with you, Mary, and you are half her mother too.

The Day My Life Fell Apart

by Mimi Reddicliffe

The start of the day my life fell apart was not dramatic. As far as I could tell by peering through the grime of the window by my bed, it was a sunny April day. I got up, took a shower, and dressed in my usual working costume of paint splattered sweatshirt and jeans. I left my apartment on the corner of Thirteenth and Sixth and headed for the studio. I had a great studio that year in Tribeca. I'd won it in a lottery. It was a huge room in an old warehouse with plenty of heat and no rent to pay. The only problem was the daily submerge into the subway to get there. But that's New York, not the studio.

Anyway, I got to the studio and started mixing up paint. I was working on a large interior. I'd dragged over a rug, a chair, some crockery, all my usual props that made a corner of a desolate abandoned warehouse look like a corner of a room in a glossy magazine. I was having trouble with some of the crockery on the table. The ellipses in the glasses were definitely off. I was pretty annoyed because fixing the drawing would take hours of work. But I started in, squinting at the shapes trying to figure out where I'd gone wrong.

Mid-squint I saw the painting. I mean, I really saw the painting. I don't think I'd ever seen one of my paintings like that. And I realized if I saw that painting in a gallery, I'd sniff and walk out. Mediocre drawing—all right, I could fix the ellipse. But the angle of the top of the table was wrong, and I hadn't even noticed. Granted, the art consultants who paraded their clients through the doors of Grant and Stein wouldn't notice either, but I was the artiste. And the harmonious, tasteful grays and reds. They were pretty.

But drawing and color, those were incidental. The big problem was that it was a totally meaningless painting. Where was the commentary on form, color, and substance the latest review of my work, in an obscure but respected journal, had raved about? Where was the exalted use of everyday objects to make said commentary on form, color, and substance?

I dragged the six paintings I'd completed since my last show out of the racks. A collection of furniture, that's what I had. A fucking collection of furniture.

At this propitious moment, my phone rang. "Sandra?"

"Uh huh. Larry?" Larry Grant's the director-owner of my gallery. Greg Stein's the silent partner.

"Sandra, we have to talk." Although Larry pours the charm on the paying customers, he doesn't waste time on painters.

"What's up?"

"When can I see you?"

"I don't know. What's good for you? I've got a dentist appointment midtown next week," I said.

"How about this afternoon? I could come down to the studio."

Not at the moment he couldn't. "No, that's okay. I've got some errands to do. I'll stop by your place," I said. We settled on the time, and I returned to the furniture. It was still furniture.

I messed with the ellipses for awhile, but my heart wasn't in it. Anyway, I needed to go home to change before going midtown. Ten years before I would've pranced into the gallery in my jeans and sweatshirt, but at forty-three I was no longer so sure that my charms would shine through my dishabille. Don't get me wrong, I could still look great. It just took a bit more of an effort. So I put on the black pants that made me look surprisingly thin and some snappy little Italian boots and trotted uptown.

Larry was busy with a client in a mink coat, so I pretended to look at the art. Rather thin, washed out looking abstractions. For a very brief second I wondered if the other gallery artists harbored such thoughts about me, but I banished the idea.

Larry ushered the mink out and kissed me with the usual perfunctory gush. He left Dierdre, the latest example of breeding and money decorating the front of the gallery, to guard the desk, and we went back to his office. "Sandra, I'm working on the schedule for next season."

"I thought we'd decided on March for my show."

"Yeah, well, that's what we have to talk about." Larry looked at me expectantly. But I didn't have anything to say. He cleared his throat. "Actually, you know that's only eighteen months between shows. I thought, you know, maybe two years would be better."

I hadn't been expecting this. "What's the deal, Larry? I always have shows every eighteen months."

Larry sat straighter in his chair. "We've only sold a third of your last show."

"I believe you've sold quite a large number of my paintings over the last ten years. And I do think my reviews reflect rather well on Grant and Stein." I concentrated on drawling rather than shrieking.

Larry furrowed his brow. "The problem is I've got a couple of new people I need to fit into the schedule. It's important to give new people a chance. And most of the artists in this gallery would love to have a show every two years. I don't think this is a big deal, Sandra."

I shrugged. "I need to think about this, Larry."

"Of course you do."

And I was out in the street. No smarmy comments about the true importance of my work or about our continued relationship, just of course you do. This was serious. It meant that Larry really didn't give a damn about whether I stayed with the gallery.

I'd walked halfway home when I realized it was colder than I thought and submerged. I needed to talk to someone about this, but that was tricky. Nothing got around faster than bad news. But Larry wasn't dumping me. I could say he wasn't doing as well as he might, and I wanted to look around. People hopped galleries all the time. The problem was Larry had the reputation of being as good as anyone else in the business. That meant he paid promptly and usually kept his promises. In fact, this was the first time he'd ever reneged on a deal in ten years—amazing for a gallery owner. I wasn't going to do better than Larry.

When I got home I settled myself on the couch and stared at the phone. If I called any painters I knew, it would be back to their dealers I was looking around and back to Larry before I made the next call. Would that give him the excuse to dump me? Ditto the collection of critics and curators on my circuit.

I lay down. There was something else nagging my soul. The collection of furniture. I surveyed my apartment. It looked like my paintings. Carefully chosen fabrics covered the couch and chairs. The blue of the walls picked up the color of a thin strip I was picking at on the couch. A few interesting objects placed on the surfaces: ceramic vases, lacquer bowls. My life. A collection of furniture.

    I sat up again. I needed to talk to someone outside the art world about the gallery problem. Someone who could be objective. My mother? No, not my mother. She regaled the entire retirement community in Florida with tales of her daughter's success. But she was the only person I called regularly outside the business.

    I fished my address book out of my purse and leafed through it. There were a number of people I hadn't called in ten years, fifteen years. Friends who'd left art for law school or decent jobs. People who'd left New York for college campuses in the boondocks. Lovers who'd found women willing to compromise to a degree. I'd survived. I'd conquered New York. And I had a collection of furniture.

    I stayed in bed for a week and considered my wasted existence. The time I could have spent creating real paintings. I didn't set out to become the foremost portrait painter of furniture in the decade; it had just happened. Sure I'd spent some energy at the right openings, parties, and bars. But I'd passed all of my days and many of my nights in studios—dreary, cold, and lonely spaces. I'd tried my best. I had. And I wasn't a great painter. Would my life have been better if I'd given up? I didn't know.

    And all those names in my address book. What if I'd told one of the men I'd slept with over the years, say Teddy Glenn—I'd liked him a lot. When he'd taken the job someplace obscure, Columbus or Cincinnati or something, I could have said that I could paint anywhere. That I could leave New York with him. How would that life have been? Teddy and I'd kept it up for a year or so after he left. Then he found someone, in Columbus it was, and married. Had a couple of kids and a New York show before tenure, then dropped out of sight. He was probably exhibiting at some gallery in Cleveland. I could've had that sort of life too.

    Toward the end of the week I called the woman who'd

been my best friend in college. Since she wasn't a painter, I hadn't spoken to her in ten years, but she was happy to hear from me. We picked up some sort of thread. Then my friend Valerie called, one of the painters I couldn't discuss Larry with, to see if I was going to this huge party in Tribeca. We made plans to go together, and I got out of bed.

Larry was there, and he gushed around me a bit to let me know he had no immediate plans to kick me out, and at least three people I knew only slightly edged up while I was talking to him, hoping for an introduction. I obliged.

I thought about it for awhile and decided that if everyone had a piece of my furniture collection, I should start another type of collection for people to buy. After considering socks and flowers, I settled on food. Larry loved the paintings, and the critic in the obscure but respected journal raved.

But I know the emperor has no clothes, and so, most probably, do they.

Authors' Notes

J. R. Carpenter is a writer and visual artist, living and working in Montreal, Quebec. She has published poetry, short fiction and essays across Canada and Europe. In 1993 she began using the Internet to integrate image and text. These web based non-linear narratives can be found at http://www.luckysoap.com. She is currently writing a novel.

Joseph M. Ditta teaches Creative Writing and American Literature at Dakota Wesleyan University. His work has been published recently in *Weber Studies, The South Dakota Review, Connecticut Review, Prairie Winds,* and the *Hernando Medic.* He has a story appearing in an anthology of poetry, fiction and memoirs about the Great Plains. He is the recipient of two Artists Grants in Literature from the South Dakota Arts Council and recently had a story nominated for the Pushcart Prize.

Annamaria Formichella Elsden lives and works in Storm Lake, Iowa, with her husband and two children. She received her M.F.A. in Creative Writing from Emerson College and her

Ph.D. in American Literature from Tufts University. In addition to writing fiction, she writes critically about issues of gender, travel, and nationalism in American literature.

Kathryn Hamilton has earned both her B.A. and Masters degrees, and is a professor of composition and literature at Columbus State University. She resides in Columbus, Georgia, with her husband and basset hound. She is currently writing a novel based on her grandfather's journal.

Tom Henighan was born in New York City and now lives in Canada. For many years he taught creative writing at Carleton University, Ottawa, where he is Professor Emeritus of English. He has published two novels and two collections of stories, three authoritative books on Canadian culture, and several academic works. Two YA novels, *Mercury Man*, and *Viking Terror* will be published in Canada in 2004.

Caitlin Hicks: "I was born into a very large military Catholic family in the United States of America. I graduated Cum Laude with a double major in English and French from Loyola Marymount University of Los Angeles. Here, I wrote weekly columns as Feature Editor of the *Los Angeles Loyolan*. My first job out of school was a writer of Camp Fund stories at the *Los Angeles Times*. I worked in radio for several years in the San Francisco Bay area for CBS and NBC, where I was Manager of Advertising and Promotion for KYUU-FM. When I was 26, I dropped out of the corporate world to follow a lifelong dream to become an actress. At the same time, I met my creative soul mate in an Improvisation class—an accomplished artist from Canada named Gordon Halloran. In Toronto, I began writing for the theatre when, as an actress working on a solo show, The Tarragon Theatre invited me to be a member of the Playwrights Unit there. My first play *Six Palm Trees*, co-written with Gordon Halloran, came out of that effort. My path as a writer has always been a personal spiritual journey, although my work is not religious. I am drawn towards stories that I don't hear often in the mainstream culture. I enjoy bringing to life personal, pivotal stories which have the kernel of transformation and which connect us all to each other."

Mike Hood is an Associate Professor of English at Belmont Abbey College where he teaches English literature and is Director of the Great Books Program. His short story, "The End of the West and Practically Everything Else," recently appeared in *The William and Mary Review* (Fall 2002).

DeAnna Jarrell was born the second child (and only girl) to Danny and Bonnie Jarrell. She was raised in Slidell, LA, a quiet community that splits the forty-five mile difference between the deepest part of rural Mississippi and the New Orleans French Quarter. Ms. Jarrell will graduate in May 2004 with degrees in theatre and mass communications from Lindenwood University in St. Charles, MO. She plans to pursue a career in acting and continue writing. "Fisherman's Daughter," written when she was a twenty-year-old junior, is the first in a series of snapshots about her childhood.

Mark Johnston is a Professor of English at Quinnipiac University in Hamden, CT. His poetry and fiction have appeared in a variety of publications, including *The Georgia Review, Rattle,* and *The Western Humanities Review.* His book of poems, *Out Into the End of Time,* appeared in 1998. He is currently working on a poetry manuscript entitled *Unvisited Cities.*

Dawn Ladds currently resides in Orangeville, Ontario, Canada with her husband, Brad and their Golden Retriever, Phoebe, who—like Morris in "Brunch"—jumps up on everybody.

Theresa Martin is a freelance writer for *Indianapolis Monthly Magazine* and *Indianapolis Woman Magazine*. In addition, she has been published in *Quarterly West*.

Jason Ockert won the *Atlantic Monthly* Fiction contest in 1999 and the Mary Roberts Rinehart National Fiction Award in 2002. His fiction has appeared in *Virgin Fiction 2*, *McSweeney's*, *River City*, *CutBank*, *Oyster Boy Review*, and *Highway 14*. He is currently at work on a novel.

Evelyn M. Perry is an Assistant Professor of English at Framingham State College in Framingham, Massachusetts, teaching literature and creative writing. Professor Perry's creative work has appeared in *Kicking and Screaming*, *Sophie's Wind*, *Sahara*, *King Log*, *Artisan*, *Scrivener's Pen*, *Pine Island Journal*, *Friends Journal*, *Salt Hill*, *Berkshire Review*, *The Cortland Review* and *Gumball Poetry* and in anthology and chapbook form (*I Keep a Sledgehammer Handy*) via Angel Fish Press.

Mimi Reddicliffe is Chair of the Humanities Department at Lasell College. She is currently working on a murder mystery.

Chris Reed lives in Columbus, Ohio, and graduated from Capital University with a degree in English. His work has been published in *Potpourri* and *Dionysia*.

Jewel Seehaus-Fisher is discovering the pleasures of the short story form, after years as a playwright. Her plays, FANNY AND WALT, GESUALDO, WILDE IN LEADVILLE, WILDE NIGHT IN THE ROCKIES and MY SISTER UNDERGROUND have been produced in New York City, San Francisco, and several theatres in NJ. She has won numerous awards, among them: Finalist: Actors Theatre of Louisville, Samuel French New Play Festival, Playing by the Lake Festival. First place: Southwest Festival of New Plays. First Place: NJ Council on the Arts Individual Artist Fellowship. She has just finished a play about the musicians Clara and Robert Schumann and Brahms, at the height of the Romantic Period, when they fell in love with each other, all three, and Robert Schumann went mad.

Evelyn Shakir was a Fulbright fellow in Lebanon in 1999 (the first since the end of the civil war). Her short stories and personal essays have been published in several journals, and she is the author of *Bint Arab: Arab and Arab American Women in the United States* (Praeger, 1997).

Ron Sheasby is an Assistant Professor of Writing at Loyola University Chicago, where he is also known as Dr. Lefty. His short stories have appeared (or will appear) in *Elysian Fields Quarterly*, *Just a Moment*, *Bibliophilos*, and *Citizens In America*. His poetry has appeared in the *Midday Moon*, the *Moon Reader*, and his 2003 chapbook *Silver Slivers*.

Jessica Somers is a new writer and "Playing With An Invisible Deck" is her first published story. She was born in Toronto but has since moved to the west coast to enjoy fresher air and better views. She is studying to become an accountant.

Mark Vogel is an Associate Professor of English at Appalachian State University. He has published scholarly articles, short stories, poems, and photographs for the past fifteen years.

Heidi Wohlwend has recently finished her MFA at San Francisco State University and hopes to publish her novel *Speaking in Tongues* some day. At present Heidi is also an actor specializing in historical recreation. For the 2003 holiday season she helped write and produce an authentic Victorian British Pantomime for the Dickens Fair in San Francisco. Heidi also wrote, produced and directed a semi-autobiographical play called *The*

Almost True Adventures of an ExMormon Stripper for the San Francisco Fringe Festival in 2003, which played to sell-out houses, and will run again in another venue in October of 2004. She resides in Oakland, California with her husband Brian, and their two cats Ingrid and Archie.

Printed in the United States
18699LVS00001B/292